MW00749085

MURDER

by

PINS & NEEDLES

ARDELLE HOLDEN

For Patrick, my love

1997

ormented by guilt, Adrian Bennett watched his bride twirling in the Jardins du Trocadèro. A band of cooing pigeons fluttered around her feet.

Lenore opened her arms and took a deep breath. "Ah, Paris in the spring." Her eyes closed as she turned her face up to the warm breeze wafting through the park. She tugged on Adrian's arm as they strolled past the *L'Homme* and *La Femme* sculptures. "Aren't these beautiful? Look how they're gazing up at the Eiffel Tower."

"Hmm," was all he could manage. Without slowing his pace, he gave them a cursory glance. *One man, one woman. Shit.*

Lenore cocked her head away from him with a quizzical look. "I want to remember this moment forever, to describe our honeymoon in Paris to our children. Wouldn't it be wonderful if we've conceived here in the City of Love?"

"You're such a romantic, my sweet. That's why I brought you here." He had to deflect the lie. "And it's actually the City of Lights."

Lenore sighed. "Whatever. It will always be the City of Love to me."

She kissed his indulgent smile. "This is our last day in Paris. Let's have supper in the Jules Verne Restaurant in the Eiffel Tower tonight. If this really is the City of Lights, I want to see them in all their splendour before we head home."

He agreed with less enthusiasm than he should have. Lenore was trying to hide her disappointment, which caused his conscience to dig its claws into his shoulder.

§

Until six months ago, Adrian had been a contented man. Then came that call from Paris.

"Hello?"

"*Bonjour.* My name is Lise Adrianne Richard. You are Monsieur Adrian Bennett?"

Intrigued by her soft, seductive voice, Adrian glanced around as if it was a 900 number, even though he lived alone. "Yes, this is Adrian Bennett. Should I know you? What was your name?"

"Lise Richard. You may not recognize my name, but my *grand-mère*, my grandmother, was Antoinette Lise Bertrand. Do you not recognize her name?"

She sounded offended. Adrian shrugged. "No. Should I?"

"Was not Henri your grandfather? He left Paris with the soldier, Private Adrian Bennett. The man whose name we both bear."

A little uneasy, he paced. *There were no stories of his grandfather having left any relatives in France when he was adopted—in fact, just the opposite.* "Are you a distant cousin then, Miss Richard?"

"*Pas possible!* Not possible, *mon cher ami.* My grandmother was ten, and Henri was eleven, when the soldier took him to Canada."

"So, your grandmother was not Private Bennett's daughter either?"

"No no no. Henri sought refuge in the church. He was an orphan, a ward of the church, and my grandmother came with her mother to bring fresh flowers. The two became *amis pour toujours,* friends forever."

Oddly relieved this exotic voice was not a cousin, Adrian pressed on. "So you are just curious to know what happened to Henri, my grandfather, then?"

"*Au contraire, mon cher.* I want to get to know you, meet you. Your soldier and your *grand-père* left two broken hearts in Paris. This unrequited love has become a family quest through the generations. The connection between us is strong. We all carry their names: my brother, Henri; and me, Lise Adrianne. And then I discover you, too, carry the soldier's name."

Adrian relaxed, sat, and put his feet up. "I guess I do, but my grandfather never spoke of his childhood during the war, and we never asked." *What secrets did Private Adrian Bennett leave behind in France? Perhaps she knows.*

Lise continued to explain her search for these long-lost loves, and her hope to reunite them in spirit through the succeeding generations. The romance of it sounded plausible in her seductive murmuring. By the end of the call, she had vowed to write pleading letters until he promised to visit her in France.

Adrian stared at his hand resting on the receiver. *That was a strange call.*

Her sensuous voice tormented him many times in the ensuing week. When her first letter arrived, he tore it open as he walked from the mailbox. He stopped short before walking into the door of his block as he read. His heart fluttered. His hand shook as he gazed at the photo that slipped from the envelope. The stunning French beauty he had imagined on the phone stared with a coquettish smile from beneath the brim of a veiled blue hat.

With guilty pleasure, he read her enticing words. The story of lost loves had permeated Lise's entire childhood. Her mother had, as she lay dying, extracted a vow from her to find Henri. And so she began her search, convinced love would transcend the generations in his bloodline.

What a dreamer. He slipped the letter and photo into his breast pocket and patted it. *Lenore can never see this.* But for some reason he could not bring himself to destroy it.

Neither could he burn the letters that arrived regularly as his wedding day approached. Lise's intimate pleas questioned his devotion to Lenore.

He frowned at his half-shaven face in the bathroom mirror. *I'm not having an affair with a voice or a photograph. I'll never meet her. What can a little fantasy hurt?*

But then she called again.

"*Mon cher.* I had to hear your voice. You have French blood; you should be able to write a better love letter."

"Love letter? I'm engaged to be married in a month."

"There are all kinds of love, *mon cher.* Come to Paris. We must meet. Tell me you don't want to hold me in your arms and make love to me."

He couldn't ignore the tug on his heartstrings or in his pants and deny the attraction, but he wasn't about to give up Lenore. That was genuine love.

"Of course I've imagined the fantasy of you, but I love Lenore, and I will marry her. But … God help me, I'm going to say this out loud. I could change our honeymoon to Paris?"

"Your honeymoon! *Mon Dieu.* That will be too late! *Tu es un cochon!*"

The pouting lips uttering the insult aroused him even more, and he imagined their furious make-up sex. "Take it or leave it, Lise. I'll be in Paris, and I'll bet you can't leave it."

He hung up. *What have I done?*

§

Later that week, Adrian arrived at the Allen residence, near Ladysmith, apprehensive but excited.

Cherry blossom petals sprinkled his windshield like confetti as he pulled into their driveway. His hand trembled on the key. Needing to steel his resolve, he let the drone of the engine steady his nerves. Lenore appeared at the door. Well, this was it. He pasted a sheepish grin on his face, loped up the steps, and gave her a peck on the cheek.

"Change of plans, my sweet! We're going to Paris for our honeymoon."

Amid the hubbub of disbelief, Lenore begged for an explanation for this sudden and dramatic shift to Paris, since Long Beach, right here on the Island, had always been their absolute favourite place to go for solitude and romance. And there was the cost.

Adrian expected pushback on that—switching from across Vancouver Island to across the Atlantic. He had rehearsed several variations of his speech until he was certain he had removed any hint of ulterior motives. He settled next to his bride-to-be on the sofa, draping his arm casually around her shoulders, hoping to mask his trepidation.

"Well, I have found the church where Private Adrian Bennett hid out to recover from his wounds. I've often thought I'd like to know more about the boy, Henri, who was my grandfather. There might still be some older folk around who remember him as a child." He grinned at the three nodding heads.

Lenore threw her arms around his neck. "I think Paris is just the most romantic place on earth, and the possibility of finding your blood relatives at the same time? Awesome. Oh, Adrian, thank you, thank you." She pecked his face with kisses. He squirmed out of her embrace, embarrassed in her parents' presence.

Mr. Allen's brow furrowed. "They would have to be extremely old, even if they were younger than your grandfather back then."

"You may be right, Mr. Allen, but I'm hoping the church records might yield some clues. And besides, what better place to spend our honeymoon?" He kissed Lenore on the forehead and closed his eyes for a moment, his face pinched with self-contempt. He loved the scent of jasmine in her hair.

His future mother-in-law frowned and shot him a suspicious look, heaping more discomfort on his narrow shoulders without saying a word.

Adrian managed a wan smile. This was reprehensible; he had just lied to his bride-to-be and her parents. They hadn't really been keen on him from the very beginning. He probably shouldn't have kept her out past her curfew so often in high school. Even after three years of dating, when Lenore announced their engagement, her parents had been less than enthusiastic. Today would surely reinforce their apprehensions. As he drove away, he patted his breast pocket. He had already purchased the tickets—lie number one, or was it ten?

§

The morning after their arrival in Paris, Adrian laid his note on the night table. *I'm off to find that church, my sweet. Wish me luck. Love, Adrian.* He smiled at his bride sleeping off her jet lag. In the elevator, a twinge of guilt crept up his neck for not waking her. The doors opened on the ninth floor. His furtive glances down the corridor further betrayed his guilty conscience. He tapped with his knuckle on the door of Room 912.

When Lise Richard opened the door, Adrian gasped. She was even more stunning than her photo. With a coy smile, she drew him into a passionate embrace. Her lips were softer than he could ever have imagined, but this was not the time. He pulled her arms from around his neck.

"Not now. We have to leave before Lenore wakes up." He kissed her and took a deep breath, her perfume almost derailing his mission. "I'll meet you out front."

He followed her at a discreet distance from the porte cochère until she hailed a cab. She gave the church address to the driver before slipping her hand under Adrian's coat. *"Mon cher,* I have waited months for this. Why did you marry her?"

"Because I loved her long before I knew you, my sweet." Adrian slid his hand between her inviting thighs.

He glanced in the rear-view mirror at the driver, who gave an indifferent shrug. *"C'est la vie."*

§

Adrian tipped the driver generously, but it seemed their activity in the back seat was of no consequence to him. Flustered and thankful for the cool morning air; he pulled his coat closed to hide his erection. It faded quickly when the elderly priest met them at the door.

Lise took his arm with an air of intimacy. "Father Ignacio, this is Adrian Bennett, the Canadian I told you about."

He lifted his arm from her grasp, flushing to think this priest might know this was not his wife.

Nonplussed, the priest extended his hand. "*Bienvenue*, Monsieur Bennett. Come in, please."

He and Lise genuflected and crossed themselves before passing the nave to the vestry. The heavy, ornately carved door creaked with age as they entered. Adrian stifled a condescending smirk as he surveyed the room. Except for the computer tower and monitor that dominated the ancient desk, this was a medieval wizard's den. Shelves of dusty books lined the vestry. The door of a small wardrobe in the corner hung by a broken hinge. Vestments dangled from hangers bent with the weight of time. The ceiling was low, forcing Adrian to dodge the oversized light fixture of naked cherubs holding fake candles.

Father Ignacio lifted a stack of papers and books from the corner of his desk and glanced around. Not finding anywhere less cluttered, he set them on his chair. He removed an imposing ledger from a stubborn drawer and placed this threadbare record of the parishioners from that time reverently on the cleared spot. He opened it facing Adrian and Lise and pointed to 'Soldat Adrian Bennett, canadien'. Much further back, there was 'Henri, enfant abandonné, deux ans?'

Lise elbowed in front of him. "*Mon cher*, look at this. Here is Annalise Bertrand, who nursed him in secret and fell in love with your namesake, Private Bennett."

He stared at the yellowing pages. "I didn't know any of this until you."

"And there is my grandmother, Antoinette Lise Bertrand. She

was only ten when Henri left. She lost her sweet *ami*. What a sad pair they made, mother and daughter."

She flipped through the pages carelessly, ignoring Father Ignacio's pleas for respect. "And here, see?"

Her voice droned on in his head while her red fingernail tapped on births, marriages and deaths of her family. Her parent's marriage was the last entry in this tired old ledger.

She closed the book. "You see? We have kept the name, Adrian, alive through the generations—both my family and yours."

Adrian stared at the pages of meticulous entries in exquisite hand, changing as each scribe came and went from the parish. "May I take some photographs?"

"*Absolument*, Monsieur Bennett."

Adrian teared up, surprising himself. "So, there is no record of any parents or other relatives for the boy, Father?"

"Regrettably, *Non, mon fils*. I came here as a young curate after the war. When Mademoiselle Richard approached me, we made the connection between the boy and the soldier. The last name led us to the Canadian Embassy, and to you."

"I guess I'll never know who my grandfather was."

"My son, he was Henri Bennett, the adopted son of a brave soldier, Adrian Bennett—a name you proudly bear yourself. That is enough."

Adrian brushed a tear from his cheek and drew himself up to his full height. He cleared his throat and slipped his camera into his pocket. "I expect you are right, Father." He glanced towards the door. "Does the outdoor kitchen still exist? My grandfather spoke of sitting with the soldier behind the church kitchen, peeling potatoes and feeding them to the pigs."

"No, *c'est triste*. It is a parking lot now. The kitchen is long gone. *C'est un garde-manger pour les pouvres*."

Adrian looked to Lise with eyebrows raised.

"It is what you would call a food bank, *mon cher*."

"Aw. I guess I'm fortunate to have found out this much about my grandfather." He made one last stab at unlocking Father Ignacio's memory. "So there were no inquiries after the child, from anyone?"

Father Ignacio shook his head. "Sadly, so many died in the Resistance, it is doubtful any of his family survived. If they had, they surely would have made inquiries. *C'est triste.*"

Adrian shook the priest's hand and thanked him again.

He had always known about his grandfather's adoption as an orphan. No one in the family had shown any interest in researching even the Bennett family tree, let alone Henri's history back in France. Despite that, he was surprised at his disappointment. After all, this had been just a pretext for the trip to Paris.

Waving goodbye to Father Ignacio, Lise pressed her blue hat to her head in the morning breeze and laughed. "Take a picture of me in front of the church, *mon cher.*"

"Not on your life, Lise. Are you nuts?"

§

Lenore had just stepped out of the shower when Adrian returned to their suite. He deserved a withering scowl, but her half-smile revealed only disappointment.

"I'm cross with you. Why didn't you take me with you?"

Adrian wrapped his arms around her waist, lifting her off her feet. Her body smelled wet, clean, and delicious when he kissed her shoulder. Her towel slipped to the floor, making her giggle like a schoolgirl. "You were sleeping so soundly; I didn't want to disturb you. And anyway, this was something I wanted to do on my own. But I took pictures of the actual page with my grandfather's name— well, his first name anyway—and Private Adrian Bennett's. It was like stepping into the past. I have to admit, I got a little emotional. I took a few photos of the church, but the garden and pigpen are gone. I guess that's understandable after all these years." He blathered on and on until, mercifully, Lenore pinched his lips shut.

Her tone brightened. "Still, I would have enjoyed sharing that experience with you. Let's go down to the restaurant. I'm starving. You can tell me all about it while we eat."

That was his Lenore—never one to dwell on a disappointment. "Sure. I've built up quite an appetite too." He sat on the edge of the bed and watched his bride dress. It aroused him. Like dandruff, he flicked his beleaguered conscience off his shoulder.

§

Lenore bounced out of bed the next morning, causing Adrian to roll his eyes beneath their lids.

"Come on, Adrian. Get up! Get dressed! I have two gardens and maybe a third on my list today."

Adrian rolled over and sat on the edge, yawning. "I need a cup of coffee." Would she always be so chipper in the morning, or was it just because they had made love late into the night?

She nuzzled his face between her breasts, teasing his morning erection. "Come with me. We'll have breakfast at an outdoor café near the park and enjoy our coffee in the sun."

Lenore read her itinerary between mouthfuls of warm croissant and fresh jam. She had chosen the Parc des Buttes Chaumont because, in the nineteenth century, it had been built in a former quarry. "Just like Butchart Gardens."

By the late afternoon, Adrian insisted they rest. He didn't tell her he never wanted to see another garden in his life. They settled on a bench in the Anne Frank Garden, overlooking a profusion of colour.

Lenore sighed. "All of this has inspired me to make a Monet garden quilt. Just look at that explosion of vibrant colour. I think I'll put the garden in the Attic Windows pattern—maybe modify it a bit." Her eyes cast to the sky with a wistful look.

Adrian put his arm around her. "Sounds beautiful." He hadn't a clue what she was talking about, but, hey, she was happy.

They sat in silence for a while, hearing only the children

squealing with delight in the playground. Lenore squeezed Adrian's hand. "Listen to that laughter, honey. I can hardly wait to have kids."

Adrian buried his face in the thick brown curls on the top of her head. "We'll practise like last night until we get it right."

Lenore elbowed him, wrinkling her nose. "Just until we get it right? Well, I guess I'll never admit that it feels perfect to me already." She stroked his thigh.

God, she knows how to push my buttons. He groaned and took her hand and pulled her to her feet. "What's the verdict on the Park des Buttes-Chaumont?"

"It's hard to beat Butchart Gardens. I think we'll skip the Tuileries Garden until tomorrow and stroll through it on our way to the Louvre."

"My god, Lenore. Another garden *and* the Louvre?"

"Adrian, I may never see Paris again. Consider yourself lucky. I read somewhere there are over a hundred parks in this city."

Adrian groaned. His feet hurt.

§

That evening, when Adrian emerged from the steamy bathroom fully clothed, Lenore had donned her most provocative nightie. She had propped herself up in a come-hither pose, making him sweat all over again. *Calm down, you fool. Where's your game face? Resist. Resist!*

She frowned. "Why aren't you in your pajamas?"

"I'm not tired, my sweet. It's cooled off, so I think I'll take a walk," he lied.

"An hour ago, you were exhausted, and your feet hurt." Lenore crossed her arms.

He sat on the edge of the bed, leaned over, and kissed her. Her perfume made his heart flutter. He squeezed his eyes shut. "I just want to walk by myself and think about the Paris my grandfather knew as a boy during the war. I wish I knew what happened to his family." That part was true, but the lies were piling up.

"Well, fine. I'll probably be asleep when you get in." She flipped on her side, turning her back to him.

Adrian ran his hand through his hair, where his conscience had delivered a heavy smack. "I won't wake you, my sweet."

§

Adrian's pulse raced with anticipation as he stood in the hall at Lise's door. What was he thinking? The way she had smiled at him in the dining room earlier reminded him of the cab ride that had promised all his fantasies were possible. A shiver ran up his spine. He rapped with one knuckle. Lise must have been standing right there, waiting.

"*Mon cher*, I saw you leave this morning with your wife."

He closed the door quickly behind him and scooped her into his arms. "What did you expect? I am here on my honeymoon."

"I know, *mon cher*. But we need to take advantage of every moment we can to be together." Lise unbuttoned his shirt and drew her hands over his chest. She pulled his shirt off his shoulders, pinning his arms to his sides. Kissing his chest, she unbuckled his belt. He smirked to himself—Lenore had already primed the pump.

"You're a minx, my sweet." He yanked his shirt cuffs over his hands as she slowly unbuttoned her blouse. Her breasts were as alluring as he had imagined. It was not long before their clothes lay around their ankles. She laughed when he playfully pushed her back onto the bed. Holding her arms above her head, he kissed his way from her neck to the inviting breasts that pressed firmly against his chest. When she wrapped her legs around him, he rolled over and lowered her onto himself. "I want to look at you. Take it slow." He fondled her breasts. "You are the most beautiful creature I have ever seen. Your photo did not do you justice."

Lise sat upright, her body undulating. "But you love your wife."

"But I love my wife." Adrian rolled back and thrust to the rhythm of her urging moan.

§

Adrian showered in Lise's suite to rid himself of her scent, but he could not drown his conscience. He walked for an hour in the cool night air before returning to his suite, feeling no less guilty. Happy couples lost in each other's eyes, strolling the streets and sitting in sidewalk cafés had tormented him enough. *What have I done?*

He slipped between the lily-white sheets beside Lenore without waking her, and he vowed that for the rest of his life he would be faithful to her. Tomorrow he would endure the Louvre and whatever gardens she wanted to drag him through.

§

The next evening, as the elevator rose above the mall, Adrian looked up into the precise geometry of the Eiffel Tower and shook his head. If he never saw another masterpiece in his life, it would be too soon.

Lenore squeezed his hand and pointed at the crowd below and a lone figure waving. "There's that woman again."

"What woman?"

"That woman who sat across from us in the hotel dining room last night."

"Where?" Adrian tensed, pretending not to see her.

"There. I recognize her blue hat. See, she's waving at us."

As they ascended, Adrian scowled, focusing on the blue hat. "She could be waving at anyone up here."

"Don't be silly; she's looking right at us."

Lenore waved to the woman. But by then, she was just a blue speck in the crowd.

The breathtaking panoramic view of Paris from the Jules Verne restaurant, as well as the exquisite meal, effectively swept the topic of the woman in the blue hat from conversation, much to Adrian's relief. Satiated, they moved to the observation deck with the other diners, who all shared Lenore's effusive praise for the maître d'. As the sun descended into a pool of lipstick red, Lenore sighed and rested her head on his shoulder. Evoking murmurs of wonderment, the sky soon turned a deep indigo—the perfect backdrop to the lights of Paris.

"Honey, this has been the perfect honeymoon. Thank you for bringing me here. There isn't a more romantic place on earth."

"Mmm." Adrian squeezed her hand.

Staring out over Paris and the sea of lights, he replayed the events of the night before. Lenore had said they would have dinner in the hotel dining room. He had protested, but had no plausible reason to object. Just as he feared, before the wine even arrived, Lise made her entrance. God, that interminable meal. *She's reeling me in like a flounder.*

Tension crept through his body, making Lenore look up at him with a questioning glance.

"Are you cold?"

"No, no. Just thinking about the cost of that haute cuisine we just inhaled. There wasn't even enough on the plate to bother chewing." He cringed. *Furthest thing from your mind, you prick. Get a grip.*

Lenore shrugged. "The more it costs, the less you get. It was wonderful though—really lived up to its Michelin stars." She spread her arms to the sky. "Come on. Just look at this view. This is one of those once-in-a-lifetime moments."

He wrapped his arms around her, cupping his hand over her warm breast. The romance of the Parisian night was bittersweet.

2018

*S*am and Ben arrived on the Island on the one-thirty ferry from Tsawwassen. It was a short drive from the Duke Point terminal to his folks' place in Chemainus. As they drove off the ramp, Sam looked up from her phone at the grey sky. "It might snow tonight. It's cold enough, and those clouds look heavy." She missed the sound of snow crunching beneath her feet at thirty below.

Ben waved to the ferryman directing traffic. "How do you know what a heavy cloud looks like?"

"You forget where I grew up. You want to bet we'll have snow for Christmas Day?"

Her husband reached over and stroked her thigh. "You're on. The usual?"

"You bet—winner's on top." Making love in her in-laws' basement suite felt like stealing forbidden fruit. She giggled. They had stifled many heated pleasure sounds under the quilts down there.

§

A few flakes fluttered around them as they drove up to Grace and Lenny's carport. Sam couldn't keep from snickering. She pointed to the sky and raised one eyebrow. "See?"

"We'll see if it has staying power before I concede."

Ben's mother stood at the door, rubbing her arms. "You're here, you're here. Come on in." She held her hand out to catch a snowflake. "It looks like we may have a white Christmas this year."

Sam looked at her husband's puckered-up face and snickered. "That's my bet, Grace."

Grace fussed around them like the mother hen she was, pulling their faces down to be kissed. "Come inside quickly. Ben, take your bags downstairs. Lenny, the kids are here."

The phrase seemed to roll off Grace's tongue, only now it no longer meant Ben and Sandra. His sister's murder had left a huge void in their hearts that Sam couldn't possibly fill.

She shrugged off the gloom and plunked herself on the sofa. "It smells good in here, Grace. Are the girls coming tonight?"

"No, but they'll be here for Christmas dinner as usual. We're just family tonight."

Grace's three closest friends were a hoot. Their constant nit-picking and witty comebacks kept Sam and Lenny exchanging crumpled smirks. All three widows lived alone in their own homes, but socially they were inseparable, partly because only one of them still held a driver's licence.

Ben popped up the stairs. "Have you got coffee, Mom?"

Lenny folded his paper. "How about a glass of wine instead?" He took four glasses out of the china cabinet. "You know, Keith sent us an entire case for Christmas. Can you imagine?"

Sam chuckled. "We've given half of ours away as Christmas gifts."

Grace fiddled with her apron in her lap. "Oh, I don't know. I'd feel guilty, giving away such a generous gift."

Ben rolled his eyes. "For crying out loud, Mom. It's not really a gift. We own nearly a third of the winery. Anyway, cheers. Merry Christmas."

Remembering the vineyard left Sam cold. That Christmas, after

Ben's disappearance, Sam wasn't even sure if she was still a part of his family. But, despite her loss, Grace had made a herculean effort to include her. *I've got to stop this stream of abhorrent thoughts. It's going to be hard enough for Ben to deal with his PTSD. Pull yourself together, Sam.*

From across the room, twinkling white lights and silver bells drew her toward the Christmas tree. Warmed by the fire, the natural pine scent made her close her eyes and inhale. The tree was festooned with ornaments commemorating holidays at the pyramids of Egypt, in Mexico, at Disneyland, and two darling macaroni ornaments Ben and Sandra had made as children. Others had been selected in memory of friends and loved ones departed. These ornaments were not tacky or macabre—they were touching family treasures.

Sam cradled a sailboat with Sandra's photo on the jib. "I love your tree, Grace. It is so unique."

Grace came up beside her, linked their arms, and laughed. "I'll never forget when she named her dinghy 'my yacht': M-Y-O-T-T."

Sam gave her mother-in-law's hand a squeeze and resolved to follow her lead and move on. Could she? She had to, for Ben's sake.

§

The warmth from the fireplace, the familiar music, and the mellow wine all made this Christmas Eve the epitome of family peace and tranquillity.

"Shouldn't you be calling your sister, Sam? What time is it in France, anyway?"

Christmas was the worst time for missing Celeste. Sam hadn't seen her since their parents' funeral. This was not helping her avoid thinking about death right now. Perturbed, she glanced at her watch. "No. I'll call them in the morning."

After that horrible crash, Celeste had returned to Vancouver for the funeral but flew back to France the very next day, leaving Sam feeling like an adult orphan, alone in the world.

Seeing the contented faces around her, she resolved never to take this feeling of belonging for granted. The fire crackled in the fireplace, and the tree lights twinkled. She snuggled up under Ben's arm, where she felt warm and safe.

Sam could hear Grace humming Christmas carols in the kitchen. Her gaze settled on the dining room table. It was truly a thing to behold. Her English Lace china rested on silver chargers, and tiny blue satin bows trimmed the stemware. Embroidered white-on-white poinsettias, with a cluster of seed pearls at their centre, adorned the crisp linen tablecloth drop. The blue satin table runner set the tableau for the crystal bowl of pearl and blue ornaments flanked by white candles in gleaming silver candlesticks.

Reaching for her phone, Sam uncurled her legs. "I've got to get a picture of the table." She took photos from different angles. "Grace, this could be the cover image for a magazine."

"Thank you, dear. Lenny wanted me to downsize when we moved to the Island, but I told him we'd still be entertaining family."

Lenny defended himself, pointing out they didn't have room for twenty guests at this table, to which Grace replied, "But dear, you haven't accounted for the 'shrinkage' when you help with the dishes."

She emerged from the kitchen, untying her apron. "All right, everybody, we're ready. Come and help me bring out the food. Lenny, set the roast in front of you. The carving tools are there? That's right." She patted his arm.

Sam carried in the bowl of mashed potatoes. "Grace, even these look elegant." She snapped a few more shots.

While Lenny carved the roast, Grace read a poignant poem written by Sandra. "If-Onlys are for Dreamers." When she had finished, she folded it and smoothed the creases. "What I've learned from this is that listening, really listening, differs immensely from hearing."

"Quite right, dear. We could use some music. Why don't you put on your Diana Krall album, *Christmas Song*? Ben, pass me your plate. Speaking of listening ..." Lenny waved his fork like a sabre as he recounted a recent hiking experience. " … and I'll bet that cougar couldn't have been more than ten yards in front of me."

"Metres, dear, metres."

"Well, metres, yards—either way, it was damn close. I gave him a blast with my horn, and he ran off. You can bet your boots I was 'listening' after that. My head was on a pivot until I got off that mountain."

Ben gave his father a stern look. "You know I don't like you hiking in the mountains alone, Dad. What if you fell? It's just not smart."

Grace and Sam voiced their vehement agreement.

Lenny paused with a mouthful of stuffing, nodding and shaking his head. "I know, I know. Your mother made me join a hiking group after that incident. Sam, did Grace tell you about her amazing find at the thrift store this summer?"

Sam stifled a smirk. That was an odd segue, but a brilliant deflection on Lenny's part.

"Shush, Lenny. It's a secret."

Ben pointed from his father to his mother with his fork. "You've got to remember, Dad, you can't steal their thunder."

Sam smiled. She looked around the table, remembering the Christmases with her mom, dad, and Celeste. She sighed, feeling blessed to be part of this family now.

Looking pleased, and deservedly so, Grace presented a tray of sticky pudding in her crystal fruit nappies. Between mouthfuls, the cook received muffled praise until Lenny announced the official end of the meal, pushed away from the table, and let his belt out a notch.

Sam stood at the patio doors with her glass of wine. The moon rested in the treetops, casting a silver path of moonlight across the bay. The stars winked in the cloudless sky. She smiled. *That's okay. Either way, I'll win this bet.*

§

After supper, Grace shooed Sam out of her kitchen. While Lenny dozed in his easy chair, Sam smiled at Ben, who was sitting on the couch with his finger to his lips. She tilted her head towards the patio doors leading to the beach. Without speaking, they ducked out. She squeezed Ben's hand. "Your folks are so cute."

Ben kissed her cold fingers and warmed her hand between his. "Cute, huh?"

"You know what I mean. We should be so lucky."

Along the beach, families gathered around their campfires as they did each year, wrapped in blankets while the young ones roasted marshmallows. Everyone had family home for the holidays. Just above the tide line, geese tucked their heads under their wings in sleep. In the bay, lights outlined the rigging of boats at anchor.

It had stopped snowing. Ben held the back of her hand to his cheek. "It looks like you will lose our wager."

Sam revelled in the tease. "The night is young. Besides, the bet is for tomorrow. But you can still practise." She took off running toward the house.

When they burst through the patio doors, Lenny was lighting the gas fireplace. "There you are. Can I interest you in a nightcap?"

"Sure, Dad. But just a short one." Ben plunked himself on the sofa beside Sam, placed his arm around her, and winked.

The fire and the wine soon had everyone yawning, although Sam was sure Grace was faking it—bless her. She was glad Ben didn't have to make any awkward excuses before taking her by the hand and leading her downstairs.

He called back from the bedroom door. "We put out the gifts at midnight, right?"

His dad grumbled, "Or whenever I have to get up."

Sam stifled her laughter when Ben bobbed his eyebrows at her and locked the door.

§

She awoke on Christmas morning to Ben's touch. Spooning like this was their thing—sometimes they even made love. He threw back the covers and rolled his eyes. "Come on, I hear Mom in the kitchen." Still aroused, he tucked himself into his jeans and groaned.

Sam giggled. "Come here. You can't take that upstairs." This was going to be one of those mornings.

§

The heat rose in her cheeks when Lenny gave them a mischievous grin, his lopsided Santa hat perched on one ear.

"At last. There you are. Get your coffee."

The fresh brew beckoned. She tiptoed into the kitchen in bare feet, leading her guilty-looking spouse. "Sorry. Slept in."

Once settled with their steaming mugs, Lenny began his Santa act, ho-hoing over every gift. He seemed especially jolly when he handed a large, ornate gift to her.

She gave Grace a quizzical look. "What's all this?" The lid slipped off to reveal a quilt nestled in white tissue. She gasped.

Sam unfolded the quilt as if it swaddled a sleeping baby, revealing a stunning pattern of flying birds outside a window. She ran her hands over the quilting in utter amazement. The lump in her throat kept her speechless.

Grace leaned forward. "It's called Attic Windows. Lenny nearly let the cat out of the bag last night at dinner. But it looks like it's never been used. I knew you needed one for Ben's office at the cottage. I hope you like it."

"Like it? I love it. Don't you just love it, Ben?" She turned to see her husband's stricken face.

He mumbled and tore downstairs. Shocked, Sam watched the pain creep over her mother-in-law's face.

Grace took the quilt from her lap. "You'd better go to him, dear." She looked from Sam to her husband. "What have I done?"

§

Ben collapsed on the bed. His head was exploding. Images of Gerry's body sinking in the river flooded his brain. He groaned in agony. *This can't be happening.* He gripped his hair in both fists.

He couldn't even acknowledge Sam when she eased the bedroom door open. In an instant, she was at his side and cradling his head against her breast. He could almost hear her heartbeat, the most comforting sound he knew.

Ben twisted his body to wrap his arms around her waist and hung on for dear life. Long moments passed until his cries subsided and he could speak. He looked into Sam's gentle green eyes, but no words came.

Sam swept the sweaty hair from his forehead. "What triggered this?"

"You had to have seen it, Sam."

"Seen what, Ben?"

"In the quilt ... in the window ..."

"What?"

"A *murder* of crows!"

§

Grace could hear their muffled voices from the top of the stairs. "How could I not have seen that? And he's been doing so well." She wrung her hands and paced. "Oh, dear. Oh, dear."

Lenny set a fresh cup on the coffee table for her. "Come and sit down, Grace. There are bound to be triggers for Ben now and then. You know Samantha will help him through this. Come. Sit."

She sat, her heart aching for both of them. "I don't know what we'd do if it weren't for Samantha. It's not as if she hasn't suffered as well."

Lenny nodded from his easy chair. "Yes. It broke my heart when she asked if she was still part of this family."

"I know. I know. How did we make it through that Christmas without our children?" She blinked away her tears.

"We made it through because you made it bearable, my dear."

"Well, it had to be as normal as possible, for Samantha's sake. And she was so worried about us, bless her heart." She put her finger to her lips when the bedroom door downstairs opened.

Her daughter-in-law appeared alone at the top of the stairs. *Her smile looks strained, poor dear.* "Samantha, come and sit by me. How is he, and how are you?"

"He's over the worst of it, but he needs to rest, so I'll take his lunch down to him in an hour or so."

"Of course. And you? How are you holding up?"

"I'm fine. I just need to keep busy. Can I help with lunch?"

"I'm so sorry about the quilt. I just never thought."

§

After lunch, Sam wanted to appreciate the quilt while Ben was sleeping, but Grace was skeptical.

"Maybe I should take the quilt back and make you one without such a sinister meaning."

"No. I love this quilt." Sam unfolded it on the coffee table and, with her finger, traced the stitching around each bird. "Do you think the quilter realized the symbolism of the crows?"

Grace hesitated, her mistake clouding her ability to think. "I'm not sure. She could have chosen any outdoor scene in a panel, but instead she's chosen an all-over pattern, and that's hard to do—to make it look like a scene through a window."

"You think she chose this pattern specifically?"

"It could be, but why?" Grace turned up the corner to read the label. "Remember me, Nicky. Love, Mom. L. Bennett, 2015 … Hmm."

Sam gazed at the ceiling. "The name 'Nicky' sounds like a young child, don't you think?"

"Yes. How odd to have chosen this fabric for a child." The timer on the oven rang, and Grace headed for the kitchen, glad to get away from the quilt. "Time to baste the turkey."

"It smells wonderful. I should put this away." Sam folded the quilt back into its box and followed her into the kitchen.

"There's something else bothering me, too. L. Bennett made this in 2015. How does it show up three years later in a thrift store, looking crisp and clean?"

"Maybe 'Nicky' never received it?" Grace drizzled the steaming, savoury drippings over the golden breast unconsciously, distracted by her thoughts. *Oh, dear. What have I unleashed?*

THE QUILT

*I*t was Mother's Day weekend. Grace leaned on the starboard railing with Lenny's reassuring hand on hers. Sun sparkles danced off the water like a symphony, in contrast to the lament playing in her head. She hadn't seen her son since Christmas. "I do hope he's forgiven me."

"Nonsense. Ben doesn't blame you for his PTSD. Sam was adamant at Christmas; he has made great strides in his recovery since ... what happened to him after Gerry's murder. He's bound to run into triggers like that quilt."

Grace sighed. "I know. I just wish I'd seen the symbolism. I never would have given it to them."

"My dear, you worry too much. I won't allow you to be miserable over a silly quilt. We are going to spend a very happy Mother's Day with our son and his beautiful wife at the cottage. Remember the good times when it was our home?"

Lenny was right, but her heart ached as she watched the wake slip past her, carrying her stream of consciousness with it. *What happened to him in those six weeks? How does he cope at the cottage where it all began?* She shivered, pulled her coat closed at her throat, and leaned her head on her husband's shoulder.

The loudspeaker blared; it was time to return to their vehicle.

§

Standing on the back stoop of the cottage, Sam put her arm around Ben's waist. She placed her hand over her heart to quell her excitement. She could see Grace smiling and waving even before their car came to a stop.

True to form, Grace had loaded the trunk so full of food it took the entire team to transport it inside. Grace seldom looked down as she navigated the steps in the path—such familiar territory for her. Behind her, Sam trundled up to the back door, watching her mother-in-law survey the overgrown backyard and the depleted woodpile.

"Son, the blackberry is encroaching on the lane. You must knock it back."

The teenager in Ben rolled his eyes at Sam as he held the door open for his folks. "Yes, Mother. And I see you checking out the woodpile. I'll have a couple of loads delivered this summer. Lots of time."

He set the groceries on the counter and grabbed two beer from the fridge, winking at Sam before joining his dad at the front windows. She smiled. *This is good—he's already more relaxed.*

Lenny stretched and slapped his chest like a silverback. "Oh, it is good to be back here. I see the water is almost over the bank. Did it come up the yard this year?"

"Just a few feet. It hasn't been up to the fire pit in years, has it?"

"No, and even then, it couldn't float our logs away. I see the crocuses are out. Your mother will be happy to see them." Lenny sat opposite his son, set his beer on the coffee table between them, and leaned on his knees. His tone changed from reminiscent to concerned. "Ben, let's talk about the elephant in the room. How do you feel about this place?"

Sam stood with the fridge door open, listening. Ben needed to have this conversation with his dad. They had far too much shared tragedy in their lives.

Ben glanced back at her and rocked his head. "The worst times are when I'm standing out there where I watched Gerry get ... you know ... shot. But every time we come out, my comfort level improves a little. I will not let this thing rob me of all my childhood memories or future happiness."

As she watched, Ben stood and faced the window. His dad rose to rest his arm across his son's shoulders. They drank their beer and gazed out at the river that had swept Gerry's body away.

Sam felt a chill and realized she still had the fridge door open. "Grace, with all this food, we'll have to eat non-stop for three days."

"I knew you wouldn't have time, dear. Slip that casserole in the oven for a few minutes to heat it through."

"I can do that. Would you mind setting the table?" Sam waited for it, a grin sneaking across her face.

"Oh! My goodness, Lenny! You walked right by this table. Ben! This is so beautiful." Grace stroked the smooth grain of the top as she walked around it, running her fingers over the salmon that swam around the skirt and stooped to touch the carved grizzly paws forming the feet of the pedestal. "It's as if he's imagining the salmon swimming around him, teasing him." After a long pause, she stood up with tears in her eyes. "When did you make this? It's truly amazing, Ben. What a work of art. The hours it must have taken."

Sam could not contain her excitement. "He worked on it all last winter. I think it's gorgeous." She caught Ben's smile as he stood there with his arms crossed, clearly enjoying the accolades.

Lenny cocked his head. "So ... octagonal, eh? I'm glad."

"Had to. Granddad would have turned over in his grave if I hadn't kept to his overall design for this place."

Ben's grandfather had built Chambers Lane Cottage out of untreated railway ties. Since they were only eight feet long, he built the central core in an octagon. As the family grew, he expanded the shape, using longer logs from the property for the outer walls.

Lenny, with an engineer's appreciation for the precision of his son's workmanship, began picking his brain about every aspect of the construction.

The timer on the oven dinged. "Okay, okay, Dad. I think lunch is ready. Let's eat."

Grace set the table with the touch of a butterfly's wing. She placed the casserole on a Douglas fir round with a felt cushion. Nothing should mar her son's masterpiece, she said.

This reveal to his parents was everything Sam had hoped for. Would it be as cathartic for them? She paused as she passed the salad. The almost reverential pride on their faces told her it would.

§

Lenny had let his belt out a notch and retreated to the sunroom with his coffee and Bailey's. "A lovely meal, Mother ... you too, Sam."

"Well, there's not much skill involved in a salad, but thank you anyway." Sam began clearing the table with her eye on Ben. "I want to spread the quilt out here."

Grace furrowed her brow. "Oh ... Is that a good idea, son?"

"It's fine, Mom. I'm not ready to sleep under that quilt, but it is a beautiful thing; so we'll bring it out for unsuspecting guests."

"You don't have to keep it. I'm sorry I didn't realize ..."

"It's all right, Mom. I'm dealing with it." Ben gave her a peck on the cheek and a loving smile.

His humour and deference to his mother over the quilt eased Sam's anxiety a little. She set the dishes in the sink. *He's gotten so much better just from making that table out here, but I don't think I'll ever stop worrying.*

But right now, she had little apprehension discussing the strange things she had uncovered in the quilt. "You know Grace, there's a lot more to that quilt than we noticed at Christmas."

"What do you mean, dear?"

"Let me show you." Sam retrieved the quilt from the bedroom closet. She unfolded it right side up at first. "Sit beside me, Grace.

Remember these?" She pointed at the border. "These three crows we noticed around the border are quilted in matching thread. You can hardly see them. Why? Why wouldn't she want the three distinct crows to be obvious—say, white thread on black?"

"I see what you mean." Grace ran her fingers over the quilted crows like Braille.

The men leaned in. Sam looked at Ben for the nod before continuing. "There's more." Sam flipped over the quilt and centred it on the table. "This got me thinking about the crows on the front.

"Look at all the crosses. And the bars on the crosses." She paused. "I read nothing into the pattern until I saw this." She pointed at the centre of the back.

Lenny took out his reading glasses. Grace was the first to see it. "It's writing." She squinted even closer.

Sam unfolded a sheet of paper. "Don't strain your eyes. I've done a rubbing—like a stone engraving. It's incredible. Listen to this."

Ben rocked from foot to foot. "Okay, Dad, we're out of here. I'm not ready for this. Let these two have at it."

Sam tried not to show her relief at their departure. The murder of crows on the top had been disturbing enough for him, and she was sure this quilt was all about murder.

She ran her fingers over the words stitched in rows and read from her rubbing. "First of all, there's the Roman numeral for *one*. Hmm? Then it says:

> *A sultry crow swept 'cross our view*
> *In veiled blue hat o'er yellow eye.*
> *Each annum as her murder grows*
> *A blue hat glimpsed is fleeting by.*
>
> *Haunting every fledgling's rite*
> *The blue hat caws in throaty songs.*
> *Flight to warmer climes evades not*
> *The blue hat crows in palms.*

And then there's this little blue hat tucked in behind these bars. Could they symbolize prison bars?"

Grace touched the label at the bottom with all the admiration and respect of a fellow quilter. "This label is quite normal for provenance. But this poem ... how strange. She embroidered this on the backing fabric before assembling the quilt sandwich."

"Quilt sandwich?"

"Yes, there's the quilt top and the backing with batting in between. She either basted or pinned the three layers together to stabilize them. Then the quilting was done by machine."

Sam nodded. "So that's how it's done? And she's used white thread on white fabric. Hidden. Just like the crows. Why? What would be the point?"

"Compelled to make this quilt but hiding oblique symbolism for her child to find or not ..."

Sam shook her head. "What if she was hiding these clues from her husband? And then 'Nicky,' her child obviously, gets rid of this quilt, or loses it, and her murder can never be solved?"

Grace was visibly shaken. "Murder again, oh dear. Samantha, I think I'd like to put this away for now. Let's look at it again tomorrow with fresh eyes." She wiped the corner of her eye.

"Of course. I'm sorry. I've been so caught up in this." Sam began folding up the quilt. *Why did I do this? Damn. She's not ready. It's too soon after ...*

Grace interrupted her train of thought. "I'm certain you've discovered something dreadfully sinister, dear, but she could be alive, and you may very well prevent a murder rather than solve one. We have to keep going with this." Grace's eyes widened with the urgency of her words.

"I'll keep looking into it, Grace. But I think maybe you shouldn't ... I mean ... let's have a glass of wine and enjoy the rest of the afternoon."

"Yes, let's. Tomorrow we can re-examine it with fresh eyes. Now, where's that glass of wine?"

It wasn't long before the men returned. Sam and Grace clipped their conversation when the men entered. While Ben was out of earshot, they had spoken freely, but neither wanted to bandy the word *murder* around in his presence.

Lenny flopped in an easy chair across from them. "So, have you girls figured out the secret message?"

Sam glanced at Grace. "Interpreting poetry has never been my forte, but we'll tackle it again tomorrow. Who's hungry?"

Later, as they watched the river flow into the sunset, Sam worried. *Am I opening a can of worms or a snake pit?* She gazed at the three people she loved most in this world—three wounded psyches. *What am I bringing to them?*

§

Saturday morning, Sam couldn't wait for Ben to do something with his dad. She tried to hide a mischievous grin. "Why don't you two go kayaking? It's a beautiful day."

Lenny soaked up the last of his eggs with a half slice of toast. "I think they want to get rid of us, Son."

"She's not very subtle, is she?" Ben wrapped his arms around Sam's waist and kissed her. "Okay, we're out of here. Be back at noon."

"Take your phone, hon. The eaglets are huge now." She gave him another quick kiss and shoved him out of the kitchen.

Before they even had the kayaks down to the shore, Sam had the quilt spread on the table.

Grace smoothed out the wrinkles. "Where are your notes, dear?"

Sam pulled the folded paper from her pocket. "Are you okay with this, Grace?"

"Of course. I am thinking of Sandra when I say we have to find this woman, no matter what."

"We?" Grace was nothing if she wasn't resilient. Sam hesitated but laid the poem between them. "Let's back away from the details for a minute and think about our first impressions of the top."

"Yes. When I saw it hanging in the thrift store, I just thought it was a beautiful example of the Attic Windows pattern. You don't see half of a bird in one pane and the other half way over here in this one. The bird would have looked way out of proportion. This woman, L. Bennett, understood that."

Sam's eyebrows shot up. "Now I know I would not have noticed that."

Grace shook her head. "If it had occurred to me that I was looking at a murder of crows, I never would have bought it."

"Well, it's a good thing you didn't think of it, then. The more we examine and discuss it, the less anxiety I see in Ben. What do you make of the grey-on-grey crows stitched in the border?"

"Well, if I had made this ... It could mean three deaths? Or three witnesses, perhaps?"

Sam tried to soften the tone of her brutal speculation. "Or three murders? Or three suspects?"

"Oh dear, are we really thinking such an awful thing?"

Sam grimaced. "Let's leave that thinking alone for now." They flipped the quilt, smoothing out the ripples. "Okay, let's examine this verse line by line:

A sultry crow swept 'cross our view
In veiled blue hat o'er yellow eye."

Sam took a sip of her coffee. "That suggests to me that L. Bennett was not alone when she saw the 'sultry crow' in the blue hat. She says 'our view.' I'm thinking a husband? And the hat had a veil. Hmm. I doubt the woman has yellow eyes like a crow, but yellow does symbolize cowardice. I'm thinking crow might have a double meaning here."

"Yes. Calling someone an old crow is derogatory. But she did call her sultry, so she also thought of her as alluring. Perhaps a threat? Maybe she could see that her husband was admiring her?" Grace tapped the words *our view.* "I think the number of crows is significant, too—six means death is nearby. How many are there?"

"Lots. That many is a murder for sure. Okay, what's next here?

Each annum as her murder grows
A blue hat glimpsed is fleeting by."

They stared at the quilt for a few moments. Grace wagged her finger at it. "*Annum* means year. Her murder grows? ... A child every year?"

Sam topped up Grace's coffee. "Could be." She paused with the pot hovering above her cup. "Maybe it means every time L. Bennett saw the crow in the blue hat, she had another kid." She snapped her fingers. "Maybe three kids? Like the three crows in the border?"

Grace's eyes lit up. She nodded vigorously with her mouth full of coffee and swallowed too fast, causing a coughing fit. Her eyes watered as she recovered, waving her finger at Sam. "I'm okay. Let me see your notes, dear."

Sam scooted the paper across the quilt. Grace read with poetic rhythm.

"Haunting every fledgling's rite
The blue hat caws in throaty songs."

Sam could hear the resolution in Grace's tone. *This is a new level of engagement for her.* Sam didn't bring it up, just tapped the quilt. "I got this one. A fledgling is a child leaving the nest, right?"

Grace nodded. "Yes, but the 'blue hat' person wouldn't be 'haunting' her own children's rites.

It had to be L. Bennett's children. Like Nicky? But how many children did she have? And how many rites per child?"

Sam looked at the clock. "Okay. What are rites?"

"Well, there are religious rites like baptism. Could be graduation or marriage?"

Sam laughed. "Right. So, there are lots of rites. Do you think this woman in the blue hat showed up at all L. Bennett's children's rites of passage? And sang, no less? Pretty ballsy if you ask me."

"My word. And if you link it to the lines above, she may have had all her children with her."

"Wow. Do you suppose they belonged to the same church, or the kids went to the same school?"

"That would explain why their paths crossed so often. Oh dear, it would be terrible if she was paranoid about someone from her neighbourhood."

"If that were the case, surely her husband would have dispelled all the fears she put into this quilt." Sam glanced at the clock again. "Why don't we go for a walk? It's such a beautiful morning."

Grace readily agreed, and they were soon strolling down the lane, enjoying the birds and the smell of spring. Sam's mind wandered back to the quilt, and she slipped the poem out of her pocket.

"Flight to warmer climes evades not
The blue hat crows in palms."

"Goodness. 'Evades not the blue hat'? Could it be the 'blue hat' followed L. Bennett to 'warmer climes'? With palm trees? Maybe on holiday—or was she trying to escape?"

Sam scowled. "Yeah. And why is this woman singing? Maybe it's a metaphor, like a stool pigeon." Sam snapped her fingers again. "What if she 'sang' to L. Bennett? Told her something."

"I don't think so, dear. I think this woman appeared at these events over the years until the accumulation ceased to be a plausible coincidence in L. Bennett's mind."

"You're probably right. But there must have been something suspicious enough for her to make this quilt, but not tangible enough to act upon it. Grace, do you think L. Bennett could still be alive?"

"I don't know. She made this specifically for her son or daughter. Why did I find it in a thrift store? Did she have a falling out with this child?"

"Well, that's a twist. As the king of Siam would say, it is a puzzlement." They wandered back to the cottage, invigorated.

Sam glanced out the window. "We have to wrap this up; the fellas are back. But there's one more thing we have to think about."

"What's that, dear?"

"The Roman numeral *one*. That must mean there is more than one quilt by L. Bennett with embroidered poetry like this."

"Yes. I wonder how many little fledglings this poor woman had?"

"Exactly." Sam quickly folded the quilt and stowed it away just as the men trudged through the front door, tracking in sand and grass on their wet shoes. Sam smiled at her partner in cahoots and rolled her eyes.

OBITUARIES

*E*ver since Mother's Day, L. Bennett had been on Sam's mind. Who was she? Where was she? Was she dead or alive?

Today, Sam returned to the apartment on a mission. Before Ben came home, she wanted to search obituaries for the maker of this quilt of many secrets. But first: toss two chicken breasts in crumbs, some new potatoes in olive oil with tarragon, and pop them in the oven to bake. The leftover salad in the fridge will round out supper nicely.

She tapped the power button on the laptop as she passed the desk on her way to the bedroom. She was out of her scrubs and into tights and a baggy T-shirt in minutes. The cursor blinked its readiness as she spun into the chair. She entered *Obituaries BC 2015. Nope, too broad. Obituaries Vancouver Island BC 2015* cut the list by pages. *That's better.* But after scrolling through the next two and a half years of obituaries, she was no closer to finding the right L. Bennett. When Ben opened the door, she closed all tabs with one keystroke and spun around. "Hi."

Ben tossed his keys into the bowl on the console table by the door. "What are you up to?"

"Nothing."

He walked over to her, bent down, and kissed her. "Why do you look so guilty?"

"I'm just doing a little research."

"Oh yeah? On what?"

"I was trying to find the obituary for … L. Bennett."

"Is this about that stupid quilt?"

Sam crossed her arms. "Ben, something sinister is—or was—going on in that woman's life."

Ben took the roast pan out of the oven. "I agree. And that's why I don't want you pursuing this."

"But Ben, this is not the only quilt. And there may be more clues in the others."

"Clues to what? An affair? Or, god forbid, an actual murder? Haven't we had enough murder in our lives?"

Sam slipped her arms around him. "This woman left these clues with her child or children, and somehow this one for Nicky wound up in a thrift store. Why? How? The least I can do is try to find him, or her, and return it. I don't even know if Nicky is a boy or a girl."

The argument continued unabated throughout supper. With the last dish in the dishwasher, Ben closed the door hard.

"Sam, if you insist on following up on this thing, promise me you will do it online, incognito; block your number on the phone, and do this anonymously. You don't know what you could uncover, and the word *stalking* comes to mind. Promise me."

She kissed him. "Promise."

Continuing with his terms of agreement, Ben wrapped his arms around her and backed her into the bedroom. "I mean it, Sam. No in-person interviews. None. Nada. No knocking on any doors. No police involvement. Agreed?"

Sam lay back on the bed, wrapped her legs around him, and smiled. "Agreed."

§

Sam spent several evenings scouring the obituaries up and down the Island for variations of the name, but no luck. On Saturday morning she sat at the computer, frowning as she scrolled through the last page. *I'm in big trouble if this quilt came from the mainland.*

She squinted at her monitor. *Facebook has no L. Bennett or Nicky Bennett that fit my criteria. Hmm. None of these Nicoles or Nicholases are a plausible fit either. Odd. Every kid these days has a Facebook page. I wonder how many children she had besides 'Nicky'. Hmm.* She opened 411.ca.

Darn it. A page and a half of L. Bennetts on the Island. Well, I'd better settle in and check them all. Wouldn't it be great if she were alive? Hmm. What would I say? This could be awkward. But better than finding her dead. She picked up her phone and began.

On the whole, people were forthcoming, but a few were harsh hang-ups. One gave her pause.

The male voice answering cleared his throat in her ear. "Yeah?"

"Hello, is this L. Bennett?"

"Who's askin'?"

"My name is Jeannette Bowers." She crossed her fingers; her middle and maiden names could pass for anonymous, more or less. "I'm looking for a woman, L. Bennett. She's a quilter."

"Well, I'm not a woman, am I? And I sure as hell don't quilt."

"No, but I just thought maybe in your family …"

"Why don't you piss off, lady? She's not here. Never was."

He hung up. *What a strange answer.* Most people just said no, no woman lived there with the initial L. Or no, L. Bennett was a man. And if a woman with the initial *L* lived there, she was either too young or too old—or just right, but not a quilter. "She's not here, never was" gave her a creepy feeling, making her shudder.

§

On Sunday, Sam persevered. Back to browsing through more recent obituaries from the Island sites, she came across one Adrian

Bennett. She plunked her coffee down, splashing it from the cup. "Oh geez."

"Ben, listen to this." She dabbed the spill with tissues as she read. "'Adrian Bennett, a prominent Victoria entrepreneur, died on Tuesday, June 11, after a lengthy illness. He leaves to mourn his passing his wife Lise, his children Henri, Antoine, and Bertrand, and two children from a previous marriage, Nicholas and Frances! A memorial took place in Nanaimo June 14 …'" She spun around, reached over the back of the sofa, and shook Ben by the shoulders. "Nicholas has to be Nicky!"

"Hey, you're rattling my teeth. So, there's your L. Bennett."

"It can't be Lise. L. Bennett was the mother of Nicky. She has to be the wife from the previous marriage. Lise's three children must be very young, and Nicholas and Frances could be our age."

Ben turned off the television. "If he lived in Victoria, why was the memorial in Nanaimo?"

"Maybe he was from up-island."

"If you were calling the L. Bennetts, that could have been Lise, the second wife, not the L. Bennett who was Nicky's mother."

"You're right. I may have called it." In fact, Sam was sure she'd called it—it was the only one that fit. But she was not ready to tell Ben. Not yet. "I have a terrible feeling about the wife from the previous marriage. It could have been divorce, but it could have been something else … Ben?" She rubbed the chill creeping up her arms. "There's no Adrian Bennett listed in 411.ca. If he was so prominent, I should be able to find him."

Ben came around from the sofa and sat at his computer. "Let me see what I can find."

Sam slid her chair next to his and kissed him. "Are you sure? I don't want you to—"

"I'm beginning to see why you can't leave this alone, Sam. That obit has me worried for her, too. I don't mind doing a little online research."

She rested her chin on his shoulder, watching his fingers fly across the keys. *He is in his element.* She kissed his neck, making him quiver and shoo her away.

ADRIAN

*M*onday evening, Sam sat cross-legged in her robe at one end of the sofa, towelling her hair dry. Between strands, she could see Ben—barefoot as usual—sitting at his computer, wearing only his jeans. His broad, muscular back still bore the scars of his captivity two years before. But they were nothing compared to the scars he carried inside—the scars that had made him recoil from this quest of hers at first. But now ...

She stared at his back. *This is a big step forward for him. He's more curious about the fate of L. Bennett than the imagery in the quilt. This is good.* "So, what have you found out about Adrian, honey?"

He spun around and leaned on the back of the sofa. "I found someone through an entrepreneur's club who knew him. He said Adrian owned a successful marine wholesale supply company, Bennett Marine, in Victoria. He also said Bennett had a major stroke a few years back, which was no surprise to him even though he wasn't even forty. Apparently the guy was a workaholic. He spent days, even weeks, on the road, checking on customers and sometimes even delivering rush orders personally. He made a lot of money, but the work killed him, according to this guy."

"Did you get contact information for him in Victoria? The company must still be there."

"No. After the stroke, he sold the company to a consortium that operates out of Vancouver. It's a warehouse now and down to a skeleton staff. He said Adrian's first wife brought him and the children up-island to her parents' place."

Sam raised an eyebrow and stuck her finger in the air with a question on the end of it.

Ben had the answer. "No, he didn't know her name. Apparently, Adrian was in terrible shape after the stroke and needed a lot of care. This guy never saw Bennett again and just recently saw his obit."

"That's interesting. Maybe I should try a fresh angle. I think I'll go over to your folks' this weekend and do some sleuthing around with your mom." Sam could see Ben stiffen.

He squinted. "Why with Mom? I should come with you."

"You don't have to. We'll just be poking around in fabric shops and talking to other quilters. They're a pretty closely knit group. Get it? Quilters? Closely knit? Oh hell—doesn't work, does it?" She wrinkled her nose at Ben's eye-roll.

Her phone rang. "Hello."

"Jeannette Bowers?"

She walked into the bedroom and closed the door. "Who is this?"

"You've been poking around in my business, and I don't like it. You will stop if you know what's good for you." He hung up.

Sam broke out in a sweat. She had to calm down before Ben saw her.

"Who was it, Sam?"

"Just some telemarketer." She stepped into the bathroom and closed the door. Her heart raced. She flushed the toilet and splashed water on her face. Opening the door a crack, she called out to Ben.

"I think maybe you should come with me, hon."

1999

*A*drian stood tall at the baptismal font. His beautiful wife stood beside him, holding his first-born son, Nicholas Adrian Bennett. The choir sang, and sunbeams streamed through the stained-glass window onto his child's angelic face. He cooed with delight as he reached for the glistening water droplets.

Lenore had worried they might never have children when the first year of their marriage passed without conception, but ever since that wonderful day when she said, "I'm pregnant," Adrian had been strutting with pride.

Nicholas nuzzled for her breast, and Adrian's heart was full. He gazed over the congregation as a king would gaze upon his subjects, but the blue hat he saw in the very last pew turned his heart to stone.

For the duration of the service, he sat, he stood, he turned pages and mouthed words. Lenore elbowed him when he wasn't following. She poked him again when the service ended. He shook hands with the priest at the door—blah, blah, blah—and ushered his wife to their car. His head spun in his panic to keep her from seeing Lise.

"My sweet, you take the car. I see a client I need to talk to. I'll catch a ride with him."

"All right, dear. Lunch will be ready when you get home."

Adrian waved as his wife drove out of sight. When the lot emptied save one, he didn't have to turn; he knew who was waiting. When the priest closed the doors, he was alone with her.

§

The morning was not hot, but beads of sweat formed on Adrian's forehead. As he approached the driver's side, Lise rolled down her window and smiled. Her long black hair nestled at the nape of her neck under a royal-blue hat. A veil covered her demure eyes but allowed her perfect skin and full red lips to glow beneath it.

"What the hell are you doing here? And why did you wear that hat? Lenore might have recognized you."

"*Bonjour*, Adrian. I wanted to get your attention, *mon cher*. You have a beautiful son."

Adrian leaned on the roof. "Thank you. His name is Nicholas."

"*Non, mon cher*. His name is Henri Adrian Richard."

Adrian's mouth went dry, and paralysis gripped his body.

"You look unwell. Get in and sit."

Adrian's rubbery legs carried him around to the passenger side. He got in, shut the door, and buckled up. "Drive," he said.

"*Pardon?*"

Adrian's eyes narrowed. "I said drive!"

Lise startled and squealed her tires out onto the street. On the highway, she ventured to say, "Look in the back seat, *mon cher*. That is your first-born son, Henri."

Adrian did not look. "You're lying. We only had sex once, and that was two years ago in Paris."

"*Oui*, we made love on your honeymoon."

"I don't believe you." Adrian glanced in the back seat for a split second, but that was enough. The child looked like an older version of Nicholas.

The woman reached into her purse and produced a folded piece of paper. "Here is proof."

Adrian unfolded the paper, and there it was. *Mère: Lise Adrianne Richard. Père: Adrian Bennett.* The paper fluttered in his fist. "This proves nothing."

"Look at the date, Adrian. You see? Nine months to the day after we made love in my room, down the hall from your precious bride. If you like, I will get a DNA test, but as you see, he looks like you. You know what the test will say."

"What do you want?"

"What do I want? I want our son to know his father. I am living in Vancouver in a small apartment, but I need a bigger place where Henri can play in the yard. Where he can have his own room, because I expect you to visit."

"We're just getting my business off the ground. I can't afford a house for you in Vancouver."

"Perhaps out in the valley, a small house in the country?"

"There's no such thing."

"*Au contraire, mon cher.* I have found something. It is near your *centre de distribution.* Perhaps you could give me a job there? *Non?*"

JONANCO

*T*he *Spirit of British Columbia* was well away from the
Tsawwassen ferry terminal. In the cafeteria, Sam and Ben
ate breakfast in silence except for the amalgam of passenger voices
and engine drone. She had been getting the silent treatment from
Ben since they had left the apartment.

The day before, Ben had spoken to Harry, the supervisor at the
warehouse of Consolidated Distributors. He was the only employee
left who had worked for Adrian Bennett. Harry had kept the wheels
of Bennett's company greased and everything running smoothly
while the boss was out of town, and that was a lot. He didn't know
how his poor wife, Lenore, put up with him. Harry said that after
Bennett's stroke, she sold the company, and that was the best thing
that could have happened to him. He heard she had died not long
after they moved up-island. And no, he knew no more about
Bennett except that he was dead now, too.

Ben broke the silence. "Now that we know her name was
Lenore, and that she is also dead, I think this trip is pointless."

"But her being dead is the point, Ben. How did she die? There is
no obituary. I want to find those kids. The only clues I have are in
this quilt, and Lenore lived and quilted on the Island. Your mother

has a lot of quilting friends. Talking to them is the logical next step."
If she had told him about the 'telemarketer' phone call, she was
certain Ben would have put a stop to her sleuthing. *Why didn't I block
my number as he asked? Stupid.*

Ben snapped at her. "And you couldn't get any information from
the funeral home? What did they say?"

"They said that if I wanted to donate to the Heart and Stroke
Foundation I could do it online, along with giving my condolences.
He wasn't about to give any information on the death certificate to
just anyone. And anyway, your man Harry didn't know her maiden
name." Sam knew this was a feeble excuse.

"So you figure Lise Bennett has Lenore's kids? So much for
thinking they were our age." Ben stabbed his spoon into his yogurt.

"Right. At the age they are now, I should be able to find them on
social media."

"Didn't you call someone who sounded suspiciously like they
knew who you were looking for?"

Sam hated keeping information from Ben. "Yes, but that was
before Adrian's obituary. If it's Lise's number, I don't want her to
know we are still asking questions. She could be the lady in the blue
hat for all I know. And maybe even involved in Lenore's death, if
our suspicions are correct." Sam cringed, waiting for Ben's reaction.

"Our suspicions? Sam, I'm only here to make sure you keep your
promise. Be careful who you talk to when you're asking around
about this dead first wife. It could get back to this woman, Lise. And
it's clear from Adrian Bennett's obit that she wrote it with no
respect for the kids. At the very least, Lenore should have been
mentioned as the late wife and mother of, et cetera."

"Yes. And that strikes me as suspicious. Why would she be so
insensitive to Lenore's kids? Ben, we were wrong. Judging by what
Harry told you, they aren't our age at all. They're eighteen and
twenty, but Lise's three boys must be very young."

She had another disturbing thought she would keep from Ben. *If
they are just kids, then who is the guy threatening me? Adrian is dead.*

She reached across the table and squeezed Ben's hand. "I

promise I will be discreet." She could tell Ben's anxiety control was tenuous.

He pulled his hand from beneath hers. "I'm going out on deck for some fresh air."

§

Sam always loved the way Grace greeted them: her arms open wider than the doorway.

"I'm so glad you came over this weekend. It is Quilt Daze at Jonanco, and everyone will be there. I didn't tell the girls who we were looking for."

Sam grinned. Grace was getting into this. She was about to warn her about the risks of this intrigue when Ben jumped in, waking her guilty conscience.

"Mom, you've got to take this seriously. Please let Sam do the talking, okay? We don't know who we're dealing with here, you know? I don't like that you're even involved in this." He hugged her and kissed the top of her head.

"All right, Son. I know all these ladies, and there's not a dangerous one among them. But don't you worry. I'll leave the talking to Samantha." She caressed Ben's cheek.

Lenny came up behind his wife. "Ben, we have to fend for ourselves for lunch."

Grace shook her head and rolled her eyes. "I've already made your lunch; all you have to do is just put it on the table, dear. Honestly. Samantha, I've packed sandwiches and some veggies for us, and a tub of cookies for the table. It'll be easiest to talk to everyone at lunchtime."

Ben gave his mom another hug. "We'll manage, Mom. We're going for a hike after lunch."

Sam kissed Ben. She needed him preoccupied, but safe, so she could focus. "Make sure you take that 'cougar horn.' I want you back in one piece."

§

Driving to Nanaimo, Sam reminded Grace that Lenore Bennett may just have been paranoid and have died of natural causes. "We only have our suspicions from the quilt, so we have to be very careful we don't imply that she was murdered."

"Yes, of course, dear. I understand. The turnoff is just past this bridge."

In the parking lot, Grace loaded her arms with their lunch and the cookies while Sam dragged her carry-on containing the quilt.

"So this is where you, Mabel, Gloria and Theresa come to quilt?"

"Yes. It's a wonderful bunch of ladies. You'll see."

A chorus of voices greeted Grace, as if a week had been too long. Her three friends jumped up to hug Sam.

"Grace told us you were coming."

"We haven't seen you since Christmas."

"How have you been?"

Before Sam could open her mouth, Theresa bellowed, "Hey, everybody, this is Samantha, Grace's daughter-in-law."

Greetings emanated from the far corners of the clubhouse, including the kitchen.

"Wow. This is amazing. What are all of you working on?"

Theresa elbowed her way between Grace and Mabel and grabbed Sam by the arm. "Come with me." She walked her charge around the room, introducing her to the ladies behind the machines —each of them happy to detail their current project.

Someone announced lunchtime, and machines stopped humming, chairs scraped on the well-worn linoleum, and the lineup began at the microwave. Grace placed her cookie tub on the lunch table with the other goodies and claimed two chairs for her and Sam.

Everyone was aware of Ben's harrowing experience two years ago and the grief it had caused Grace. They had celebrated his rescue with a cake. Sam admired the friendship between these women, thinking she could be part of it one day if they ever moved to the Island.

"So. What brings you to the Island, Samantha?"

"Well, last Christmas, Grace gave me a quilt she'd bought in the Ladysmith thrift store. The label says it was made by L. Bennett for her child, Nicky." Sam studied every face around the table, not letting on she knew *L* was Lenore. Only one kept her head down and did not react. Sam tensed. *Please don't let her be the conduit to Lise. I've got to watch that one.*

Jillian interrupted her thoughts. "I think I remember her coming a few years back. Not very sociable. Doesn't anyone else remember her?" Murmurs came from around the table.

Jillian called to the suspicious character with her head down. "June. *June?*"

June raised her head and cupped her ear.

"Did you know an L. Bennett?" Jillian almost shouted.

Unfazed, June shook her head and went back to studying her grapes. *Mission compromise averted.* Sam grinned to herself.

The bell on the microwave sounded, and Sherry emerged from the kitchen with a steaming bowl of pasta. "What'd I miss?"

Mabel piped up. "Samantha is looking for anyone who knew L. Bennett."

Sherry sat down across from Sam. "I knew Lenore. She passed away four years ago. What about her?"

Sam's heart sank … but now, the possibility of a suspicious death was more plausible. She explained to Sherry how Grace had given her this amazing quilt, and since L. Bennett was on the label, they thought this was the place to start in their quest to find her. "I'm sorry to hear she's passed away. I would have liked to meet her."

After lunch, Sam and Grace held up the quilt for all to admire with much oohing and aahing. A few vaguely recalled the woman working on it, but they hadn't remembered her name. Sam packed it away without pointing out the embroidery on the back.

Sherry leaned in to speak to Sam. "Bring coffee and sit beside me so we can chat."

"Go on, dear. I'll work with the girls." Grace hadn't brought a project, so she flitted from squaring up blocks for Gloria to pressing seams for Mabel and unsewing for Theresa.

Excited, Sam grabbed her coffee and pulled up a chair next to Sherry. She had to lean in to hear her over the hum of machines all around them. Their conversation was not meant to be overheard.

"Sherry, did you know Lenore well?"

"For years. She grew up in Ladysmith, and she and Adrian lived in Nanaimo before they started the company in Victoria. After Adrian had his stroke, it looked like he wouldn't recover fully, so she moved him up here to live with her parents and sold the company. That was the best move she ever made. That Adrian was *away on business* half the time." Sherry made air quotes. "Lenore always suspected he had a mistress somewhere on the Island or in Vancouver. And by the looks of things, she was spot on. Adrian married that woman less than ten months after Lenore's death. Why would any woman with three kids marry a disabled man unless he had gobs of money or he was the father of her kids?"

Sam shook her head. "Wow."

"You know, she told me about this woman in a blue hat she would see in the most unlikely places. She said the first time she remembered seeing her was on their honeymoon in Paris. Then she saw her with a small child in the back of the church at Nicky's baptism and again at his graduation."

Sam scanned the ceiling. "This makes so much sense now. Adrian's obituary claimed he left a wife and three children and two children by a previous marriage. We just assumed Nicholas and Frances were older and Lise's were very young."

"Exactly. It didn't say stepsons, did it? And the oldest one is older than Nicky, so you know what that means."

Sam whistled through her teeth as she did the math. "You think he knew Lise before he married Lenore?"

"Not necessarily. That first boy of hers is about a year older than Nicky, and Nicky was born in their second year of marriage. Did I mention Lenore and Adrian honeymooned in Paris, and Lise Richard is French?"

Sam's head spun. "So. Her surname is Richard. She's French, and Adrian and Lenore honeymooned in Paris. Wow. That explains a lot. Poor Lenore. That couldn't have been easy: suspicious but still caring for him until her death."

"I wouldn't say she knew all along, but as the years rolled by, she saw the pattern of coincidences. How she put up with that ornery bugger after his stroke, I'll never know. He couldn't drive, so he wasn't able to visit this other family anymore, not that Lenore knew that was the reason he was such a belligerent old fart. You know, she told me she saw this woman and her three brats at their resort in Mexico on spring break one year. It was their tenth anniversary."

"She recognized her?" The lines from the verse were making more and more sense. Sam squirmed with excitement.

"Yes. She once told me she was getting paranoid about women in blue hats." Sherry moved to the ironing board, and Sam followed.

"It sounds like he took both families on the same holiday. He had balls."

Sherry thumped the iron on a seam. "Yeah. The bastard."

Sam held the trailing quilt off the floor as Sherry pressed the seams open. The sound and smell made her think of her mother ironing and Lenore making the quilt. "Odd that I couldn't find an obituary anywhere for her."

"Figures. That bitch handled everything for Adrian, I suspect. She moved him and those poor kids into her place right after Lenore's death. God, that must have been tough on Nicky and Franny."

"Sherry, what did Lenore die of?"

"Well, she developed diabetes, and she wasn't managing her insulin very well. The first time she almost went into a diabetic coma, Adrian called the public health nurse. It was a close call. Another time, they took Lenore to the hospital in an ambulance. She swore three nurses came to the house that day wearing three blue hats. God, did we laugh about that." Sherry huffed. "It's not so funny now."

"Do you think she died of an insulin overdose?"

"That's what they say. But who knows? The next time it happened, she didn't make it."

Sherry's machine whirred. When she looked up, her eyes glistened with tears.

"I'm so sorry, Sherry. That is so sad."

"That's okay. It was a long time ago. Now about this quilt. This one was Nicky's, but that year, the year she died, Lenore made one for Franny too."

Sam's heart fluttered. "Really?"

"Yes. She called it *The Sewing Room*. Some piecing she did here, but she finished it at home. She wasn't feeling up to going out towards the end. I assume Franny has it."

"How do you suppose this one for Nicky found its way into the thrift store?"

"That witch probably cleared out all Nicky's belongings the day he left for UBC."

"So that's where he is? But Franny must still be here. How old is she now?"

"Let me see. They got married in '97, Nicky was born in '99 ... so he's twenty. That makes Franny eighteen. She would have graduated just last month."

"So, with their father's marriage to this woman, how did that affect Nicky's education?" Sam fidgeted, wishing she could take notes.

"That's the one good thing that came out of Lenore's paranoia. She had Adrian set up a trust fund for the kids after the sale of the company." Sherry snorted with derision. "That blue-hat bitch can't touch it, and I'll betcha it frosts her ass."

HENRI

$\mathcal{A}$ s they hustled out to the car, Sam could not contain herself. "What a stroke of genius, coming here. I don't know why Ben and I were uneasy about this. Except for the two minutes when I thought June might be an emissary of the wicked stepmother, I enjoyed that. Thank you for bringing me here."

"You're welcome, dear." Grace sighed. "Yes, poor June, bless her heart. She wasn't always deaf. But it looked like you and Sherry were having an intense conversation."

"You have no idea." They climbed into the car and Sam took Nanaimo Road out to the highway. "Here, take my phone and hit the microphone icon. I don't want to forget a word."

On the road back to Chemainus, she recounted her conversation with Sherry Baker in short bursts of facts, afraid she would forget some important detail. An eerie thought kept distracting her. The creep who spat out the words 'she's not here, never was,' and the telemarketer, must have been Henri Bennett. He was an adult, not a child. This changed the whole timeline Sam had imagined based on Adrian's obit.

In the driveway, Sam switched off the engine and turned to her mother-in-law. "I think I know which number was Adrian

Bennett's. I have to call. With Nicholas at university and both their parents dead, Franny is basically an orphan, living there with ..." Sam shivered at the possibilities.

"Oh dear, do you think that's wise?"

"Probably not, but I have to talk to her. I don't know how safe she is, now that Henri knows someone's looking into this. And if she still has the *Sewing Room* quilt, I'll bet that's where we'll find the Roman numeral *two*."

"Yes, but this could be dangerous. I mean, couldn't he be ...?"

Sam put her hand on Grace's arm. "I know. I promised Ben I'd be careful." She didn't enjoy deceiving Grace. Remembering the threatening call, she knew anonymity was impossible. He may not have had the right name, but he had her number.

"The boys aren't home yet. Let's get in, and I'll make that call."

§

Pacing with her phone in hand, Sam wrestled with her conscience while Grace dithered.

"Oh dear, oh dear. Don't you think you should wait for Ben to get home?"

"No. Ben might want to call himself. And two alpha males on the phone will get me nowhere." She took a deep breath and hit the number.

"Hello, is this Henri Bennett?"

"No, Henri Richard. Who's askin'?"

Sam took a second to register the name. "This is Jeannette Bowers again."

"You don't listen too good. I told you to fuck off."

Sam looked down at her phone—she had blocked the number. So. She was right. He was the 'telemarketer.' "I just want to talk to Frances Bennett. Is she there?"

He paused, then spoke through clenched teeth. "She's gone. They're all gone now, and they aren't coming back."

Sam heard the click. Her hand shook.

"What is it, dear?"

Still hearing that vile man's voice in her head, Sam didn't respond.

Grace touched her arm. "Samantha?"

At that moment, the men walked through the door, exhilarated and laughing.

§

Sam cringed under Ben's steady gaze as he shed his boots and came at her like a lightning bolt. He grabbed her by the shoulders. "What's happened?"

She didn't answer, trying to collect her thoughts. What had she just heard?

"Samantha learned some disturbing—"

"It's okay, Grace, I'll explain."

"You're damn right you will. Who was that on the phone?"

"Henri Bennett, uh, Richard. Henri Richard."

"I was looking for Frances and ..." Sam turned away from Ben. "Let's talk downstairs."

Ben spun her around. "No, Sam. This is their home; you've brought this down on them. Whatever's going on, they should know."

Grace signalled for Lenny to come with her into the kitchen.

"No, Mom. Stay here. Samantha?"

Sam perched on the edge of the couch. "You remember when I called all the Bennetts on the Island?"

"I do. Go on."

"Well, one of them had a strange reaction to my question. He said, 'She's not here, never was.'"

"And?"

"And ... I got the impression he knew who I was talking about, so I kept the number. After meeting Sherry Baker today, I was sure Frances was still living with Adrian's widow—the second wife—and her boys. And that the number was theirs."

Her eyes followed Ben as he paced around the room while the clock on the mantel reproached her second after interminable second. *Damn clock.*

"So, he knows who you are? That is just great."

"No, I used Jeannette Bowers, but he had my number from the first call last month."

"I thought you called him just now."

Sam covered her face with her hands. "I did ... this time. But that 'telemarketer' the other day? It was him." She sighed. "I didn't tell you because I knew you'd want me to stop looking and I knew you'd worry."

"Too late, Samantha Jeannette Bowers Chambers. I'm more than worried, I'm pissed off."

"I can see that, Ben. I'm sorry, but this guy makes me think we can't ignore ..."

"We can't ignore what?"

Sam scowled, shaking her phone at Ben. "He's creepy, Ben. His exact words were 'She's gone. They're all gone now, and they aren't coming back.' We have to find Frances and her quilt. I believe there is something to this. Her brother is at UBC. He'll know where his sister is." She dropped to the sofa. She couldn't make eye contact, but she could hear his heavy breathing. Her mind raced. *What have I done?* She glanced up at Ben with apologetic eyes.

Ben sat beside her, rubbing his thighs, his expression a mix of hurt and fear. "If you insist on following up on this ludicrous quilt thing, I'm going to ..."

Self-reproach gnawed at her conscience. *This is going to trigger an episode if I don't diffuse the situation.* She took the sting out of her response. "You're going to what, hon?"

Ben sighed, then nodded. "I'm going to ..." He put his arm around her shoulders and gave her a gentle squeeze. "Have your back. But—and it's a big 'but'—we do this together. I mean it, Sam."

2001

From where he stood at the baptismal font, Adrian stared at Nicholas squirming on Grandmother Allen's lap. Sweat ran down his neck; Lise was there again. How did she know this was the day of Frances's baptism? *She must have overheard me on the phone with Lenore. And she brought Henri and the baby, too. Damn her.*

Lenore elbowed him—it was over. Adrian took Nicholas onto his lap as they settled in the pew. Lenore leaned in to whisper. "Did you see that blue hat in the very back? Where have I seen it before?"

Adrian whispered back. "You're asking me about a hat?" His head filled with muffled Charlie Brown whah-whah-whahs from the congregation and the priest.

At the end of service, Adrian's heart pounded as he watched Lenore craning her neck to see over the parishioners who chatted as they slowly filed out of the church. *God help me if she gets another glimpse of Lise's blue hat. Damn it.*

Lenore pulled on his sleeve. "Do you see her? I'm sure I know that woman, but I can't remember from where."

Adrian made a pretense of checking the crowd. "Sorry, I don't see any green hat."

"It was blue, a bright royal blue."

In the parking lot, he spoke to his father-in-law. "Chris, can you take them home? I want to talk to the pastor about those food baskets."

"Sure, Adrian. See you back at the house. It was a lovely service, wasn't it?"

"Yes, it was."

Lenore rolled down the back window. "There she is, over by that car."

"Who?"

"The woman in the blue hat, Adrian!"

"Where?"

"Over there with the little boy and the baby. I know I've seen her before."

"Must be at one of your groups."

As Chris drove away, Adrian could see Lenore through the rear window, pointing out Lise to her mother. *Shit.*

§

Adrian exhaled a long, slow breath when his car rounded the corner and disappeared. He watched the last vehicle but one, pull out onto the street. His eyes narrowed as he strode over to Lise's car. *Damn her.* He climbed in the passenger side and slammed the door.

"What the hell are you doing here, Lise? Don't you realize how risky this is for me? Lenore saw you. Thank god she didn't remember where she'd seen you before." He motioned for her to get on the road.

"I wanted to see Frances and to give you the good news."

"What good news?"

"You will be a father again."

"Dammit, Lise." He clenched his fists.

"Daddy, you swore."

"You are right, Henri. Daddy must watch his language, mustn't he?"

"Yes, Daddy. The baby's not supposed to hear stuff like that."

"I'm sorry, Henri. I'll be careful." Adrian glared at Lise. "You take care of this."

"I will ... in seven months."

"That's not what I meant, Lise, and you know it. Stop the car."

"*Sacré bleu*, Adrian."

Adrian got out and slammed the door.

Lise put the window down. "We'll see you next week for Henri's birthday," she said, and sped away.

FRANCES

*B*en and Sam stayed the night in Chemainus and caught the early ferry Sunday morning. With the school term over, young people swarmed the decks.

Sam watched a group of girls taking selfies along the rail, their long hair blowing in the wind. She smiled to herself. "You know, Frances would be about their age. From Adrian's obituary, I just assumed she and Nicholas were much older. I searched for Henri and Lise under the name Bennett, but their surname was Richard. It never occurred to me he alternated sowing his seed in two pastures."

"Why would it? When we get home, you'll find Frances, and I'll find Nicholas through UBC, although he may live off campus."

"Good. He should have just finished his third year of law school if Sherry Baker is right about his age." She sighed. "Even though she said Lenore created a trust fund for them, it's got to be hard, going to university and taking in your teenaged sister."

"I know what you mean. I can't help wishing I had been there to protect Sandra that last year of college."

"Ben, don't go there. You did all you could." She wrestled with a bad feeling about his PTSD for the rest of the crossing.

§

That evening, as they sat booting up their laptops, Sam's phone rang. She reached for it, but Ben's hand came down on top of hers. "Check it."

It was the Bennett's number. She gladly relinquished the task to him.

"Hello."

It was a woman's voice. "You've been calling for Lenore and Frances."

Ben pressed speaker. "Yes, that's right. Do you know where they are?"

"Why are you looking for them?"

"An old friend saw their father's obituary and asked us to get in touch. This is Lise Richard, isn't it?"

"Lise Bennett. That friend of Lenore's is in for a shock, because my husband's first wife is dead."

Ben grimaced. "I'm sorry to hear that. How did she die?"

"Diabetes, I think."

Sam scoffed under her breath. *I won't be taking her word for that anytime soon.*

Ben's tone remained nonthreatening. "Does her daughter, Frances, live with you, then?"

"No. She's gone to live with her brother in Vancouver, and *pas assez tôt*—not soon enough."

"Do you have a phone number or an address for them?"

"No, I don't."

Ben's voice chilled. "I imagine losing both parents would be difficult at their age. Oh, and tell your son, Henri, to stop making threatening calls to my wife. Is that clear?"

"*Mon Dieu!* You are lying! *C'est faux!*" She hung up, still spitting derogatory epithets.

Ben smirked. "She would have slammed down the receiver if she could have."

"Yeah. But, whatever else she's done, she has just lost her

husband and the father of her children. We should have at least expressed our condolences."

"Did she sound grief-stricken to you?" Ben huffed.

"Even so, she pursued him because of Henri and then stuck by him for twenty years, bearing him two more sons. During all that time, she couldn't have been under any illusion he was going to leave Lenore. Anyway, I'm glad you took that call." She turned back to her computer, a little shaken by the encounter, but she had to refocus on finding Lenore's daughter on social media. She'd begin on Facebook, just in case.

"Look at this. There are dozens of variations of Frances Bennett here. I'll start with any that could be about the right age from Vancouver Island, or Vancouver." An hour later, she yelped. "Here's one! Fran, from Ladysmith. She lists Nick as a brother, not as a friend." Sam gave Ben a playful punch in the shoulder.

After searching for Nicholas with no luck, she crafted her private message to his sister.

Hi Fran. You don't know me, but I saw your father's obituary on the Internet. I'm so sorry. I met your mother's friend, Sherry Baker, at Jonanco yesterday. I wanted to get in touch with you because I came into possession of a quilt made by your mother in 2015, for Nicky. I'd like to meet you and your brother and return this quilt to him if he wants it. Sherry tells me you received one, too. I'd love to see it if you still have it. Please friend me if you are interested. A Friend, Samantha Chambers.

§

The week it took for Frances to accept the Friend invitation felt like a month. Sam was lolling in front of the computer with her morning coffee when the message popped up. "Ben! Come here. Listen to this!

"Frances has friended me on Facebook! She and Nick—she calls him Nick—are in France. She says she moved in with him in Vancouver right after she graduated. Since their father had passed away, they wanted to get as far away from that *crow*—yeah, she says 'crow'—and her *spawn,* as possible. They are spending the summer touring France, but especially Paris, where their parents spent their honeymoon. Ben, Lise is from Paris." She read the rest to herself.

Ben scooted his chair over beside her. She squeezed his hand and fought back tears. She didn't realize how stressed she had become about Frances. "She signs this 'Fran.' They want to get together as soon as they're home. That's only three weeks away."

She smiled up at him. "Listen to this part: Nick is thrilled you found his quilt. Lise took all the stuff he had stored in the garage to the thrift store when he left for law school." Sam slumped in her chair. "Isn't that exactly what I told you?" She sat upright again and continued reading. "She says, 'He put it away when Mom died because she often said the crows signified death, but he loved it because she made it.'"

Ben stood behind Sam's chair and rested his chin on her head. "So ... Lenore planted the seeds of suspicion in them 'often.' Sam, I don't want you to even hint to them what you suspect regarding their mother's death, not even when they're back. We need to tread carefully here."

She pulled Ben's arms around her. "Give me a little credit, Ben. I'll just ask her to keep in touch when they're back. Do you think I should hook them up with Celeste?"

"I can't see why not."

Every morning before leaving for work, Sam checked Facebook for messages from Fran. Even though their age difference was closer to that of sisters, he teased her for sounding like a meddle-some mother. She didn't mind. She was growing fonder and fonder of Fran and Nick with each exchange. All she cared about now was their welfare. She worried about the inevitable emotional crises they would face on their return. *I want to be there for them. Whatever may or may not have happened to their mother will have to wait.*

When Celeste connected with the kids, they met at the China Town Belleville Restaurant on rue du Buisson Saint-Louis. Fran posted a video of the three of them chatting and enjoying the summer sunshine at an outdoor table with a red-chequered table-cloth. When the food arrived, she pouted. "Oh, we gotta go. Can hardly wait to meet you." She made the heart sign between her and her brother. "Bye."

Sam blinked away her tears. "Celeste looks good, doesn't she?"

"She does."

"And Nick and Fran seem like nice kids, don't they?"

"They do." Ben massaged her shoulders. The lump in her throat kept her silent as she scrolled back and read their account of the last two weeks spent hiking in Fontainebleau Forest and biking from Orléans to Tours, Angers, and Le Croisic.

Ben's gentle hands were doing their magic.

Fran described their nostalgic ride up in the Eiffel Tower. From childhood, their mother had told them about the last day of their honeymoon in Paris, watching the sunset and the City of Lights from the observation deck.

Sam leaned back into Ben's arms, imagining what it must have been like up there. "Mmm. That feels so good, hon. Don't stop." *He knows I'm in a funk. What a gem.*

He kissed the top of her head as if he'd read her mind.

Every day, Fran had uploaded exquisite photos of castles and scenery throughout the Loire Valley. It had been ten glorious days on their own, with no guide.

Sam read aloud the caption under the photos. "'Nicholas and me looking out at the exact same view of Paris Mom remembered from their honeymoon twenty-two years ago.'"

She sighed. "They look so happy. I worry about them crashing emotionally when they get home."

Ben kissed Sam on the top of her head. "Of course you do. That's what my wife does; she worries about everybody else. Come on, let's get to work. We'll be seeing them in a couple of days."

NICHOLAS

$\mathcal{S}$am received frequent emoji-laden texts from Fran as they progressed from Toronto to Calgary to Vancouver. Their arrival time at YVR was 2:45, and could they 'please, please' come to their condo that afternoon?

She replied with an emphatic 'Of course!' Sam and Ben left the apartment at three and stopped at a deli en route. Sam assumed, since they had been away the entire summer, their fridge was bare. She loaded the cart with a frozen shepherd's pie, a roast chicken, two large salads, a tray of fruit, two loaves of bread, butter, juice, and milk.

"They probably have coffee and tea, right?"

"I would think so, Sam. For crying out loud, what are you doing?"

"Their fridge will be empty, and they'll be jet-lagged."

Sam checked out, and Ben loaded the car. For a few blocks, neither spoke.

Sam stroked Nick's quilt folded on her lap. "I thought I'd be more upset giving this up, but I'm not."

Ben took his eyes off the road for a second. "You know, I've never really liked it. In fact, *loathed* isn't too strong a word. I'm rather glad you're doing this."

"I know, Ben." She reached over and squeezed his shoulder. "Depending on what Fran's quilt looks like—if it has the Roman numeral *two* and the rest of the poem on the back—we will have to weigh our suspicions against their curiosity."

"It's agreed, then. Neither of us will bring it up unless there is no mistaking their mother's intentions. Right?"

"Or if they voice any suspicions themselves."

Ben nodded. "That would be a game-changer."

"Ya think?" Sam pointed. "There, that's the building." She looked up at the tiered balcony facade. "That must be some trust fund."

§

Sam resisted the urge to give Nick a big hug when he greeted them at the door. Fran's pictures on Facebook and video didn't do him justice. Yes, he was tall, and his blonde curls gave him a boyish charm. But his smile? It exuded the warmth and caring of an old friend. "Hi, welcome home" was all she could say.

"Thank you. Come in, come in. We haven't even unpacked yet. Fran had to rush over to the university and deal with some crisis in her schedule, but she should be along shortly. Have a seat. What's all this?"

Ben handed Nick the shopping bags. "Sam figured you'd come straight from the airport."

"Good call. Thanks."

He held out his hand and smiled at Sam. It took her a moment to realize he wanted the receipt. She tried to protest, but he insisted.

He glanced at the amount and opened his wallet, fishing his Canadian bills from behind the French francs. "Can I offer you coffee or a glass of wine? We brought back two bottles from the Bordeaux region."

"The wine would be nice." Sam laid his quilt on the coffee table and sat. Nick hardly took his eyes off it as he poured the wine.

He handed her and Ben their glasses and sat opposite. "Salut." After savouring the wine for a moment, he set his glass aside. He stared at his quilt through glassy eyes and rubbed his thighs.

"Mmm. The wine is lovely." Sam perched on the edge of the sofa as Nick unfolded it. His restrained emotions told her this had been the right thing to do.

"You know, I never thought I'd see this again. When I went back that first Christmas, I planned to bring back some boxes that I had stored in their garage, but they were gone. I confronted Lise. She said she'd taken some of them to the thrift store. I was livid. What with Dad being sick and all, I lost it. Henri and I got into a fight. That was enough for me. When Dad died in June, I had to get Fran out of there, so we stayed in my grandparents' house—well, my house now—until Fran wrote her exams. God, that was tough on her, but she did it. We came right over here after her grad, and we planned our trip."

Just then the intercom buzzed, and Fran was home. She burst into the room. "Sam! Ben! You're here!" She hugged them like long-lost friends. "It feels like we've known you forever. Nick here was over the moon when we read your friend request message." She looked at her brother and the quilt. "And there it is." She knelt on the carpet beside the coffee table and smoothed the quilt with her hands. "I felt so guilty. She must have gotten rid of Nicky's stuff while I was at school."

With his finger, Nick traced a crow quilted into the border. "So how did you come by this, Sam?"

Taking Ben's hand for reassurance, she explained how they had received it from Ben's mother for Christmas last year and because of the label, they thought they should try to find 'Nicky.' "At that point, we couldn't tell if Nicky was a boy or a girl, or how old you were. It wasn't until we read your father's obituary online that we realized. We're so sorry."

Fran squeezed her brother's hand. "It's okay. Dad had been unwell for a long time—since before Mom died. We weren't that close because he was away a lot, and then when he was sick, he was not very nice to Mom. We resented the way he treated her. And then he marries this witch before Mom's body is barely cold? I hated her, and I hated him."

"Come here. Sit by me." Nick put his arm around her shoulders.

He turned to Sam and Ben, frowning. "You know, that woman moved Dad out of our home immediately after Mom died. It was my grandparents' home, where Mom had grown up, and she left it to me. But Dad insisted Fran and I move in with them. I think Lise thought, since I'd inherited the house, I'd stay in the house and keep Fran with me, but that just wasn't possible since we were both still minors. That was two years of hell, living there. I spent most of my time in the library or crashing at a friend's." He gave his sister a quick shoulder hug and grinned at her. "Fran had her own room, but I had to bunk in with those three guys. Henri and I locked horns a lot. Ten months later, Dad and the witch got married."

When he mentioned Henri's name, Sam saw the stony look on Fran's face. After a few moments of awkward silence, she managed a weak smile. Nick hadn't even noticed. *What was that about?*

Fran piped up. "Sam, you want to see my quilt too, don't you?"

"Yes, I've been dying to see it all summer—ever since Sherry Baker told us about its existence." She watched Fran dash down the hall. *I guess it was nothing.*

In seconds she was back, spreading her quilt on top of her brother's. Sam could see why Lenore had called it *The Sewing Room*. The fabric print had images of every conceivable item you could find in a typical sewing room: pins, needles, thread, sewing machines, tiny quilts draped under the needle. The quilting meandered around every item, including a blue hat. A floating black border had the same three quilted crows that bordered Nicky's. She spotted another blue hat hiding in plain view among the notions. And another one. Sam's eyes locked onto Ben's. Should she turn the quilt over? *No. Not yet.* "Oh look, there's a blue hat. You can hardly see it."

Fran leaned over the quilt, running her hands over it. "Yeah, I noticed one once, but I thought nothing of it. Oh, there's another one, and another one. That's funny. Why would she do that? What does it mean?"

Nick refilled his glass and gulped half of it. "I know exactly what it means."

§

Sam projected only attentive curiosity while struggling to restrain a volley of questions as Nick told his story.

The tension showed in his flexing jaw. "I remember it well. It was Mom and Dad's tenth anniversary, and we were on holiday in Puerto Vallarta. I was nine; Fran was seven. At the pool, there were kids everywhere; it was great. I got to horsing around with these three boys, and we started diving—doing crazy stuff.

"I waved at Mom and Dad when they came down, and then I dove into the pool. By the time I surfaced, Dad was holding his head and leaving. It didn't seem significant, but late that night, I woke up hearing Dad's angry voice in the other room.

"Mom said that she had seen a woman in a big blue sunhat with three boys ushered out to the beach from the pool area. She thought the woman looked familiar but couldn't be sure from the back.

"She asked Dad if he had seen her. He really got his back up, then. He told her to quit with the twenty questions, and something like, 'I'm not ogling other women at the pool,' and 'there were lots of hats there, you expect me to remember a blue one?'

"Mom backed off, but said this person reminded her of a woman she'd seen on their honeymoon, and at our church a couple of times. The hats were different, but they were always blue.

"Anyway, Dad said, 'You are paranoid, my sweet.' He always called her that. He went down to the bar, and that was the end of it. It seemed like an overreaction to me, but Mom had said earlier he had a headache, so I thought no more of it at the time."

Fran looked mesmerized by her brother's story. "How come you never told me any of this?"

"What for? It was between Mom and Dad. It had nothing to do

with us. Anyway, the woman and her kids never showed up at the pool again, and I forgot all about it until Lise started coming around after Mom died. Then I realized she was the woman in the blue hat and those boys were Henri, Antoine, and Bertrand."

Sam rubbed the goosebumps on her arms. Nick had lifted the veil.

§

It was time to share what Sherry had said about their mother's suspicions and how she had cleverly hidden these clues in their quilts—clues that might only be interpreted if her fears came to fruition.

Sam cleared her throat. "Nick, Fran? There are some things we need to share with you about your quilts that you might find disturbing. How do you feel about that?"

Nick nodded. "I've always felt there was something there, and if you've found it, I want to know what it is."

"I feel the same. I'd rather know than not know."

"All right, then. I want to point out some unusual things, besides the blue hats, in these quilts that you may not have noticed. They may be important, but I think we need to look at them objectively and discuss them. The symbolism here needs considered inter-pretation."

Sam peeled off Fran's quilt, put it behind her on the sofa, and looked at the two siblings sitting across from her. "Okay?"

Nick nodded, but Fran threw her arms in the air. "What? What's the big mystery?"

Sam waved her hands over the quilt. "What do you see here? It's not just a bunch of birds; they're crows—a flock of crows." She waited for them to grasp the concept.

Nick's face grew pale, his voice a deep whisper. "A murder of crows."

Fran knelt on the carpet and pored over the quilt. "That's right, and we're seeing them through a window."

Nick pulled her back by the shoulders, allowing Sam to continue.

"And you see the quilting in this grey mottled border? These are crows too. There are three distinct crows repeated all around it."

Nick looked up at Ben. "Henri, Tony, and Bert."

"Let's turn the quilt over." Sam and Nick flipped it together. "What do you see?"

Fran got up and stood back. "It's all black and white. It looks like ancient hieroglyphics with a bunch of crosses cutting through them."

"I think that was your mother's intention. This black-and-white striped fabric looks like tiny bars and they make up these crosses and *double crosses* this way and that. And see here at the bottom?"

Nick shook his head. "A blue hat behind prison bars."

Sam took a deep breath. He was beginning to grasp the meaning, and he hadn't even seen the poem yet.

"I want you to examine the stitching here and here."

Fran wrinkled up her nose. "It's writing. I can't read it."

Sam took the poem from her pocket. "I've got it here. Let me read it to you.

"There's the Roman numeral *one* that you see there. Then it says:

> *A sultry crow swept 'cross our view*
> *In veiled blue hat o'er yellow eye.*
> *Each annum as her murder grows*
> *A blue hat glimpsed is fleeting by.*
>
> *Haunting every fledgling's rite,*
> *The blue hat caws in throaty songs.*
> *Flight to warmer climes evades not*
> *The blue hat crows in palms."*

Ben looked askance at Nick. "Nick, I've been skeptical of Sam's interpretation of this, but I have to say that this is everything you've just told us, in poetry."

Sam patted the sofa beside her. "Fran, come and sit beside me. When we read this, we knew we had to find 'Nicky.' We didn't know there would only be two quilts until we saw your dad's obituary."

She looked from one to the other. "Shall we have a look at your quilt again?"

Tears welled up in Fran's eyes. "Okay."

Running her hand over the quilt, Sam pointed out the five blue hats inside the floating border and the one outside it near the bottom. "We don't know its significance yet, but I'm thinking now the five inside the border represent the times your mom thought she'd seen her throughout her marriage—and the one outside might represent the unknown. Look at these crows quilted in the border itself. They are the same three crows that appear on Nicky's. Now, let's turn it over."

This time Nick and Fran flipped the quilt. Before they could examine it as a whole, Fran had her nose within an inch of the stitching. "Here's the Roman numeral *two*, but the writing is impossible to read. It's all black on black."

"Fran, I did a rubbing of Nick's quilt. Can you get some paper and a soft pencil?"

"Yeah." She jumped up and disappeared into her room.

Sam could see Nick was looking at the entire picture, not just the writing. "What are you thinking?"

He traced the crosses with his finger. "The same double crosses as mine. A play on words? And a blue hat. How did we not see this?" He sighed and rolled his eyes.

Sam rocked her head from side to side. "I think she didn't want the symbolism to be obvious; she had no idea who might see them. As it turned out, her suspicions were correct, and Lise has seen both quilts. But how likely was she to examine a gift clearly labelled from your mother? Case in point: she sent yours to the thrift store!"

Fran was back. She laid the paper over the stitching and rubbed the high points with the pencil lead. "It's coming, it's coming."

When she had finished, she read,

Home alone suspicions shadow
Obsession patches stitched in rows.
The blue hat cunning now emboldened
With courage of a murder of crows.

Fever, visions seen in treble,
Blue hats pecking at my vein.
The crow perched on his grieving shoulder
And my tombstone bears my name.

"And then there's the label: 'Remember me, Franny. Love, Mom,' and then 'L. Bennett 2015.'"

Fran sat back on her heels, tears streaming. "Did Mom think Lise was going to kill her to marry Dad?"

Nick dropped his head into his hands. "Something about that relationship between Dad and Lise has been tormenting me ever since Mom's death—even more so since Dad's passing. But, without seeing—really seeing—these quilts, I never would have allowed myself to consider it."

Sam knelt on the floor and hugged Fran. "Your mother went to a lot of effort to hide her suspicions in plain sight, hoping that if you had any inkling of foul play, you might connect the two. If those suspicions were unfounded, then these would just be pretty quilts."

Fran sniffled. "If you hadn't found Nicky's, then, then ... that's all mine would ever have been." She gathered her quilt in her arms.

Ben rested his hand on Nick's shoulder. Sam could see the creeping anxiety building in both of them. She covered her mouth with her hand. *And this is just the beginning.*

Nick stared into space. "Poor Mom."

2008

*A*drian sat in his wingback leather recliner, watching the news at noon. He pointed the remote at the television and turned down the volume. "That's better. What are you saying, my sweet?"

Lise came out of the kitchen, looking chic in her heels and an apron that hugged her figure to great advantage. "I said, I wish you weren't going away for spring break. You'll miss Henri's birthday. *C'est très important pour lui.*"

"You know Lenore wanted a vacation away for our tenth anniversary last June. I promised her and the kids a holiday in Mexico this year."

Lise tapped the toe of her red stiletto. "I know when it was: exactly nine months before Henri's tenth birthday."

Adrian rose and slipped his hands around her waist, pulling her against him—her allure still captivated him. Especially when she was trying to get her way. "There is no way around it. How about I take you and the kids to Vegas for the convention in September, hmm?"

Lise untied her apron and took the clip out of her hair. When the silky strands fell over her eyes, she tossed her head. "Vegas is no place for children. Why don't I join you in Mexico, *mon cher?*" She took his hand and led him into the bedroom.

"Don't be absurd, my sweet." *Damn, this woman can push my buttons.* "There is no way in hell that will happen." He closed the door with his foot.

§

At home on the Island, Adrian sat in his frayed floral recliner, watching the news at noon. Annoyed, he pointed the remote at the television and hit the power button. "That's better. What are you saying, my sweet?"

"I said, what was the name of that resort?"

"Vista de la Isla Santuario. It looks out over an island bird sanctuary."

Holding up her wet hands, Lenore emerged from the kitchen in her T-shirt and jeans in bare feet. She pushed the stubborn curls off her forehead with the back of her hand, as she had done countless times before. *She has no idea how endearing these little habits of hers are. And how I love the predictability of my life with her.* A surge of contentment made him sigh.

Lenore dried her hands and flung the tea towel over her shoulder. "I wonder if they have tours to the island."

"I don't know. We'll see."

"I think Nicky and Franny would enjoy that." Lenore came over and pushed the foot of Adrian's chair down with her toes. The chair popped Adrian upright. She climbed into his lap and nestled in his arms.

Adrian relished moments like these. No longer annoyed, he stroked her thigh. "It's going to be great. Just you, me, and the kids.

Lenore undid two of Adrian's shirt buttons and toyed with his chest hair. "Not exactly the second honeymoon you promised me last year, but you really need a getaway from work."

Adrian slipped his hand under her T-shirt. Lenore arched her back and closed her eyes in response to his caress. As he led her to the bedroom, he thought her choice of words apropos. It wasn't the office from which he needed an escape, but the sword of Damocles that was Lise.

§

On their third day in Mexico, Adrian stood in his robe on their balcony overlooking the pool, the beach, the ocean, and the sanctuary island. He breathed in the warm sea breeze. He hadn't felt so relaxed in years. The office, the clients, and Lise—banished from his thoughts for an entire week. He closed his eyes. *This holiday is exactly what I needed. Life is good.*

His wife slipped her hands around his waist and rested her face on his back. "Be careful the breeze doesn't open your robe, or everyone will see what we've been up to."

Adrian turned and pulled her to him. "I love making love to you, Mrs. Bennett." He kissed her forehead.

Lenore sighed. "We'd better get down there and make sure the kids are putting on sunscreen. Come on. Put on your trunks, Mr. Bennett."

Like two teenagers, they walked holding hands through the hotel lobby and out onto the pool deck. A cacophony of exuberant voices muffled the waves drumming on the beach.

"Let's sit over here." Adrian dropped his towel and book on a lounge.

"Oh? You don't want to sit up front where the kids can see us?"

Adrian stretched out, crossed his legs, and opened his book. "I want the shade, Mrs. Bennett. Besides, they couldn't care less if we're here. Look at them, they're having too much fun." He looked up at the two boys on the diving board and dropped his book.

He clapped his hands over his face. "Oh, damn, my head is splitting. I'm going back to the room to lie down."

Lenore rushed to his side. "Adrian! Raise your arms."

He pushed her away and got up, still holding his head. "Stop that. I'm not having a stroke."

She took him by the arm. "I'm coming with you."

Adrian raised his voice. "No. Stay here. I'll be fine." He walked off, shielding his eyes as if from the glare on the pool.

Just inside the lobby entrance, he looked back, scanning the crowd before approaching the front desk. Panic gripped his throat. "Do you have a Lise Richard registered here?"

"No, *señor.*"

"Are you sure? I thought I saw her at the pool."

"She may have walked up from the beach, *señor.* We can't keep them out."

"I see." Despite the cool breeze flowing through the lobby, sweat dripped from Adrian's nose. "I'm Mr. Bennett, room 604. Do I have any messages?"

"Yes, *señor.*" The clerk handed him a folded piece of paper without making eye contact. "A lady left this for you earlier, with explicit instructions. I was to give it only to you."

Adrian mumbled thank you and headed for the elevator. The occupants had punched 4 and 11; his finger hovered above 6 but then pressed 7. He stared at the note gripped in his hand, trembling with rage. As soon as the doors closed behind him on the seventh floor, he paced the hall while he read.

Mon cher, I am on the beach at Los Condominios. Meet me at the bar tonight at nine.

"That bitch." Adrian crumpled the note and tossed it into the wastebasket in the elevator alcove. He looked at the lights above the doors and took the stairs to six.

§

When Nicky and Franny bounded into the suite, Adrian was nursing a drink in one hand and choking the balcony railing with the other, wishing it was Lise's neck. He released his grip and flung his anger, metaphorically, onto the concrete below. He muttered under his breath. "I'll deal with you later."

Franny ran up behind him and hugged his leg. "Daddy, Daddy,

you won't believe this. We were playing with these kids, and ..."

Nicky talked over her. "I was doing tricks with this guy, Henri. You should have seen us, Dad. He could do flips and everything. He said tomorrow is his birthday. He'll be ten."

Adrian thought he might retch off the balcony when he heard Henri's name.

Lenore poured herself a drink and joined them on the balcony. "How's your head?" She glanced at his glass.

Adrian gave his wife a noncommittal smile and turned to the kids. "So, it sounds like you two had a lot of fun today."

"That's for sure, but those guys won't be back."

"Oh, why not?"

"The pool guy noticed they didn't have wrist bands and kicked them and their mother out." Nicky headed to the bathroom with his clothes, and Fran dashed into their bedroom.

"Don't let Nicky, like, come in here."

"Just lock the door, Franny." Lenore rubbed her husband's back. "You know, I saw them escort that woman and her kids out today. She was quite indignant. My god, you're tense, dear. You could use a massage."

"You can give me one tonight." Adrian could not remember being wound this tight since Franny's baptism. *I must deflect the focus from Lise and the boys.* Knowing he was going to disappoint her, he wrapped his arms around her waist and lifted her above his head. She squealed with delight as she slid down his chest to a tender kiss.

With a wistful sigh, Lenore pulled away to pick up the kids' wet towels and hang them on the back of the balcony chairs. She slipped her bathing suit down from under her cover-up and flipped it to him with her toe ... and a sly smile. "The kids have had a lot of sun today. Probably an early night?"

Adrian feigned objection with an exaggerated groan. "You're incorrigible, my sweet. I'll have to see if I'm up for it."

§

Even knowing Lise was not staying at their hotel, Adrian was nervous at supper. Tiny birds flitted between the tables on the terrace, giving him the opportunity to check out the other diners. By the time the kids had finished their key lime pie, he was a wreck. He didn't have to fake a residual headache.

Back at the suite, Nicky flopped onto the sofa and grabbed the television remote. "Boy, was that pie ever good. I'm so full I could bust." He patted his protruding stomach.

Franny flopped down beside her brother. "Did you see the server light that guy's bananas on fire? That was, like, outstanding."

"You two get into your pj's before you watch TV."

Adrian mixed them each a drink and settled on the balcony, where a cool breeze off the ocean made the evening perfect. "Come and sit, my sweet."

She sat beside him, leaned back, closed her eyes, and sighed. "Honey, this is the best anniversary gift you could have given me. Thank you."

"Better than Paris?"

They watched the sun sink into the sea, throwing crimson clouds across the sky.

Lenore nodded. "Yes. That's the same perfect sunset but now we have the children I could only wish for in Paris."

As nine approached, Adrian looked for a reason to leave. "My headache won't budge. I think I'll go for a walk on the beach."

"Oh. I was hoping we could go down to the bar and dance for a while once the kids are in bed."

"Not tonight, my sweet." He kissed her.

"I could come with you?"

"No, I think I'd just like to be alone and clear my head." Seeing the disappointment in Lenore's eyes, he kissed her. He left blaming the sting of conscience he felt on Lise.

§

From the pool deck, Adrian looked up at the balcony and waved to his wife. He strolled out to the beach, knowing Lenore would watch him until he was out of sight. As he walked, he gathered the anger he had flung over the railing: pebbles, then stones, and then rocks, heaving them into the surf with all his strength.

How had he come to live this lie? In the beginning it was fear. Fear that Lenore would find out about Paris. Of course, it was blackmail, but he had grown to love Henri, and the flames of Lise's passion consumed him. As each precious son was born, he forgave her, and settled into the routine of this comfortable double life. The risk of betrayal had faded, or so he thought.

I had it all. But now, she is getting more and more demanding, threatening I must leave Lenore. She's waited long enough. The boys are asking unanswerable questions. She's been faithful to me. She deserves a husband. They deserve a father.

Adrian kicked up a cloud of sand that blew back into his face and teeth. He sputtered. He could feel the noose tightening.

The bar of Los Condominios spilled onto the beach. As he approached, there was Lise, sitting barefoot at a table in a lace cover-up, nursing a drink. She waved to him. "I thought you might not have got my message, *mon cher.*"

"Don't you *mon cher* me. Have you paid for this drink?"

"Yes, why?"

Adrian grabbed her by the elbow and lifted her out of the chair. "Come with me."

"But Adrian, I can't leave. The children know where I am."

"That's just the point." He hustled her through the lobby and into a taxi parked in the porte cochère.

"*¿A donde, señor?*"

"*El Solar, por favor.*"

Adrian sat back and ignored Lise for the duration. Once settled at a table on the beach, he ordered drinks.

"*Mon cher,* I don't understand. Why did we come here?"

Adrian slammed his fist on the table and made her jump. He clenched his teeth. "I don't know if you are just the stupidest bitch in the world, or if you are deliberately trying to wreck my marriage."

Lise's eyes narrowed to slits. "You can be certain I am not stupid."

"So you sent the boys down to our pool hoping they would see me and call me Daddy?"

"No, that was just a lucky coincidence. I only went to leave you my note."

"And how did you plan on explaining my presence if Henri had seen me today?"

"I would leave that up to you, Daddy."

"What is it you want, Lise? You want me to leave Lenore and the kids and marry you?" He felt his blood pressure rising.

"Yes. It's time. I carried your first-born. He has a right to have you as a father."

"You're giving me an ultimatum?" His words escaped his clenched teeth. "He has that now."

"I need you for my husband, to give our children your name. It is not enough to live as a family, one week here, one week there. It is not enough. Henri already questions where you go. I need my self-respect."

"Lise, you lost your self-respect the first time I asked you what you wanted. You got a home, you got a job, Henri got a father. I grew to love you, Lise."

"There is such a fine line between love and hate, *mon cher*."

"Yes, and you've crossed it. If I lose my family, I will not marry you. And no matter what the courts award you, the children will never see me again. You gain nothing by hurting me. That's not what you want, is it?"

Lise wept. "No, *mon cher*."

How could he deny those oh-so-French lips quivering with tiny sobs? Adrian's tone softened. "I have given you everything I could possibly give you without hurting my family. I can give you no more."

"*Oui*, I'm sorry. It's just that … Henri is getting suspicious about your work. Why it keeps you away so much."

Adrian dreaded the day the boys would learn the truth. He was not so naïve to think they need never know. "You must always claim ignorance, Lise. It is too easy to get our stories crossed."

Pouting, Lise wiped her tears. "Maybe you're a fisherman?"

Adrian snorted and dropped his head, almost smacking his forehead on the table. "That sounds fishy to me."

Their anger and resentment dissolved into laughter, which normally would have landed them in bed. Adrian's last defences crumbled when Lise drew her bare foot up under his pant leg and the mariachis drew closer.

"Oh, Lise. What am I going to do with you? I don't love hating you, and I don't hate loving you."

LISE

*B*en and Sam were kibitzing in the kitchen after supper when her phone rang. She held Ben at arm's length. "Behave yourself." She checked the call display before answering. "Hi, Nick. What's up?" She put her phone on speaker and held it between them.

"I can't help thinking Mom must have been frightened when she made our quilts. I can't focus. Classes start in a few days, and with this being Fran's first year, I was wondering if we could get together again this Saturday?"

Ben said, "Of course we can. We'll be there in the morning. Have the coffee on."

"Great. We can do some brainstorming. I want to do something, but what? So many questions are hanging over me, like daggers."

Sam hung up. This was what she had feared most. "Ben, we have to discuss how we are going to approach this. If we want to help these kids move forward, we need a plan for Saturday—one sensitive to their vulnerability."

"I can't judge their apprehension by mine. I have my answers; they don't. How much do they want to know? Was their mother murdered or just paranoid? It seems she had plenty of reason to be paranoid. But murdered? What if it's neither? It could still be accidental. I don't know."

Sam sighed. "Nick is realizing his mother might have been afraid for a long time. He hasn't even articulated his questions yet. That's why he's reaching out. Let's just find out what kind of resolution he's looking for."

"This won't be easy. They both suspect Lise's involvement somehow. But ... we must be very careful not to accuse anyone of murder, even hypothetically; and don't even mention getting the police involved."

Sam scowled. "Do you really think I would suggest they walk into a police station with two quilts claiming Lise murdered their mother?"

§

Nick was enjoying the view and his coffee on the balcony when Sam and Ben arrived. The anxiety he felt regarding the quilts had decreased significantly just knowing they were coming. He had purposely planned for Fran to be out. She was still his little sister, and he didn't want her to hear the speculation he expected to voice today.

He waved as they approached the entrance. "Come on up. As requested, I've got a fresh pot of coffee brewing."

A few minutes later, Ben handed Nick two paper bags. "Lunch. I hope you like Thai?"

"Superb. Why don't we take our coffee out on the deck?" Nick hoped the fresh air might energize him for what he expected to be a tough conversation. He needed to organize his thoughts as if this were a case study.

Sam made it easy for him by getting straight to the point. "Nick, I guess Ben and I need to know two things: What is your greatest concern? And what can we do to help you resolve it and put your mind at ease?"

He took a deep breath and looked out over English Bay. Her

questions had clarified his thinking. He laid his hands flat on the table in front of him. "My biggest fear is that my mother was not paranoid—that they murdered her and I'm letting that bitch get away with it. I need your help, but I don't want Fran to know about this until we have some clear answers."

Ben held his hand up and paused before he spoke. "Sam, tell him. I need a refill." He went inside with his cup.

Sam nodded. "It's a bit of a long story, Nick. Bear with me. What you need to know about Ben and me is that our experiences over the last few years made us acutely suspicious when we saw your quilt ... and it made us cautious. Ben lost his sister to murder. I was falsely accused of another. And Ben, well, he still suffers from PTSD because of his last brush with death. We have learned more than we ever wanted to about murder.

"Consequently, when Ben's mother gave us your quilt for Christmas, the murder of crows was an instant trigger for him. He did not want me getting involved but gradually came to realize how vulnerable you and Fran might be. And so here we are, committed to helping you through this. Whatever it is."

Nick leaned on the railing, not able to make eye contact with Sam. He felt a chill creep up his back. When he turned, there was Ben, standing in the doorway. "I'm sorry, Ben. I had no idea. Maybe we should drop this."

Ben rubbed his face with his hand. "I don't think you should. We want to help you, but it's not without potential risk."

"Well. After what you've just told me, are you sure?"

Sam and Ben nodded vigorously. "We needed you to make the first move."

Nick couldn't speak for a moment as he struggled to keep his emotions in check. "All right, then. Here's my first move." He leaned in, wanting them to hear every word. "I've been recalling things Lise has said, things I've been trying to suppress. She boasted about a family connection that goes back to WWII. Apparently, our great-grandfather, Henri, pledged everlasting love to her grandmother, Antoinette Bertrand. It was bizarre. They were just kids."

Ben noted the names on his phone. "I've done some genealogical research with my mother. I could look into this. What do you know about your family's history?"

"Fran had a family tree project at school—maybe sixth grade—and Dad said we only go back to great-grandfather Henri Bennett. And that's not even his name. He was an orphan that Private Adrian Bennett had taken under his wing in Paris in 1943. When this private returned to Canada after the war, he brought Henri with him and adopted him. We know nothing about this soldier except that he became our great-great-grandfather."

"That's useful, Nick. I can do something with that information through his military record." He turned to Sam. "We'll need Celeste's help with this."

A sickening feeling made Nick's face turn pale. "It can't be." He looked from Ben to Sam and back again, shaking his head. "Shit. It's always bothered me that the names have carried on through the generations. Even Fran's middle name is Adrianna. Then there are the Henris. Coincidence? You don't suppose Henri and Antoinette were siblings, do you? I mean, what if the soldier and Antoinette's *mother* were the item, not the kids, and he was supposed to bring that family over later on?"

Sam raised her eyebrows. "I guess it's a possibility."

Nick covered his face with his hands. "Adrian Bennett did marry my great-grandmother soon after he returned with Henri." He paused. "We can't be blood relatives with Lise. We just can't. Ben, do the research. I need to know."

FAMILY TIES

*E*ver since Ben had asked him to come over, Nick had been on edge. He nodded to the doorman as he entered the elevator. Ben didn't sound like he had bad news, but still that uneasy feeling crept up his collar. *I'd better not be related to Lise.* The thought of it made him feel physically ill. He shook his head as the doors opened on the tenth floor. Before he could summon the courage to knock, Ben opened his door.

"Perfect timing, Nick. Come on in. Thanks for coming here. I need to monitor the office today, so we have to work around that." Ben spun around at the computer. "Have a seat. I want to show you a little family tree I've built for you."

Nick hesitated, his mind racing. *Here we go, the moment of truth.* He looked up at Ben. "Do I want to see this?"

"You do. On your side of the family, it starts with Private Adrian Bennett, who, in 1945, brought your twelve-year-old great-grandfather, Henri, to Canada and adopted him. This much you already know. His surname is unknown. He's listed as an orphan, his family assumed to be dead. That was a common assumption with young orphans after the war."

"You're telling me Lise's ancestors were *not* his family?"

"No, absolutely not. When young Henri was twenty-two, he had a son named Lucien, your grandfather. And when Lucien was twenty-one, your father Adrian was born."

Nick buzzed his lips as he exhaled. "Well, that was relatively painless. Were there other siblings on this tree that could mean cousins?"

"Yes, and no. Henri had a daughter, Anna, but she went back to France after a nostalgic visit, and the trail disappears. That's the trouble with girls. They lose their name. We could search further, but she obviously didn't keep in touch."

"Did you dig up anything on Lise Richard?"

"Yes. Because we could prove that you are the legitimate stepson of Lise Adrianne Richard, we could access genealogical records in France. Notice her middle name—Adrianne?"

"That's amazing, Ben. What does all of this prove, though?"

"Hold on; you'll see. Lise's father was Adrian Claude Richard, and his mother, Antionette Lise Bertrand, was the daughter of Annalise Bertrand."

"Ha. The love of my eleven-year-old great-grandfather's life really was Lise's ten-year-old grandmother, Antionette? Incredible. And he was an orphan. Not her brother." Nick slumped in his chair with a loud huff. "I've not got a death wish for a cousin. That's a relief."

"Right. But, just to amplify all the longing in the air back then, I wouldn't doubt her mother, Annalise Bertrand, was in love with the soldier, Adrian Bennett. After all, they were the adults in the room. Judging from the continuity of names, a desire to find Adrian and Henri's descendants has burned in the hearts of every generation since, which culminated in Lise tracking down your father at around the time of his marriage to your mother."

"So they hooked up in Paris on my parents' honeymoon, and nine months later—bingo—Henri Adrian Richard was born."

"That's about the size if it, Nick. No wonder she immigrated to Canada."

Ben's pat on the shoulder did little to comfort him. He didn't know who he hated more at this moment, Lise or his father. But how do you get angry with a dead man? He sat, staring at the screen, the full spectrum of emotions battling in his brain. "What a spineless coward."

§

When Sam opened the door, Ben and Nick were staring at the monitor in silence. She hurried into the kitchen with an armload of groceries. "I'm glad you're still here, Nick. What do you think of your family tree?"

"Ben did an amazing job. The good news is, we're not related to Lise by blood, but the rest of it is pretty disturbing." He got up and put his jacket on, extending his hand to Ben. "Thank you for doing this."

"You're welcome. We'll keep in touch?"

Nick nodded.

Sam stopped unloading the groceries and pulled a file from her bag. "Oh, you're leaving?"

Nick rolled his eyes. "Fran's waiting at home. We both have a lot of coordinating to do before classes start on Monday. Was there something else?"

"Ten minutes; just give me ten minutes. I'll just go over these documents quickly, but you can take them with you. This will connect some dots, but it's not exactly pleasant news."

Nick sat on the sofa beside her and peered at the folder in her lap.

"I was at the Land Titles Office today, and there have been some interesting transactions in both your father's name and Lise Richard's." She handed the documents to him one at a time. "He purchased this house in Vancouver in 1999 when Lise had one child. He sold that in 2001 and bought this larger house when Lise had two children. You can see, this one he put in joint names. In 2015—the year your mom died—they sold that house, and she bought the one she has now on the Island." Sam handed him the empty folder. "I'm sorry."

Nick leaned back, stuffing the documents back into the folder. "So ... when he was away for a week out of almost every month, that's where he was? Playing happy family with her in Vancouver? Not at his warehouse. Not at a conference. Not in meetings with clients or suppliers ... for twenty fucking years." Nick's expression changed from anger to rage. "That bastard."

2013

*L*enore stood at the kitchen sink, gazing out over the Salish Sea. The Coho ferry from Port Angeles was heading for the Victoria harbour. Sailboats dotted the horizon, enjoying favourable winds. A dragon kite soared in the clear blue sky, swirling and lunging as only a dragon could.

She held her hand in the running water, her mind wandering through a distant memory of herself and Adrian standing across the road, admiring this house. She had been pregnant with Nick and, they could not have been happier. Her cell phone buzzed, startling her. She grabbed a tea towel before fishing it out of her pocket.

"Hello?" It was their manager at the Island warehouse.

"Hi, Harry. Did Adrian get back from Vancouver?"

"Yeah. Lenore. Listen, I think Adrian's had a stroke. They've taken him to Victoria General. You'd better get over there."

Panic constricted her throat. Her hands trembled as she texted her neighbour, Denise.

Lenore: *Adrian's in VGH, can you keep the kids after school?*
Denise: *Yes!!*
Lenore: *TY.*

To Nicky, she texted: *U2 go to Denise's after school.*

She dropped her phone in her purse and ran out the door. Although Nicky was a responsible fourteen-year-old, Franny was a precocious twelve and could wrap her brother around her little finger. Lenore didn't need the added worry of the kids being home alone for god knows how long.

Knowing the traffic would be heavy on the highway, she took Craigflower to Helmcken, arriving in the Emergency parking lot in twenty minutes. Her anxiety level rose each time her phone buzzed.

As she rushed towards the emergency entrance, she called her son. "Nicky, your dad is in the hospital. I just got here, so I know nothing yet. You will take Franny to Denise's after school?"

"Okay, Mom. For sure text me?"

"I will, dear. As soon as I know something."

She ran up to the intake window in Emergency. "My husband, Adrian Bennett, just came in by ambulance?"

"Yes, Mrs. Bennett. They are working on him now. Please have a seat. I'll let them know you are here."

"Can't I see him?"

"Not right now, Mrs. Bennett. Someone will come and get you."

She phoned Denise. "Hi. I don't know anything. I'm stuck in the ER waiting room." She cupped her hand over her other ear to block out the PA.

"Hang tight, Lenore. As long as they know you're there. Do Nicky and Franny know to come here after school?"

"Yes. I promised I would text Nicky as soon as I knew anything. Denise, I'm so scared. This can't be happening. I've told him so many times, he burns the candle at both ends. The business is doing well. Slow down. But no. He has to have his finger in every pie. He spends far too much time on the mainland. Surely to god, that warehouse can run itself. And he's constantly checking in on our clients. I swear he counts every damn box shipped between this warehouse and that one."

"Calm down, Lenore. I know he's like that. But doesn't he always say that business is booming because he works that hard?"

"Well, there should come a point when he can admit it's running like clockwork. That it's time to delegate. I think that's the doctor. I'll call you back."

The doctor approached her. "Mrs. Bennett?"

"Yes?"

"Your husband is stable. You can see him now."

Lenore followed the doctor through. Murmuring voices and that distinct clean-hospital smell filled her senses.

"Your husband has had a major stroke. It occurred on the left side of his brain; therefore, his right side is impaired."

Adrian lay under a blanket, with tubes running everywhere. They had cut off his clothes. She walked around to the other side of the bed and held his left hand. She thought she felt a weak squeeze.

"Can he speak?"

"He may have speech and language problems."

She raised his hand to her cheek. "What else can we expect, Doctor?"

"He may have sustained some memory loss, and even with extensive rehab, he may never regain full physical functionality."

"Doctor, we own a distribution company. He manages all the operations at both warehouses—Victoria and Vancouver."

"Is there anyone who can step into his shoes?"

Without taking her eyes off her husband's face, she spoke directly to him. "We built the company together. In the early years, our babies came to the office with us, didn't they, honey?" There was no response in her hand. Her voice faltered. "We hired a nanny, but at some point, you just have to say, 'I'd rather be there when my children come home from school.' So we hired an office manager to take over from me." She tried to blink away her tears. "Adrian and I still make all the major decisions together, and I still write up all the reports."

"Mrs. Bennett, I think you will need to take over the reins for the time being. Your husband will require home care and rehab daily."

"For how long?"

"For as long as it takes. There is no way of knowing. We are taking him up to the stroke unit now. If you take the elevator up to the eighth floor, we'll see you there."

Lenore was numb. She found the elevator, pressed eight, and phoned Denise on the way up.

"I'm going to stay here for a while. I don't know how long they will let me stay. Can you keep ..."

"Lenore, the kids can stay here as long as need be. They're right here. Nicky wants to talk to you."

"Hi, Mom. How's Dad?"

"He's had a stroke, Nicky. I will stay with him for a while. You and Franny will sleep at Denise's tonight, okay?"

"Okay. Franny wants to talk to you."

"Hi, Mommy. Is Daddy going to die?"

"No, honey. He's just very sick. You're going to stay with Denise tonight."

"Okay. Give Daddy a hug and a kiss from me."

Lenore tried hard to hold back her tears. "Okay, dear. Put Denise back on." She snuffled. "Denise, I'm going to call my folks and ask them to drive down tomorrow. I'll probably be spending a lot of time here and at the office for a while."

"Oh."

"I'm afraid so. Don't let on to the kids."

"Understood."

"Thanks for doing this, Denise. Bye." The elevator doors opened, and she stepped into the silent hall to wait.

Somewhere between five minutes later and forever, the larger elevator doors opened, a bed emerged and turned toward her. As it passed, Adrian stared blankly at the ceiling. She choked back her tears and followed.

§

Lise did not hear from Adrian between visits. She had neither his phone number nor his email address. She didn't like it, but it had to be that way. From the warehouse, she could call him at the office without arousing suspicion.

The day after his stroke, the word came from head office. Five o'clock couldn't come soon enough. As usual, her boys were already at home when she arrived.

"Henri, I have to go over to the Island. Your father is ill, and I need you to watch Antoine and Bertrand until I get back tomorrow, *d'accord?*"

"What's wrong with Dad?"

"I think it's a stroke. You'll be fine, *oui?*"

"Yeah, text me when you get there."

Lise caught the last flight to the Island. Even at that, she had the pilot call ahead for a taxi to be waiting at the terminal. Charging up the ramp, she caught her heel in a crack. It broke off when she wrenched the shoe free, but it hardly broke her stride. She ran on her toes to the waiting cab.

"The general hospital, *s'il vous plaît.*"

At the admissions desk, she asked for Adrian's room number.

"Are you a member of the family?"

"I'm the mother of his three sons."

"He's on the eighth floor in the stroke unit."

"*Merci.*"

In the elevator, Lise produced a compact mirror, applied her lipstick, and straightened her hair. She scowled at her heelless shoe. "*Sacré bleu.*"

She was about to ask for his room number at the nursing station when she spotted Lenore coming out of a room down the hall. She stepped around a corner and held her breath.

"Good night, Mrs. Bennett."

"Good night, Carole. I'll see you in the morning."

"All right."

Lise heard the elevator doors close and stepped out. The nurse had left the station, so she hurried past, to the room his wife had just left. Adrian lay still, surrounded by hissing and beeping machines. She rushed to his side and took his hand. His eyes opened a little and then a lot. He mumbled and trembled.

"Shush, *mon cher*. I am here." She kissed his limp hand.

Adrian became more and more agitated until one machine did, too. Within seconds, a nurse flew into the room to Adrian's bedside, checking monitors and shutting off the alarm. "You cannot be here. Who are you?"

Lise dropped Adrian's heavy hand and backed away from his side. "I am an employee of Monsieur Bennett."

"Well, you must leave."

"But ..."

"*Now.*"

Lise tore from the room in tears, limping on her broken heel, all sense of decorum abandoned. The beeping machines, the tubes, and Adrian's twisted face would be the last images she had of that night, and they would haunt her for months.

§

Lenore hated leaving her parents with Adrian, not the other way around. Despite health issues of their own, there had been no hesitation when she had called. Before he was even discharged from hospital, they had settled in the spare room. Home care came and went, but for the rest of the day, they were at his mercy. Lenore stopped and took a deep breath before she opened the office door. Except for quarterly reports and year end, she hadn't set foot in the office in a managerial role for ten years.

"Good morning, Andrea."

"Good morning, Mrs. Bennett. I'm so sorry about Mr. Bennett."

"Thank you, Andrea. I'll be managing things until Mr. Bennett gets back on his feet." She hung her coat on the back of his office door. "If you would give me a rundown of all orders pending, and any other unfinished business sitting on his desk and yours, that will get me up to speed and save me a lot of time."

"Yes, Mrs. Bennett."

"Oh, and Andrea, I'd like a list of the clients he saw on his last trip to Vancouver. I want to follow up with them."

"Yes, Mrs. Bennett."

"Thank you, Andrea."

Lenore spent the day reviewing everything Andrea put in front of her. By noon, she felt up to speed and relaxed a little. She called the three clients Adrian had visited and discovered that his follow-up visits were very much appreciated. Any problems with their orders they had had over the years he had always 'nipped in the bud.' They were distressed to hear of his stroke and hoped his recovery would be swift. The last call was to Mr. Delmar.

"Thank you so much for your kind words, Mr. Delmar. I will give Adrian your regards. I won't be able to make these trips to Vancouver as he has—because of the children and managing his care, you understand. But if you find the slightest issue with your deliveries, I want you to call me immediately. I assure you, I will 'nip it in the bud,' as you say."

At four thirty, Lenore asked Andrea to have the warehouse employees come to the office at the end of their shift. When they arrived, she invited them into Adrian's office.

"Harry. I haven't had the chance to thank you for calling me when Mr. Bennett had his stroke, so thank you.

"As you all know by now, Mr. Bennett has a long road to recovery ahead of him. Most of you may not know that I am familiar with the day-to-day operations of the company he and I started so many years ago. Therefore, I don't anticipate any changes going forward. I cannot leave the children and Adrian to visit the warehouse in Vancouver. Therefore I was thinking—Harry? You are familiar with their operation, are you not?"

"Yes, Lenore—I mean Mrs. Bennett."

"I'd like you to pay them a visit and combine that with a video chat with me. What do you think?"

"I can do that. Ralph here can step into my shoes anytime."

"Good. So it's business as usual. Does anyone have questions?"

"I do, Mrs. Bennett."

"Yes, Jean."

Her voice quivered. "It's not a question, actually. I just want you to give our very best wishes to Mr. Bennett. We're all rooting for his swift recovery."

Lenore made a stoic effort to smile. "Why thank you, Jean. Thank you all."

§

As the weeks grew into months, Lenore could see that she needed to hire a caregiver. She could not expect her parents to stay in Victoria for the children and drive Adrian to his daily therapy sessions indefinitely. She could see they missed their home and friends. They never complained, but she knew.

But, one after the other, the people she hired found their job as childminder/nursemaid/taxi driver/cook 'not a good fit' or 'not what they'd expected' or, more pointedly, 'more than they were willing to put up with.' Lenore came home from the office early and sat with Adrian after the latest departure. She took his withered hand.

"Honey, what happened this time?"

Adrian's voice was improving, but his temper wasn't. He stamped his cane on the floor. He still slurred his words together. "Don't like being treated ... like a ... child. I told her to ... fuck off."

Lenore sighed. "I'll bet you did. What you need is another wife. You didn't want to go to rehab?"

Adrian's eyes grew wide, and he stammered. "Yes, yes, yes ... I mean no. I'm sick of it ... sick of it. As good as ... as good as I'll get."

"I know, Adrian. But the point is, it keeps you active. Otherwise, you aren't working on your speech and memory."

When he spoke, Adrian couldn't control his spitting. "My speech fine ... so is memory."

"Well, who were the last three clients you saw in Vancouver?"

"There was ... um, that fellow on Kingsway ... and, what's his name, and that other guy over on ..."

"Adrian, we don't have a client on Kingsway. You aren't remembering much about the business."

"Dammit … maybe if you took me … to the office with you … it would … all come back."

"I took you there last week, Adrian. You didn't remember Andrea's name."

Adrian chucked his cane across the room. It landed at Nicky's feet as he came through the door.

"Is Dad okay?"

"Why … you asking … her for? I'm sitting … right here."

"Sorry, Dad. Mom, can I go over to Brent's?"

Lenore looked at the floor, hiding her face from her son. "Yes, Nicky. Just be home in time for supper."

Franny stuck her head in for a quick "I'm home" and dashed off to her room.

Lenore's gaze followed her daughter and back to her bitter, frustrated husband. *They are not coping with his outbursts. He's chased off the last caregiver. I am out of options.*

§

Lenore sat at her desk, reviewing the month-end payroll, when her phone rang. "Lenore Bennett."

"Hello, Mrs. Bennett. This is Don Brandt of Consolidated Distributors. We missed Adrian at the convention. I'm sorry to hear about his stroke. I thought I'd get in touch to see how he is getting on."

"Thank you for your concern. Adrian has regained much of his speech and walks with a cane, but he still has some right-side paralysis, and his memory is spotty."

"I'm sorry to hear that. Are you managing the company now?"

"Yes. I helped Adrian build the company, so there isn't much I don't know about it."

"So, you are managing all right?"

"Well, there are some issues juggling home care for Adrian, the children, and the business, but I'm muddling through."

"That must be frustrating. Listen, if you find it becomes too much for you, Mrs. Bennett, call me. We wouldn't be averse to expanding on the Island."

"I must confess, the prospect of selling has crossed my mind. I'll keep your number handy."

"That's just fine, Mrs. Bennett. And please give Adrian my very best wishes."

"Thank you, Mr. Brandt. I will. Goodbye."

Andrea poked her head in. "Mrs. Bennett, you'd better go down to the floor. Harry says Mr. Bennett is down there and he's fallen."

"What? How did he get here?"

"Harry said a taxi dropped him off."

Lenore grabbed her jacket and purse on her way out.

Near the loading dock, Adrian lay on the floor, yelling at Harry, who was hovering over him.

"What's happened?"

"He tripped over the forklift and fell, Mrs. B."

"Adrian, are you hurt?"

"How the hell should I know? This arm is useless. Who parked this, this, whatever this is, here anyway? It's a safety hazard."

Lenore and Harry exchanged worried glances and helped him to his feet. "The forklift is always parked here, dear. Let's get you home."

"I want to see if the delivery for Gleason is ready."

"Adrian, Gleason hasn't been a client of ours for four years. Now let's go home." Lenore looked at Harry and shook her head. The sadness she saw in his face mirrored her own.

§

Two months later, Lenore and Andrea stood on either side of Adrian as he struggled to sign his name with his left hand. Exasperated, he threw the pen across the dining room.

"It's fine, Adrian. Andrea will witness our signatures."

Andrea quickly signed beside Adrian's squiggle and Lenore's neat hand. "I'll have these couriered to the lawyer as soon as I get back to the office." She held the file against her chest with both arms. "So, that's it, then. It will be sad to see the Bennett Distributors sign come down. And thank you so much for that reference. It's been a pleasure working for you, Mr. and Mrs. B. Do you know when the new manager arrives?"

"Mr. Brandt is bringing him over on Monday. I'm sure it will be a smooth transition. After all, he will have you as an assistant."

"Do you think they'll keep me on?"

"They've promised no major changes for a year, and even then, it doesn't mean they will downsize staff."

"Well, I hope not. Will you be coming down to the office to say goodbye?"

"Oh yes, Andrea. I still have to clear out this house." She waved her arm at the boxes stacked everywhere. "The moving trucks will be here on Monday."

"You're moving back into your childhood home."

"Yes. Mom and Dad don't want to downsize, so it will be best for everyone if I can look out for them."

As soon as Andrea left, Lenore knelt by Adrian's knee and looked up into the saddest eyes she'd ever seen this side of the mirror.

"I could use a cuddle. Do you think I could climb on your lap?"

Adrian's face brightened with a half-smile. He held out his left arm. Lenore climbed into his lap, pulled his right hand around her waist, and nestled her face against his chest.

"Now, we'll have all the time in the world for this."

§

Months after their move up-island, Lenore came home from the doctor's office and walked right past the living room without saying a word to Adrian or her parents. In their en suite bathroom, she closed the door, turned on the shower, sat on the toilet, and cried.

Adrian had suffered a stroke. She'd sold their company—a company they'd built together, from scratch. She'd sold their beautiful home in Victoria and moved in with her parents. True, they had no worries financially. But … today she could add diabetes to her list of miseries.

She heard Adrian's shuffling footsteps, a rap on the door, and his slurred words. "My sweet. All right?"

She yanked on the toilet paper too hard. It popped off the spool and rolled across the floor. "That figures," she whimpered. "I'll be out in a second." She shut off the shower and splashed cold water on her face.

When she came out, Adrian was sitting on the bed. She tried to smile. "Well, it's official. I'm diabetic, and I have to go on insulin right away."

Adrian droned in his unsympathetic monotone. "You be fine. They have groups for that."

"Thanks a lot. You're a fine one to talk. Of course 'they have groups for that.'" She scratched air quotes at him. "Just like the stroke support groups *you* won't go to."

§

Adrian sat at the kitchen table with documents spread out in front of him while Lenore scrubbed the flowers off the tired old linoleum.

"I just don't know, my sweet. Will we have enough to live on?" Adrian's voice was improving. He felt confident using complete sentences now.

"Adrian, if we live to be two hundred, we couldn't spend half of the money we now have. Look at these investments. With half of that and your disability pension, we could live very comfortably and even go on vacations. Think of it this way—we'll only be putting my half into the irrevocable trust for Nicholas and Frances's education and a kick-start to life on their own. Why should they have to wait until we die?"

He wondered how Lise would manage if he died. He missed his boys. When she had shown up at Dallas Road, he nearly had another stroke. Luckily the caregiver, if she could be called that, was out. Lise had been laid off, and the dummy company 'LR Transfer' was no longer receiving monthly payments for 'storage.' So she'd had to sell the house and move to the Island to make ends meet. She railed against him for abandoning her and his boys. It was a travesty!

He couldn't hen-scratch the documents fast enough. He had to get Lise out of there before the caregiver or, god forbid, Lenore came home. *Yes, yes, okay, have someone 'witness' my signature later, just get out of here.* When Lenore got home that night, they were so concerned about his agitated state they almost called an ambulance. He'd had one hell of a time convincing them he was just stressed from getting to the bathroom on his own. He blamed the good-for-nothing caregiver for leaving him alone.

Since then, it had been a constant worry that Lise would phone the house or appear on the doorstep. But he missed his boys.

He sighed and pulled his wife onto his knee with his good arm. "So I will be supporting you on my half, have I got that right?"

Lenore put her arms around his neck and kissed him. "Yup. I'll be a kept woman."

He smiled his lopsided smile. "Where do I sign?"

§

Lise slipped each wineglass between the cardboard dividers of the liquor box and folded the flaps. "Put this box in the dining room pile."

Henri slid off the counter. "I don't see why we have to move. All my friends are here."

"You know very well we can't afford to stay in this house since I've lost my job. The houses are cheaper on the Island, so we will have some money left to tide us over until I find another job."

"Why did you get fired, anyway?"

"They did not fire me, Henri. I was laid off when the company sold."

"You always said you had job security because you knew the owner."

"Yes, well, he's not the owner anymore." Lise put up her hair in a topknot.

"Why couldn't Dad help us out? He's not so sick that he can't write a check."

"Why? Why? *Pourquoi?* Constantly, Henri, you are giving me a headache. Make yourself useful and bring the boxes down from your room. You boys will have to sleep on the mattresses tonight. I want to be ready when the truck arrives tomorrow morning. Hurry. *Vite. Vite.*"

Lise didn't know how much longer she could keep up the pretense. Henri was fourteen, and in eighteen months would have his driver's licence and be capable of visiting his father on his own.

After his stroke, transfers from Adrian had dried up. Luckily, the equity from this house was more than enough for a down payment on a small place in Nanaimo. She had to make do with the difference until she could find a job on the Island. The new owners had given her an excellent reference considering her record with the company, so finding one would not be a problem. They were very sympathetic when she gave her notice. An invalid relative on the Island needed a live-in caregiver, so she couldn't possibly transfer to the Victoria warehouse.

She emptied the contents of her desk drawer into a box and had almost closed the flaps when she noticed the file that had been at the bottom of the drawer was now on top. Pouring herself a glass of wine, she settled on the sofa with the file. There was Henri's birth certificate, with Adrian Bennett's name beside hers. "*Mon cher*, why would you never sign this?" She drank far too quickly and sputtered. Beneath the birth certificate was a life insurance policy she had taken out on Adrian. He would never know he had paid the premiums all those years. She suddenly downed the last of her wine. "*Sacré bleu.* Now I must pay the premiums myself."

THE HEIST

$\mathcal{S}$am and Ben were canoodling in the kitchen when his phone chirped. She squirmed out of his arms as he juggled his phone.

"It's Nick." Ben tapped speaker. "Yeah, Nick. What's up?"

"I've been thinking"—there was a long pause—"about all those years my father kept up this elaborate hoax, and it's really messing with my head. What is a family anyway, if it isn't your parents and your siblings?"

Sam leaned on the counter beside Ben. "Nick, when you were growing up, did you feel like you were a happy family whether he was there or not?"

"I didn't think about it. We were happy. Well, probably Mom wasn't, but she didn't show it. We missed him when he was 'on the road.' But he always phoned. I just can't get my head around those three guys being my half-brothers. You know?"

Sam shrugged at Ben. "You had no suspicions? When you, Fran, and your dad moved in with them, didn't they treat him like he was their father?"

"In hindsight, sure. But, when they would call him Dad, I just thought they were being presumptuous or goading Fran and me.

And it worked. It felt like they were horning in on my territory. And it was their house."

Sam pressed him. "Did they seem to love him?"

"Well, Bert, yes, but that didn't seem abnormal for a kid his age. The other two didn't adjust well to having Fran and me move in. Henri and I clashed a lot, and neither of them had patience or respect for Dad. He always seemed to be overcompensating. Like a stepdad trying to fit in."

"And he never told you they were your half-brothers?"

"Nope. Well, Lise would make wild gestures about us being one big family now. I always thought Dad married her ten months after Mom died because he wanted a caregiver for himself and a 'mother' for us. Now I see it for what it was. Dad wouldn't divorce Mom for all those years but now, with her diabetes, Lise could see the possibilities. And that's why I want to retrieve our family albums. I want to look at our family in light of what we now know to be true. I think it might be quite revealing. I know they're stored in the garage."

Ben shook his head. "That's not the best idea. You don't want to tangle with Henri."

Sam waved her arms as if to stop a train. She couldn't have agreed more.

"I don't intend to. I have a key. I'll wait until they're all out, get the boxes out of the garage, and be out of there in two minutes."

"When are you planning on doing this?"

"Tomorrow. It's Sunday. She drags them to church. It should be simple enough."

"And if you aren't certain the house is empty? What then?"

"I'll speak to the police. I have a right to retrieve my belongings from what used to be my home, such as it was."

Sam put her hand over the phone and whispered to Ben. "What if there is some unexpected confrontation?" Just remembering Henri's voice made her shiver.

Ben gritted his teeth and nodded. "Nick, we're not comfortable with you doing this on your own. I'm coming with you."

"That's not necessary, Ben. They won't even know that I've been and gone."

"It's not up for negotiation, Nick. I'll pick you up at six."

The call ended, and Sam peppered Ben with what-ifs. "Shouldn't we talk to the RCMP?"

"No. That's up to Nick. I'll be there to make sure there is no confrontation."

"*We'll* be there, you mean."

§

Nick left a note for his sister before tiptoeing out the door. The click was imperceptible. If Fran woke up, she would beg to come, and that was out of the question. As he made his way outside, he reproached himself for misleading Ben and Sam. This might not be the walk in the park he had led them to believe. He checked the time on his phone. They would be pulling up any minute. The first ferry had left Tsawwassen, but they would make the 7:45.

And there they were. "Good morning." He had one foot in the car when he paused. "Wait a minute. I've got the door key, but I should take the garage door opener from my car." Within minutes he was back from the underground parkade. "Sorry about that."

All during the crossing, Nick had to reassure Ben he would not take any chances. Sam was on his case too. Should she stay in the car and keep watch or come with and help?

They were making him nervous. "Okay, you guys. Two minutes, that's all I need."

Sam persisted. "What is your plan, Nick?"

"I will block my number and phone the house. Lise still has a land line—can you believe it? If there's no answer, I will ring the doorbell. Simple."

"And if someone answers the phone?"

"I'll hang up, and we'll leave."

Ben wouldn't let up. "And if someone comes to the door?"

Nick held his hands up in surrender. "I'll ask for the damn albums! Geez, Ben."

"And?"

Nick tried to hide his impatience. "And walk away from a confrontation and go the legal route. I know what a confrontation could do to my future as a lawyer. Satisfied?"

Sam got in his face. "Don't be flippant, Nick. Ben is right. Remember, this guy has threatened me more than once."

"You're right. I'm sorry. If it's all clear, I'll open the garage door or the side door, grab the box, and get out. Okay. There's the house on the left, with the red front door."

Ben parked and nodded to Nick in the rear-view mirror.

Nick made the call. No answer. "Okay, here goes nothing."

Ben scowled in the rear-view mirror. "Wait. What are they driving?"

"Lise had a … what was it? A red Nissan, I think. Just honk twice if you see any red car." Nick jogged across and onto the front step. He knocked hard on the front door and listened. Nothing. He triggered the garage door, and it opened. *Perfect.*

Heavy boxes crushed lighter ones, leaning in uneven stacks. The whole thing could collapse. So much for not leaving any sign of being there. He checked the labels for something he recognized. There it was: *photo albums.* It was second from the bottom. He groaned. This would take some work, but considering Lise's penchant for purging his family's treasures, they had probably been safest there on the bottom. After taking down the most precarious boxes, he lifted it out, knocking the lid off the box on the bottom. It contained a jumble of files for Bennett Distributors. Nick flipped the lids off the other unlabeled boxes and found the same thing, including miscellaneous office supplies. He signalled for Ben to come help.

Ben trotted across the street into the garage. "I thought you said one box?"

"I did, but these three are Bennett Distributors records. We have to take them."

"Are you sure they are yours to take?"

"Well, they sure as hell don't belong to Lise! Come on. Grab those two."

Nick had just lowered the garage door when Sam leaned on the horn twice. "Shit. Run." They were across the street in a second and threw the boxes in the open hatch. Nick jumped into the back and Ben into the driver's seat. He peeled away before Lise swung into the driveway. An enraged Henri was out of the car and running in their direction.

Nick's heart was pounding. He looked back at Henri standing in the street with his fist in the air. "Whew. That was close."

The whites of Sam's eyes flashed at him. "That was too close. What happened to the plan?"

Nick leaned forward between the front seats. "I'm sorry, but I found boxes of company documents. I couldn't leave them with Lise." He could actually smell Ben's sweat. "I'm sorry."

Nick stopped muttering his apologies when Ben snapped his hand up like a crossing guard. "How the hell did I let this stupid kid talk me into this hare-brained scheme?"

MEMORIES

*O*ver his shoulder, Nick could see Henri put his phone to his ear. "Get ready, he's phoning."

Despite the warning, Sam jumped when her phone rang. Ben shook his head, and she hit *dismiss*. His scowl in the rear-view mirror kept Nick quiet. Their acrimony was evident in their silence.

Sam's phone buzzed like an angry wasp every few minutes, putting them all on edge. Nick was relieved when she shut it off. On the ferry, conversation was awkward. Ben excused himself and went out on deck.

"Is he all right, Sam? I feel awful having put you through this."

"He'll be all right. He'll meditate, watching the water slip by. Don't worry."

Sam bought a book, and Nick spent the rest of the crossing thinking about the fury that awaited him at home.

As Ben pulled up in front of the condo, Nick ventured to speak. "I hope you'll come up and go through these with me. Besides, I think I'll need you to defend me when we get up there."

Ben laughed with a hint of reproof. "Sure. We'll come up, but you deserve whatever Fran hurls at you."

Sam whispered as she climbed out of the car. "We're not so innocent."

As predicted, Fran was furious.

"You should have taken me. I wanted to get things out of that house too, you know. Like Mom's things in the attic. I stashed them there so that witch wouldn't throw them out. You have to take me back."

"There wasn't time to get into the attic, Fran. I barely got out of there before they came home. They saw me, and they've been calling Sam ever since. If you'd been up in the attic, we would have been in an awful mess. Would you really want Henri standing at the bottom of the ladder? Huh?"

"Fine. I'll just phone her and ask for my stuff. She doesn't know anything about the quilts, or what we suspect. We lived with her for three years, not knowing. She won't want to act suspiciously. She'll be her regular, obnoxious self. You'll see who has the better strategy."

Nick was first in line with his objections. "After I've just poked the hornet's nest? Get real."

Sam jumped in. "That's foolhardy. You can't go alone. I'll go with you."

Ben swept all argument off the table with a stroke of his hands. "No, you won't, Sam. Everyone, take a breath. There will be a lot of resistance because of this stunt, so everybody just settle down for now. End of discussion." He scooped up his coffee cup, then grasped it in both hands.

Nick flinched, watching Ben's hands shake and the coffee splash from his cup.

§

Nick set the family albums on the coffee table, arranging them in numerical order. His hand rested on the photo of his parents on the cover of the first album. *Will I find a sense of family in these?*

Fran dropped her indignation and plunked herself on the sofa with Sam. "Come and sit between us, Nick."

He winked at Ben and opened the first album on his lap; it was their parents' wedding and honeymoon. When the girls leaned in front of him for a closer look, he waved over their heads at Ben, who stifled a smirk. *Maybe I'll be forgiven for this escapade after all?*

The formal wedding photo of their mom and dad filled the first page. Fran touched the photo and rested her head on his shoulder.

"Mom was so beautiful," she said. When he came to the end of the honeymoon photos, when she squeezed his arm. "Look at that, Nick. Didn't I tell you? That is the exact same photo we took from the Eiffel Tower! How many times did Mom describe that day to us?"

One glance at the smug look on his father's face and Nick knew he'd already hooked up with Lise. Now he could see through the facade. *Poor Mom.*

The last picture in the album was of them posing on the grand staircase in the lobby. Mom looked happy. Off to the side was a trolley loaded with luggage. Fran jabbed at the photo. "That's Lise's hat box! I'd recognize it anywhere. It's up in the attic where I put Mom's stuff. Son of a bitch. That pompous witch. She was there! On their damn honeymoon!"

Nick shifted uneasily. He dreaded having to tell her the whole sordid truth.

He opened the next album and pointed at their pregnant mother standing in front of their new home on Dallas Road. "That was just two months before I was born."

That brought Fran back from her tirade.

He leafed through many birthdays and Christmases where their father was present. He was either in the picture or taking it. Nick pointed out the year they both got the chicken pox for Christmas. "I remember feeling so cheated because we recovered just in time to go back to school."

Then there were the Christmases they spent at Grandma and Grandpa Allen's. Nick looked forward to those trips even though their dad couldn't be there. It was like an adventure. Now Nick realized those were the times when Adrian was 'away on a business trip.' *I wonder what Henri, Tony and Bert were told when it was our turn to have him home for Christmas?*

Envelopes containing their baptism certificates were tucked in the back of the baby books. And much to his relief, the photos taken at the font didn't show the blue hat that Nick was sure would be there in the congregation.

There were a few selfies Adrian had taken in more recent years while he was away on business trips. Mostly they were in hotel rooms, but occasionally, it would be in the warehouse or at a client's place of business. There was one page Nick tried to flip past. Adrian had taken the selfie in a hotel room; it looked like a convention somewhere. A hatbox sat open on a chair behind him—with the infamous blue hat inside.

Fran almost ripped the page out. "That's the blue hat in Lise's hatbox. She's definitely the blue hat crow on our quilts." She stabbed the photo with her index finger like an ice pick. "Mom put these albums together. She knew! This has to be why she made those quilts."

Nick could feel Ben and Sam looking at him. He exhaled through pursed lips. *It's time Fran knew.*

2014

*L*enore heard Adrian dragging his leg upstairs. She sighed. *Better put this away.* She stashed her quilt blocks in her basket and folded up the sewing machine. "Who was that on the phone?"

"Sherry. Checking to see if you're going to Jonanco today." Adrian stood puffing at the top of the stairs. "So, are you? Gonna leave me with him all day?"

Lenore rolled her eyes. "It's only for a few hours." She had always quilted at home, but Sherry was insisting Jonanco was more than a bunch of ladies quilting—it was also a social gathering. "Trust me," she had said, "you'll enjoy it. Get out of the house. Away from ... you know who." Lenore knew who, but it was difficult.

"I'll be back before the kids get home from school."

Adrian grumbled as she lugged her sewing gear downstairs and set them at the door. Her dad sat in his chair, staring out the window. She sighed. "I won't be gone long, Dad."

Sherry was sitting across the room, and waved when Lenore entered. "There you are. Set up at this table beside me. Everybody, this is my friend Lenore Bennett."

A chorus of voices greeted her, some even emanating from the layout room and the kitchen. Everyone showed genuine interest in her quilt project. It had been a long time … Actually, she couldn't remember ever feeling so welcome and comfortable. The stress rolled off her shoulders so suddenly, it left her feeling emotional. *Pull yourself together, girl.*

But her mind kept wandering back to Adrian and her dad—together—alone. Lenore found herself unsewing a seam for the second time. Sherry's machine hummed beside her. She leaned back and sighed. "I don't know what to do about Dad. He's really gone downhill since Mom died."

Sherry lifted her foot off the pedal. "It's only been four months, Lenore. Give him a chance to grieve."

"But he's not eating. He's wasting away. I'm afraid he wants to die too."

"Well, you know, sometimes when a couple has been together as long as they have, they do tend to go within months of each other. I think you should prepare yourself for that possibility."

"Sherry, I am on edge all the time, what with Mom dying and all the bloody paperwork, and now Dad's despondency." She sighed again. "And Adrian is getting worse. He's pissed off because he can't drive, but he has nowhere to go anyway. He has no hobbies. It's no wonder he's miserable. Even the kids are walking on eggshells around him. It's like it was when he first came home from the hospital—only now he can talk."

Sherry laughed. "Why don't you call the Lodge? Maybe one of the old gang will take your dad out for a coffee."

"That is an excellent idea. So, what do you suggest I do with the sourpuss?"

§

A slight sense of guilt irritated Adrian as Lenore pulled into the driveway after her father's funeral. He resented Lenore holding the door open for him as he manoeuvred his bad leg over the threshold. It might take him a minute, but he could open a damn door.

She carried two bouquets of flowers into the living room, placing one on the mantel beside her father's clock and the other in the window. "I think I'll take the rest over to the hospital and just keep the cards. It was a nice service, don't you think?"

Adrian took off his coat with his good hand and hung it on a hook behind the door. "As nice as a funeral can be, I guess." He sank into his recently dead father-in-law's easy chair. "Bloody nosy neighbours have inundated us with those damn casseroles. Why don't you thaw one? I'm hungry."

"Why do you say things like that, Adrian? People are just being kind. I swear, you need to go to the doctor and get some antidepressants. You're just so unhappy."

"I'm not depressed! Goddammit!" *If she only knew.*

"Well, then get them for *me*! And shush. Quit yelling."

"Why? There's no one here to hear me. They're both dead." He instantly regretted barking at her. He hadn't seen Lise and the boys since before the stroke, except for signing those papers for her, and it was killing him.

Lenore teared up. "Adrian, you can be so cruel." She went into the kitchen and put a frozen casserole in the oven. "I'm going to bed. You can eat when the timer goes off."

His conscience hung over him like an anvil on a thread. It had been a tough week. The day Lenore's father's obituary had appeared in the paper, Lise called. He thought his heart was going to leap out of his chest. Her new job wasn't paying anywhere near what he had been paying her for far less work. Could he see his way clear to send her some money? But how could he? Lenore would know. But what about that account he had on Lougheed? He didn't remember that. Couldn't he do a wire transfer? He had forgotten how.

She said, "I'll come over and help you. Phone me when Lenore is out." He dropped the phone in his scramble to write down her number. Even that had made him panicky. Memorizing it had been out of the question.

The day after the funeral, Lenore had a multitude of errands to run after she dropped the kids at school. As soon as her car was out of sight, Adrian phoned Lise, and within minutes she was at the door. He dragged her in by the arm. "We have nosy neighbours. Couldn't you have parked down the street?"

No, she could not, and anyway, this would only take a minute. She had brought the account number with her and she helped him change his password. "We must delete this email from your trash." He had forgotten about that.

There was a substantial balance in the account, which surprised him and set Lise off on a tangent. Why hadn't he been giving her a better allowance when he had this much money just lying around? He had forgotten why.

His confusion and assumed guilt allowed Lise to set up automatic monthly transfers before Adrian realized what she was up to. He grew angry. "Now leave before someone sees your car."

"*Mon cher*, you must come and see the children. Can you remember the address? You can come by taxi when Lenore is out one day."

She stroked his cheek and kissed him. Adrian withered at her touch, although he had missed that. But he missed the boys more. He would find a way.

Adrian grew agitated on Lenore's regular quilting day when she made no move to leave. She said she really didn't want to go, but he hounded her, making her so miserable that she left in a huff, leaving him with the kids. That scenario had not played out exactly as planned, but he called a cab anyway and left Nicky in charge. He was fifteen. He could take care of Franny for a few hours.

Adrian retrieved the crumpled scrap of paper with Lise's address from the bottom of his pocket. He read it to the cabbie, but closed his fist around it when he waved to Nicky in the window.

He struggled with his cane as he climbed out of the cab and scowled as he navigated the overgrown path to Lise's front door. The house was a far cry from their home in Vancouver. The postage-stamp yard disappointed him too. The boys need more space than this.

The two hours he had with them were less than ideal. They sat like twitching lumps, staring at him, asking him a lot of aggravating questions. Henri mouthed to be excused by his mother, then left muttering platitudes. Even Bertrand wouldn't give him a hug. *Shit.*

§

Adrian was very late. The children were already in bed, and Lenore had waited supper for him. He could see her standing in the window with her hands on her hips when the taxi pulled up to the house.

"Here we go. I will never hear the end of this. Keep the change, Bob."

"Thank you. Have a good night, sir."

Adrian stumped up the front steps. He was getting better at opening the door and getting inside. He hung up his coat and turned to face his steaming wife. "I know what you're going to say. Where have you been? Why didn't you call? Yada, yada."

"Well?"

"Well, what? I'm not an invalid, and I'm not a child. I don't ask you where you've been when you go out with your friends. Get a grip, Lenore." Although he hadn't, Adrian said, "I've already eaten. I'm going to bed." He scowled and thumped up the stairs. *Shit. I've just cheated myself out of supper.*

He shut the bedroom door with more force than he intended. He knew his wife could see right through the feigned indignation reflected in the bedroom mirror. Angry and frustrated, he ripped through two buttonholes and flung the offending shirt to the floor. He had to find some other way to see Lise and the boys.

§

A week went by, and Adrian made sure he behaved himself. But

Lenore was still giving him the cold shoulder. She announced at breakfast she was off to Victoria—no explanation. She reassured Nicky and Franny she would be back before suppertime.

Her steely eyes bore into his. "You can handle that, can't you?"

Her words stung. No sooner than the kids left for school and Lenore pulled out of the driveway, he called Lise. "She's gone to Victoria for the day. Come over. For Chrissake, park down the street this time."

He watched for her at the window. There she was, glancing around as she hurried along the sidewalk and up the driveway. Adrian scowled. She would be less conspicuous if she just wouldn't wear that damn blue hat. She slipped through the open door without hesitation.

"This is craziness, *mon cher*. She grabbed him by the arm. You must come back home with me."

Adrian leaned on his cane and yanked his arm out of her grasp. "You've got two good legs and a car."

She stood, tapping her foot. "I will not make love to you in your marriage bed."

The argument ended with a long-sustained honk from the driveway. Adrian flung open the door to see Lenore slumped over the wheel. "Lise! For god's sake, help her!"

Lise hesitated before rushing down the steps. When she opened the car door, Lenore slumped off the horn, almost falling out. "Adrian! *Vite!* Where is her insulin? She needs insulin."

Wide-eyed, Adrian headed for the bathroom cabinet where Lenore kept her insulin supply. Never had he swung that dead leg with as much fury. He stumbled down the steps and landed on his bad arm a few feet from Lise.

"*Mon Dieu!* Are you all right?"

"Yes! Here! He tossed her the kit. Inject her belly."

"*Oui, oui.* Get up. You must call an ambulance."

Adrian used the car bumper to pull himself to his knee and then hoist himself upright with his good arm. He stooped to retrieve his cane and dragged his bum leg up the steps. *Where is my phone?* He spotted it by the window—where he had left it after calling Lise as his poor wife drove away. *Shit.*

"Hello, I need an ambulance. My wife is diabetic." Adrian gave them the address. Unable to hold the phone and his cane, he hung up. He stomped down the steps with more care this time.

"I must go, *mon cher.*" Lise ran to her car just as a neighbour pulled up.

"Adrian. What's the trouble?"

"It's Lenore. Her diabetes. I called for an ambulance. Help me hold her up. She's falling out."

Adrian regretted every harsh word he had ever uttered to her. "Stay with me, my sweet. I hear the ambulance."

The paramedics had her out of the car and on the stretcher in seconds. As they checked her blood, they questioned Adrian. No, she hadn't eaten breakfast before she left. But she may have eaten on the road. No, she didn't have her kit with her. He told them how she had arrived and collapsed on the horn, that she had asked for insulin, and that he had administered it. The lie slipped from his lips as easily as all the others.

Lenore's insulin kit lay open on the ground. A paramedic picked up the empty syringe and examined it. "You say she asked for insulin, not glucagon?"

Adrian's mind swirled. Had she? It was Lise who had heard her. It was Lise who had given her the shot.

"No. I'm sure that's what she said: 'insulin.'"

Lenore was lifted into the ambulance with an IV drip in place. The doors closed and within seconds the ambulance was out of sight, leaving only the screaming siren to chastise him.

§

A week later, Lenore stood at the door, checking her purse. This time she did not intend to leave the house without her diabetic kit. "I'm off to Jonanco with two hundred dollars' worth of fabric." She grinned at Adrian.

He had been so remorseful after that day in the driveway, he was a different man. He was back to the loving husband he had been before his stroke. However skeptical she was regarding the reasons for his change in disposition, she thought, *if I nearly had to die to get him back, it was worth it.* She pulled into the parking lot and just sat for a moment. *But is it an act?* She couldn't shake the fuzzy image of a blue hat hovering over her that day. She glared at herself in the rear-view mirror. "How many times have you seen that blue hat since Paris?"

When she laid out her fabrics for cutting, the other quilters came around one by one to admire her choices and ask what pattern she would use.

"This one will be Attic Windows. I'm making it for my son's birthday." That was as much as she intended to tell them. They joked about the murder of crows in the window, but she let it go without comment. As she drew the three crow templates for the border quilting, she hoped Sherry would remember watching her.

Her friend looked up from her whirring machine. "How are you feeling? That was quite the close call."

"I'm fine now. I don't know what I was thinking that morning. I was miffed with Adrian and left without breakfast, thinking I'd stop at Timmy's in Duncan. But I forgot my kit again, and I felt dizzy and nauseated, so I decided I'd better go back and get it. I just made it and collapsed in the driveway. I guess I terrified him, because he has been very attentive since I got out of the hospital."

"Well, it's about time. You've put up with a lot of crap from that man since his stroke. He has been the quintessential ingrate if you ask me."

"It seems I didn't have to ask." The two friends smirked at each other.

Adrian told her he had administered the insulin, but she didn't remember it that way. Her suspicions deepened when her neighbour greeted her on the street. He had asked if the lady in the blue hat that helped Adrian that day was just a passerby, since she had left in such a hurry before the ambulance arrived. Lenore agreed she must have been, but that blue hat crept through her memory.

Steam rose from the ironing board as she pressed a small scrap of fabric with hats of many colours. The one that interested her most was the blue one, the word *Mademoiselle* emblazoned across it. She thought of Paris.

THE ATTIC

*I*t was Saturday afternoon, and Fran sat alone at the
condo. She wanted it that way. She did not need Nick
hovering over her, miming his objections while she was massaging
Lise's ego. She needed to get into that attic. It would be hard enough
being conciliatory toward the woman who may have killed her
mother. She stared at her phone for a moment before picking it up.

"Hello, Lise?"

"Oh, it's you."

"I'm coming over to the Island tomorrow to visit some friends,
and I wondered if I could come around and get some of my stuff out
of the attic."

"You have nothing up there."

"Well, I put some of Mom's things up there for safekeeping. You
wouldn't throw out my mother's things, would you?" Fran smirked
to herself, remembering Nick's quilt.

Lise sputtered. "Of course not. I would not do such a thing."

Fran visualized Lise crossing herself and looking at the ceiling as
she spoke.

Her backpedalling continued. "I had Henri put some boxes up
there when you moved in, but I've never gone up there myself." Lise

hesitated. "I suppose you'd better come after one, when Henri is not here. You two are like oil and water."

"Thank you, Lise. I appreciate this." The words were hard to say, but Fran was glad she didn't have to ask about Henri. She had no wish to encounter him. After Nick moved into the condo, Henri had begun sneaking into her room. She shuddered to think he had known all along she was his half-sister. Her stomach lurched.

"I'll see you after one tomorrow, then." Her lunch was coming up.

§

The next morning, the snowy peaks above Vancouver glowed like gold in the morning sun. Ben and Sam arrived at the condo at six. Only this time, Nick was not sneaking out on her. Fran climbed into the back seat ahead of her brother.

"Hey, morning. Will we make the first sailing?"

She saw Ben wink in the rear-view mirror. "No problem, it's only booked at seventy percent right now."

Over breakfast aboard the ferry, Fran recounted how she had manoeuvred Lise. "I just hope I can keep myself from gouging her eyes out."

Sam turned to her. "I'm coming in with you. As long as Henri isn't there, Ben and Nick will stay in the car. They'll only be a split second from the door."

"Do I need you to keep my temper in check?"

"It's not you we're worried about—it's her. And what about Tony and Bert?"

"Those two? I wasn't afraid of them." The words weren't out of her mouth before she wanted them back. She crinkled up her face.

Sam looked at Ben and back at her. "You were afraid of Henri?"

She laughed. How was she going to bluff her way out of this? "Lise said we were like oil and water. He's gone to Tofino today, anyway." One look at Sam's face, and she knew she hadn't heard the end of this. She wanted to bang her head against the window.

§

Sitting in the car in front of Lise's house, Fran was losing her nerve. She was glad Ben and Sam had insisted on coming, otherwise she would have turned chicken right now.

Sam got out first and opened the back door. "Come on. Henri's truck is not here. You've already arranged this, so let's do it."

Nick turned and reached over to squeeze her shoulder. "You know I'd do this, except Lise would go ballistic."

"It's okay. I know what I'm looking for; you don't." Fran took a deep breath and hopped out of the car.

At the door, Sam held her hand. When it opened, there stood Lise, hands on her hips, scowling like the twentieth person in line for a two-stall bathroom.

Fran shrugged. "Well, here I am."

Lise leered over her head. "That brother of yours must stay off my property."

"He will, Lise. Now can we come in?"

"Who's this?"

"She's my friend, Sam. I brought her to hold the ladder."

"You'd better get it out of the garage, then."

They found it hanging on the back wall and manoeuvred it through the doorways and down the hall without chipping any paint. Fran climbed up and pushed the hole cover aside. Once crouched in the attic, she called to Sam.

"Stick your head up here."

Sam climbed halfway until her head and shoulders were in the attic. "What's up?"

Fran could hear Lise circling below, sputtering how this was the last time she would ever allow her in this house. Mouthing the words 'your phone,' she pointed at the infamous hatbox and her empty pockets.

Sam checked for Lise hovering around her ankles and slipped her phone out of her pocket. She leaned into the attic, blocking the view from below, turned on the flash, and handed it to Fran.

Lise was sounding increasingly agitated. "What are you doing up there?"

Fran dragged a box around on the floor. "Just getting these boxes out of the eaves." She unzipped the hatbox, took a photo, and zipped it closed again. Beside it was a box labelled *Papiers*. She cringed as she opened the flaps for fear Lise would hear. Digging through the mix of file folders and envelopes, she spotted one marked *Henri*. It contained photos, report cards, certificates, and his birth certificate. There it was in black and white: *Pere: Adrian Bennett*—just as Ben had discovered when building their family tree. She hesitated.

Sam cleared her throat and mouthed, 'Let's go.' In a louder voice she said, "Push that one over here, and I'll take it down."

Fran photographed the birth certificate, put it back in the folder, and closed the flaps. She raised her voice for Lise's benefit. "Take this one. Be careful." As she pushed one of her mother's boxes toward Sam, the sound of Henri's voice from below sent a chill through her. Despite the shivers, clammy sweat trickled down her back and made her shirt cling.

§

Ben was standing in the open doorway when Henri turned into the driveway at high speed, stopping within inches of the garage door. The look on his face when he slammed his truck door told Ben this was not good.

Henri bounded up the front steps. "Who the hell are you?"

"I'm Jeannette Bowers's husband."

"What are you doing here?" Henri appeared a little unnerved.

"My wife is helping Fran retrieve some of her belongings. We're not looking for any trouble, Henri. We'll be out of here in just a few minutes." Ben towered over Henri, causing him to duck through the doorway and confront his mother.

"She just wanted her mother's things, *mon fils*. Go. Sit in the living room until they're gone." She backed him into the living room, where he slouched on a chair with one leg over the arm.

Ben moved to the foot of the ladder without taking his eyes off Henri. His contempt for these two grew as he watched Lise tapping the toe of her black stiletto. Sam stood halfway up with her head and shoulders in the attic. "Get down here, Sam."

When he saw Nick approaching the open door, Ben motioned for him to stay out and keep quiet, but he entered anyway, glaring at Lise in the living room archway and Henri laughing behind her. The situation was volatile enough as it was, but Nick ignored his gestures.

"Get Fran down from there, Ben. Hey! That's my grandfather's mantel clock."

Ben was holding the ladder for Fran as she climbed down with a box perched precariously on her hip. "No. Nick. Wait. Leave it." But it was too late. Nick had already brushed past Lise and was heading for the clock.

Henri threw a sucker punch to Nick's head, sending him sprawling against the sofa. When he lunged for Nick, a sharp kick to the kneecap made him crumple to the floor, howling in agony.

Lise screamed and struck Nick in the head with a heavy cane as he scrambled towards the clock. He lay semi-conscious on the hearth.

Ben pulled Fran off the ladder and shoved her out the door after Sam and their boxes. He had just enough time to intercept Henri limping towards his quarry, cursing. Ben spun him around, decking him with one punch.

Lise dropped to her son's side, the cane clattering to the floor. "What have you done? You've killed him! Henri! Henri!" He mumbled and rolled his eyes.

Ben knelt beside Nick. Rousing him took a few moments, making it necessary to keep a wary eye on Henri and Lise. Once Nick was upright, Ben scooped up the cane near the rubber foot like a baseball bat and tucked the clock under his arm, supporting Nick with the other. As he passed Lise, she made a move with her eye on the clock. But Ben shook his head. "Don't even think about it."

Lise screamed at them from the doorway. "You owe me. That

clock is mine. Everything is mine. The pittance he left me? And the boys have to wait? *Merde!*" She spit. "You killed your father, you, you little slut. Go! Go live off your precious trust fund. I will never forgive your father for what he's done to us. I curse his soul to hell!"

§

Sam could hear Lise screeching from the car. She put her arm around Fran, who was covering her ears. "Fran, it's over. You're safe. She'd like nothing better than to poison you with her words. It's all she has."

Ben placed the cane on the dashboard and tucked Nick into the passenger seat with the clock on his lap. He almost vaulted over the hood of the car to the driver's side. Sam touched his arm when she saw the blood on Nick's collar. Their eyes met in the rear-view mirror, but she said nothing.

A chilling thought occurred to her. "Fran, have you got my phone?"

Fran stopped snuffling and patted her pockets. A look of horror drained the colour from her face.

"Tell me you didn't leave it in that attic."

After one of those long moments of dread, Fran let out a deep breath of relief. "No, I dropped it in a box. I figured Lise would see it in these jeans."

Sam exhaled and flashed her eyes. "You're sure?"

"Yes. I know I did."

Nick groaned. Sam turned her attention to him. "How's your head?"

Nick felt the back of his head and winced. "Big goose egg."

Ben laughed. "And I almost don't feel sorry for you. We should have had the police with us."

"Yeah, I'm sorry. Ironically, that's my father's cane. I know this clock was still on the mantel when Fran and I left in June. I meant to put it in storage but forgot. It was a gift to Grandad Allen from the community. She must have snatched it before Dad's body was even cold. I need to change the locks on the house." He turned his head and winced. "Are you okay, Fran?"

She shivered and shook, as if shedding her skin. "Scared shitless, but I'm better than you. Where are we going?"

Sam smiled, seeing Fran's buoyant personality bob to the surface again.

Ben pulled away from the curb. "We're going to my folks' to regroup. I've got to stop letting you three talk me into doing this insane shit." Ben pointed at the cane on the dashboard. "But we do have her fingerprints and Nick's blood on that."

Sam raised her eyebrows at Ben in the rear-view mirror. *He seems to have weathered that stress.* She glanced at his knuckles on the wheel. *Maybe slugging Henri was therapeutic.*

§

Grace was eager to meet 'those poor children.' As Sam expected, she had prepared a lavish lunch and greeted Nick and Fran with open arms.

"Come in, come in. Oh dear. What's happened to you?" Grace spotted the blood on Nick's collar.

Ben stepped in. "Nick had a run-in with a hard object. I'll just show him where the washroom is and get him looking presentable." He ushered Nick down the hall.

"All right. You know where the first-aid kit is in the cabinet." She fidgeted. "Oh my. Do you think he'll need stitches, Samantha?"

"I don't think so. The head tends to exaggerate when it bleeds. I think he'll be fine." Sam redirected Grace's attention. "Fran here has the second quilt, and there are no others."

"Oh yes. We knew there had to be more than one because of the Roman numeral. I'd love to see it. Can you Instagram a photo to me?"

Fran raised her eyebrows at Sam. "You betcha."

Sam chuckled. "Yes, Grace is getting to be quite the social media butterfly." She made a mental note to suggest Fran send it by private email, just in case. Discussion about poetry, blue hats and crows was truncated when Ben and Nick returned. Nick had removed his shirt and was wearing one of Lenny's white T-shirts.

Sam looked him up and down. "You clean up pretty good."

Grace circled him as if checking for damage after a fender bender. "Yes, well. That looks fine. Let's eat." She took Nick's arm and walked him to his place at the table, taking another close look at the back of his head as he sat.

During lunch, Fran recounted the drama of the morning, much to Grace's dismay. When she lifted Ben's hand to examine his knuckles, Sam cowered inside. This could have ended so badly. Her mind wandered down a rabbit hole of what-ifs.

When the rescue of the clock came up, Lenny mentioned he knew Nick's grandfather. "I remember when the community gave him that clock. It symbolized the time he'd put in over his years of service. He was a fine man."

Grace, ever the consoler, said, "We were so sorry to read of your dad's passing."

Sam placed her hand on Fran's arm. She fought the tears welling up in her eyes. "But, if we hadn't seen his obituary, we wouldn't have found the two of you. You know, that label on Nick's quilt was the only clue we had."

"That's true, Nicholas. I am a quilter too, but until Samantha suspected the symbolism, I thought it was an ordinary quilt. You really must follow up on everything your mother has worked into both of them."

Nick leaned back, looking at ease. "You're right, Mrs. Chambers. The thing that convinces me that Mom wasn't just suspicious or paranoid is the fact she left the house to me, not Dad. It didn't really make sense to me until the quilts."

Lenny leaned forward. "Is the house sitting empty, Nick?"

"Yes. We had thought of renting it, but the move into Lise's place was a big strain on Dad, and we never got around to it. After Dad died, Fran and I crashed there until she graduated. To her credit, she wrote her finals in the two weeks following his death, and we left for Europe immediately after. We just had to get away."

This empty house piqued Sam's interest. "Would you ever consider selling it?" She shrugged at Ben's quizzical expression.

"Maybe, if neither of us wind up working over here after university."

Fran swiveled her head and shoulders like she was dodging punches. "Not me. I don't want to live within a hundred klicks of those crazy people."

§

Without equivocating, Ben laid out the new ground rules during the drive from the Tsawwassen terminal to Kitsilano.

The condo was within sight. Sam needed to press the point before they arrived. "Here's the thing. You two must focus on your courses. I want you to leave the digging to Ben and me, and we'll connect on the weekends, all right?"

Nick looked a little relieved. "Go for it, Sam." He looked at Fran. "That a deal?"

Ben stopped in the porte cochère and Fran stepped out.

"Sure," Fran said. "As long as Sam doesn't mind me calling her in the middle of the night." She lifted one of her boxes out of the back. "I wonder how much of this stuff was worth all that grief."

Sam caught a withering glare from Ben as he held the door for them.

Cradling the clock in his arms, Nick hip-bumped his sister in the elevator. "I better not have gotten this goose egg on my skull for nothing." They shed their nervous tension in giggles on the way up.

He hung his keys on the hook by the door as they entered and walked over to the fireplace. "I guess it was worth it." He placed the clock on the mantel and stood back. "There. How about a coffee?"

Sam waved him off. "No, I think we've had enough stimulation for today. And don't you think I should take those boxes of company documents with me?"

"Well. I wanted to go through them again before—"

"I thought we had just agreed you'd focus on your studies and Ben and I would do the research?"

Ben got between them. "Look, Sam, if he wants to keep them here, that's his prerogative."

"It's okay, Ben. She's right. I will concentrate better if the stuff isn't even here." Nick brought the boxes out of his bedroom.

On the drive home, Sam got the giggles. "Is this the stress level we can expect when our kids are their age?" She glanced at the boxes in the back seat.

Ben squeezed her thigh. "God! I hope not."

That night in bed, Sam snuggled against him, kissing his chest. He reached across her for his phone on the night table and turned it off. He smiled down at her. "We do not need any more interruptions or drama from *the kids* tonight."

DIARIES

*A*fter that fracas with Henri, Nick promised Ben and Sam he would never pull such a reckless, stupid, asinine stunt again—Ben's words, not his. Thinking about their brutal class prep and study group commitments, it was prudent to leave the sleuthing to Sam and Ben during the week and reconnoitre on the weekends. He nodded to himself as he closed the fridge door. This week had been so much less stressful.

He set the cereal box and milk on the table. "Fran. Breakfast. They're coming this morning. Get your ass in gear." He poured their coffee.

Fran emerged from her bedroom, stretching and yawning, her tawny curls in disarray. "Oh crap, I didn't pick up any orange juice yesterday. I'm sorry." She plunked herself on the chair opposite her brother.

"Never mind, I have to shop tonight anyway. Eat up and get dressed."

By the time Ben and Sam arrived at ten, Nick had the coffee table cleared of the previous night's takeout cartons and ready for its intended purpose: coffee. He opened the door just as they emerged from the elevator. "Come on in."

Fran had showered and now looked fresh and eager. "Hi, guys."

Nick wished he had Fran's resilience. The apprehension he had suppressed all week now settled between his shoulder blades.

Sam threw her coat over the back of the sofa. "Hi to you, too. Coffee smells great, Nick."

"Right. I'm on it." He delivered steaming mugs to the table before sliding Fran's boxes into the centre of the room. "Do you remember what you squirrelled away in these?"

Fran crossed her legs and sat on the floor. "I grabbed her jewellery, her insulin diaries, and any other small things I thought might get thrown out. I grabbed some scarves and a sweater when I saw Lise ramming her clothes in garbage bags for the thrift store. We had a big screaming match." She popped the flaps on the first box.

Nick clenched his jaw, seeing the way their mother's sweater lay crumpled on top. *Where was I when she had to do this?*

Before lifting it to her face, Fran stroked the sweater. "I can still smell her perfume."

Tears welled up in her eyes, and he squeezed her shoulder. A feeling of helplessness coursed through him.

He opened the second box. Stacking the papers and books in neat piles on the coffee table, he placed the knick-knacks upright beside them. These he recognized. His mother had lovingly dusted and displayed them in their living room for as long as he could remember. He looked at Ben, whose steady gaze bolstered his spirit. He needed that; this would be a tough day.

Fran tossed various accessories by the fistful on the coffee table. A battered red jewellery box had tipped over, and the contents lay loose in the bottom. She lifted out a tangle of chains and beads and fished out a few stray earrings from under the flaps.

Sitting back on her heels, she sighed. "I didn't do a very good job of packing, did I?"

Nick scoffed. "Are you kidding me? You were fourteen. I was a sixteen-year-old guy who wouldn't have thought to grab these things in a million years. You did good, Fran. I'm proud of you."

Sam agreed. "Nick, I think you should sort through those papers. Get an idea of what's there. Ben, would you hand me those insulin diaries, please?"

Fran was already untangling the clump of chains and necklaces and lining them up on the carpet beside her in a neat row. As she matched up the earrings, she placed them back in the jewellery box along with her mother's pins and bracelets.

Nick blinked back tears when Ben slid off his chair to sit cross-legged beside Fran. He picked up a pair of pearl earrings and held them in the palm of his hand. "Tell me about your mother. Do you remember when she wore these?"

Nick did. They had been a belated Christmas gift one year when their father had returned on Boxing Day from an 'unavoidable business trip.' *Bastard.*

§

Sam surveyed the orderly arrangement of Lenore's meagre possessions on the coffee table. She watched Fran place her mother's bric-a-brac in a neat row on the mantel, knowing this ritual was helping her process her conflicting emotions of grief and anger. While Sam lingered over her coffee, she drew Nick into conversation about the positive aspects of all of this. Fran's instincts had served her well, and Nick agreed, he needed to reinforce that confidence in her.

Ben was in the kitchen, heating their lunch. "Let's eat before we get into this." He placed four steaming bowls of wonton soup on the table. "There's nothing like a hot bowl of soup on a cool September day." He winked at Sam when she sat across from him. "So, Nick, how are you finding third-year law?"

"I'm settling into a routine with the same study group from last term except for one guy. But I'm no help to Fran, reading her incomprehensible papers."

Fran scoffed. "I'll bet there are just as many Latin terms in legalese as health science. If you had listened to the nurses who came around for Grandpa's and Grandma's health problems, Dad's stroke and Mom's diabetes, you would recognize a lot."

"You may have been listening, but I sure wasn't."

This was the perfect moment for Sam to ask her about that. "Do you remember the occasions when the public health nurse came to help your mother with her insulin administration?"

"I do. I hung on their every word and watched them tend to Grandpa's dressings and Grandma's pain meds at the end. The nurse taught Mom to inject herself. The whole mystique fascinated me. Those visits made me dream of a career in medicine."

Sam put down her spoon and opened one of Lenore's diaries. "Listen to this nurse's notes: 'Dec. 10th, 17:30. Adrian called. "Lenore is having one of her spells." Arrived 18:05. Administered U-500. Patient recovered.'

"There are several comments like that in these diaries, and on two occasions, an ambulance took her to the hospital. But on the day she died, there are no nurse's notes. Your mother had recorded her food intake, blood-sugar levels, and dosages four times without incident, then at eight in the evening, she overdosed. Do either of you remember that night? Did the nurse not come?"

Fran stabbed a wonton. "I don't know. I didn't see the nurse at all. When the ambulance arrived, Dad saw me crying at the top of the stairs and hollered to go back to my room. They didn't tell me anything, but I guessed. I heard a first responder say 'diabetic coma.' I ran into Nick's room and woke him up. He told me to lock myself in my room, so I did. The ambulance didn't use the siren, but the flashing lights lit up my bedroom ceiling. I just knew they had taken Mom away. There was a lot of yelling after that, so I covered my ears."

"That would have been me." Nick paced. "I'm a sound sleeper; I can sleep through just about anything. It's a good thing Fran woke me up. From the top of the stairs, I saw this guy arguing in Dad's face. When he shoved Dad, I went ballistic. I didn't know who Henri was at the time. He was bigger than me, but I was stronger. I wrestled him out the door. A woman was standing there, yelling at Dad in French. It was Lise. She grabbed Henri by the arm and berated him all the way to his truck. She got into her car and sped off after him.

"When I asked Dad who that was, he mumbled something about a friend who came over to help Mom." Nick went quiet for a few moments. "Mom died shortly after they got to the hospital, and ten months later, he marries Lise? How could I have been so blind?" Nick punched his palm again and again. "That son of a bitch." He paused, placing his hand on Fran's arm. "You know, neither of us got to see Mom that night. What a shitty way to remember your fourteenth birthday."

Ben got up and grabbed his coat. "Come on, Nick. Let's go for a run."

Sam smiled. Ben always knew the right moment to defuse a situation. She placed her hand on Fran's. "He'll be all right." They sat, staring after her brother.

Fran blew her nose. "Poor Nick. He's just remembering this now because of these diaries?"

"No. Nick is just realizing the significance of what he remembers."

"So that's why he and Henri never got along. They were always at each other's throats." Fran began clearing the table.

Sam moved to the sofa and picked up the poem. "Remember this line from your quilt? 'Fever, visions seen in treble / Blue hats pecking at my vein'?"

"Yes—what does it mean?"

"Well, when a person is going into a diabetic coma, their vision can become impaired. And Sherry Baker said your mother told her the same story about a previous incident with her insulin. At the time they thought it was funny—that your mom was hallucinating, paranoid about the woman in the blue hat. But still … she did put it in your quilt."

Fran scurried off to her bedroom. Sam watched her, berating herself. *Too soon, too much, too fast. I've got to let them lead.*

Interrupting Sam's self-reprimand, Fran trundled down the hall, wrapped in her quilt. Teary-eyed, she snuggled up beside Sam and snuffled. "I miss her."

2015

*H*enri sat in his pickup across the street from his father's house, smoking. How many nights had he sat here, his anger and resentment building? Their car pulled into the driveway. The girl popped out of the back seat with a bunch of balloons—her birthday, no doubt. She and the boy jostled to be first through the door, the woman calling after them. "You two get straight to bed, it's a school night." His father dragged his useless leg up the steps behind her.

When his father closed the drapes in the living room, did he recognize the truck? Henri hoped he did. That would rattle the bastard. He watched for a while longer before flicking his butt into the street and pulling away without lights.

Antoine and Bertrand were playing Halo 5 in the living room when Henri got home, his rage smouldering. "Where's Mom, you morons?"

"She's upstairs, asshole."

He grabbed Antoine by the arm and sneered into his face before shoving him back onto the sofa and taking the stairs two at a time. He jerked his mother's bedroom door open without knocking and slammed it behind him. "I know."

Lise continued to brush her hair at her vanity. "You know what, *mon fils?*"

"I know Daddy, dearest Adrian, is not in a home for invalids. He lives fifty K from here with his *wife* and *two kids!*"

"Henri. Let me explain. Your father is …"

"Is what? Is not my father?"

"*Non!* He is! How could you think such a thing?"

"Those kids are younger than me. Why did he leave you?"

"He didn't know about you when he married Lenore."

"So, you know this woman?"

"I've always known, but your father and I have tried to keep our family together."

"Family? What family? He drops in once a month to screw you and breed another bastard, and then he has a stroke."

Lise raised her arm to strike Henri, but he grabbed it and threw her to the floor. He spit out his words. "You're his whore, Mother. This?" Henri circled his finger in the air and glared at her, disdain dripping from his words. "This fucking farce will end tonight."

He bulldozed his way between his brothers eavesdropping on the stairs, with Lise close on his heels.

"Henri, *mon fils.* Do nothing foolish. I beg you."

Henri flung her off his arm and slammed the door in her face. Squealing tires echoed his rage.

§

Lenore knew she'd drunk too much wine with dinner and, of course, a small piece of birthday cake, so what dosage of insulin should she take? She consulted her log through bleary eyes. Why couldn't she inject herself without bruising? She had always been able to avoid stabbing herself with sewing needles, and now here she was, doing it deliberately. She winced a little and snickered to herself.

Ah. She was feeling better already. She'd just relax on the bed for a bit. *This was so much better for Adrian, taking over Mom and Dad's bedroom downstairs. It's so much easier for him with his bad leg.*

What a lovely dinner. Franny was so tickled with her quilt. What a fuss she made, pouting when Nicky got his. She closed her eyes when the room began to spin. *I'm so tired. I wonder if she ... or Nicky ... will ever need to see the meaning ... in their ...*

§

Adrian was in the living room, watching the late news, when headlights shone in the front window. He got up and parted the drapes. Lise was rushing up the steps. He almost pole-vaulted with his cane to the door. "What the fuck are you doing here?" His pulse pounded in his ears.

"It's Henri. He knows. He attacked me tonight, *mon cher.* He was in a rage when he left, threatening you, and maybe ..." She cast a furtive look past him.

Adrian looked down the hall towards the bedroom. "He threatened Lenore and the kids?"

Just then, Lenore cried, "Adrian. I need ..."

He snapped a warning at Lise. "Keep quiet. The kids are sleeping." Turning, he swung his leg in sync with the quick taps of his cane. Lenore was trembling. She held her head and moaned. Her body teetered as she tried to sit up. "It's you, isn't it? Where's your blue hat?"

Adrian spun around, wide-eyed, to see Lise standing behind him. "Get out!"

Lenore clasped his wrist. Before collapsing, she said, "Adrian, my insulin ..."

He fumbled for a new syringe and vial from her kit. "Damn it. Lise, help me." She took them from him and drew up the dose while he struggled to bare his wife's abdomen with his shaky good hand. Lise steadied his hand and administered the injection. She laid the empty syringe on the night table beside another one.

From the doorway, Lise pulled him back from her bedside. "You see? She is much calmer already. Let her sleep."

Adrian agreed, wiping the sweat from his brow. His leg dragged like a ball and chain down the hall. He paused to glance up the stairway. In the living room, he pulled back the drapes. Standing squarely in full view with Lise by his side, he waited for his eldest son.

LEGWORK

*M*onday morning, Sam sat at the counter across from Ben. She spun around with her morning coffee clutched in both hands. She stared at Nick's banker boxes of company files and the papers Fran had rescued from the attic.

"I know what you're thinking, Sam. You leave that alone until tonight."

"I was just going to have a peek."

"You'll be late for work." Ben cleared their dishes and took her by the hand. "Come on. Get dressed. I'll help you." Sam couldn't resist a chuckle as he bobbed his eyebrows.

That evening, she arrived home before Ben. Popping a casserole in the oven, Sam poured herself a glass of wine and flopped on the sofa. Nick's boxes beckoned.

When Ben walked in, she was sitting cross-legged on the carpet, surrounded by stacks of files and papers.

"Whoa, that didn't take you long. What's all this?"

Sam waved her arms and grinned. "This is almost everything we need to know about Lenore and Adrian's marriage, their business, their health, their finances, and their deaths. Well, not everything about their deaths, but we'll get to that."

"Okay, but can it wait till after we eat?"

Throughout dinner, Sam couldn't help herself from talking non-stop. It wasn't until Ben had cleared the dishes and poured the wine that he signalled for a time out.

"All right already. The first thing we will do is scan and create a spreadsheet of the files, including those photos Fran took in the attic: Henri's birth certificate, the hat, and whatever."

"Right. And I should include photos of the quilts with the poem and our interpretation of the symbolism."

"I don't think the police will consider the quilts hard evidence."

"Maybe not, but it might give the coroner pause in Lenore's case."

"True." Ben started scanning documents as Sam handed them to him.

"This is the irrevocable trust fund. I'll bet Lise didn't even realize she had this in her garage."

Ben stood in front of the scanner. "You know, we've been looking for evidence she murdered Lenore. What if Lenore's death really was accidental but Adrian's was not?"

The thought gave Sam a chill. "As disturbing as that is, I think she had motive for both. She certainly feels cheated."

"Ya think?" Ben shook his fist in the air. "I curse his soul to hell!"

§

Sam interrupted the rhythmic kathunka-thunk of their scanning assembly line with her usual quip. "Listen to this."

"Come on, Sam. Get with the program. Time enough for analyzing and strategizing later." Ben was all about logic, procedure, and order. "We have five evenings to get this job done."

"Okay, okay. But look at this employee list from the warehouse."

"Whoa. Lise Richard, Receptionist?"

"Exactly. Lenore had no idea she was paying Lise's wage." Sam unstapled a document attached to the list. "And look at this. A receipt from an LR Storage Service for six hundred dollars. And there's a red question mark circled around the name. I wonder if Lenore was questioning this for some reason."

Ben examined the two sheets and whistled. "Clearly someone was associating this receipt with this employee list. Flag this on the spreadsheet to follow up." He placed the document on the scanner.

By Friday night, they were ready to print the four-page spreadsheet summary.

Sam put her feet up on the coffee table. "You know, this all looks innocuous on the surface, doesn't it?"

"True, but we have to pull together those facts that, as a whole, would be evidence enough to get these deaths re-examined."

Sam held her finger in the air. "But first, another list—one of documents we don't have."

Ben spun around in his chair. "You're right. I'm sending you the notes I made in my interview with that warehouse manager at Consolidated Distributors. You know, the one that used to work for Bennett?"

"Right. And I have that recording of my meeting with Sherry Baker at Jonanco." She set her phone beside her laptop, turned on the app, and hit play. She added, without looking up. "We didn't find Adrian's or Lenore's wills either. I need to add those to the list. I wonder if Nick has a copy."

"He may not have Adrian's if he didn't figure to inherit anything from him." Ben looked up at the mantel. "We should list that cane, since it has Lise's fingerprints on it." He sighed. "You know, if we find enough circumstantial evidence to back up our suspicions, this is going to get messy."

Sam crossed her arms and took out her frustration on Ben. "Don't you think I know that? I'm scared to death Fran might have to face Henri in a courtroom. Haven't you noticed the aversion she has to even the mention of his name?"

2016

*I*t had only been a few weeks since Nicky and Franny had buried their mother. They were leaving their grandparents' home, their home since their father's stroke made it necessary to move in with them. Nick sat at the kitchen table next to his sister.

"Come on, Franny, it won't be that bad." His voice echoed in the room. "I have to go over to Vancouver with the truck to open the condo for them. I'll be back tomorrow on the first ferry." Nick looked through to their once-homey living room, which was now stripped of furniture for the condo and devoid of any accoutrement that had made this their home except for Granddad's mantel clock.

"But why do we have to leave our home and live in her house with those three creepy boys?"

"Besides the fact that Dad is going to marry Lise, I'd rather put up with them at their place instead of having them here in our home. Wouldn't you?"

"I guess."

"Anyway, you should feel sorry for me. I have to share a room with those guys until I graduate. It's like an army dorm with bunk beds." He gave his sister a shoulder bump. "You'll have your own room."

"I don't see why we can't live here, since Mom left it to you."

"Because I'm still a minor, Franny. I'm trying to talk Dad into maybe renting it out. It would cover the condo fees. Besides, we have to give him a break. You know how hard it's been, managing this house without Mom."

Lise appeared at the door. "Come on, kids. *Vite, vite.* The truck is leaving, and we want to get home ahead of it. You want to show them where to put all your things, don't you? Come, come. This will be fun. A new home for you." She looked at the truck pulling out of the driveway and sighed. "I suppose I'll have to store most of that in my garage."

Nick huffed. How could she be so insensitive? *Her* garage? *I'm pretty sure Dad bought that house. Bitch.* He had to rein in his contempt before he spoke. "I'll bring Franny in Mom's car, Lise. You go on ahead. We want to say goodbye to our home."

"*Tres bien*, you are all packed?"

"Yes. The furniture I need is on the truck. I want to catch the same ferry."

"Well, all that old stuff will look very shabby in your lovely new condominium in Vancouver—such an expensive neighbourhood. Your father spoils you, Nicholas." Lise tossed her head as she left.

Fran rolled her eyes and sneered. Nick struggled to hold his tongue. He rubbed his sister's back affectionately and muttered expletives as soon as Lise was out of earshot.

THREATS

*L*ise noticed the dark clouds snagged on the mountain peaks to the west. The light was fading, even though it was midday. She switched on the light over the sink.

"*Mes fils?* Boys? It is going to rain. Bring the cushions in off the deck, *merci.*"

Lise's cell phone rang in her apron pocket. "*Mon Dieu.*" She wiped her hands on a tea towel and answered on the third ring. "*Bonjour.*"

"Lise, this is Nick."

"I forbade you to call."

"Forbid all you want. I've got a few of questions for you."

"I don't have to answer your questions."

"Maybe not, but you will want to hear them."

"*Quelle?* What?"

"Why were you and Henri at the house on the night Mom died?"

Lise sat on a kitchen chair and twisted the tea towel in her lap. She could not tell him the truth. Never.

"Lise?"

"I was a friend of your father's, and ..."

"Bullshit. You were his mistress."

"*Alors?* Your mother was having one of her *episodes*, and he needed my help," she lied.

"Why didn't he call the nurse?"

"It was late, and he was having trouble, with only one hand." She dug herself in deeper.

"So *you* gave her the insulin injection?"

"No, of course not. We called the ambulance." She wiped the sweat running down her neck with the tea towel.

"That's a lie, Lise. Dad said you did."

Lise focused like a lioness crouched in the grass. "How dare you."

"How long after you injected my mother did you call 911? I wonder. But don't you worry. There are records. We know. Remember, I saw you. You weren't wearing your signature blue hat, but it was you. They'd already taken Mom away when I heard Henri and Dad fighting, and you may recall that I threw Henri out. I can't help but speculate why Dad was so angry."

Lise sputtered.

At that moment, Henri entered from the garage, complaining about the rain as he shook his coat over the mat.

Lise waved him into silence. "You saw nothing, *ingrat*! Your father was upset, he took it out on his eldest son!" Her feigned indignation wasn't as convincing as she'd hoped.

"So. Eldest son and heir apparent, eh? See you in court, Lise."

§

One look in Henri's eyes told her he knew. "*Mon fils*, that was Nicholas. *Assis-toi.*"

"I will not sit." He shook his mother by the shoulders. "What did he say? What did he want?"

Antoine and Bertrand appeared at the bottom of the stairs.

"What's everybody yelling about?"

"Don't do that to Mama!"

Lise shooed them back upstairs with her tea towel. "It's nothing.

Go play your games, Bertrand. Don't you have to get ready for something, Antoine? *Vite! Vite!"*

Lise and Henri sat in stony silence at the bare kitchen table, listening to a warlike din emanate from Bertrand's room. Antoine left, giving Henri a glare before slamming the door.

Lise took her son's hand. "Henri, I think they know."

He stood so suddenly his chair clattered to the floor, making Lise jump. As she spoke, he paced between rooms, clenching and unclenching his fists. When she mentioned the fight, he waved his fist in her face.

"What did you say?"

"Nothing. I said nothing."

"Bullshit! I heard you say, 'He took it out on his eldest son.' That's not nothing!"

"What are we going to do, Henri?"

"You leave this to me."

§

Henri sat in his truck in the driveway, his mother in the kitchen window, fear in her eyes. *There is no way in hell I want her staring at me right now.* He backed out and drove to the park at the end of the street.

It's time to play the ace. There has to be zero chance of losing the hand they dealt me that night. He lit a cigarette and watched the three teenage girls on the swings, smoking. They swung high enough to lift their skirts and tease him.

Ironic, considering the photos he was scrolling through on his phone. He snickered and made the call.

"Franny, my sexy little half-sister. How are ya?"

Henri could tell she was running. "You're breathing heavy. You trying to get out of earshot of your big brother? Or are you just excited to hear from me?"

"As if. What do you want?"

"You know what I want, sweet cheeks."

"Where are you?"

"Not far."

"I swear to god, Henri ..."

"What are you going to swear, hmm?"

"Why don't you leave me alone?"

Henri could hear her sniffling. "Because, *ma chérie*, your fucking brother is poking his nose in where it doesn't belong. You will get him off my back or else."

Fran whispered, "You wouldn't."

"Don't try me, Fran. They could find their way all over campus. Or the Internet. I know men who will pay big money for these, and don't forget your weasel of a brother."

When Fran screamed, Henri held the phone away from his ear.

"Okay! I'll talk to him, all right? You are fucking evil, Henri. You fucking piece of shit!"

Henri dropped his phone on the passenger seat, smiled at the girls on the swings, and winked.

ME TOO

The tide was turning, but Fran could not feel the water swirling around her ankles. She looked out across English Bay as it crept up to her knees. *If I stand here long enough, will it wash me out to sea and out of this miserable existence?* But it was not to be. Someone grabbed her arm and dragged her back to shore. He was talking, but she heard nothing. She just wanted to run—to outrun her fear.

The frantic squeak, squeak, squeak of her runners pierced her ears like the cries of a small, trapped animal. Her hand trembled as she fumbled with the key to the condo.

Thank god Nick was out. She turned on the shower full force and stripped. Would she ever stop shaking? She was cold, angry, and afraid. How long did she cry? She didn't know. The knock on the door startled her.

"Hey, did you fall asleep in there? I felt like clam chowder, so I dashed out." He knocked again. "Fran?"

Fran mumbled something and threw her clothes and runners into the hamper wet. Wrapping her hair like a turban, she dashed across the hall, clutching a clingy towel around her. She scrutinized her miserable face in the mirror and practised smiling.

It didn't work. Nick took one look at her and said, "Whoa. What happened to you?"

"Oh, I was running on the beach and waded in too far. I got chilled down, so it took a while to put some heat back in my core. The soup smells really good, and it's hot. That'll help."

"Are you sure? You look like you've been crying."

"It's nothing. Let's just eat already."

Her brother circled her as if she were a wounded animal. Was he trying to spot her weakness? If he only knew … only he could never know … never. Her phone rang. She froze with her hand poised above it, as if it would bite. It was him. In two clicks, she dropped the call and shut it off.

"Who was that?"

"Nobody."

"It wasn't nobody, Fran. You look freaked out. Who was it?"

"All right, all right. It was Henri."

Nick sat beside his sister and squeezed her hand. "You didn't even speak to him. What did he say that's got you so rattled?"

"It's nothing."

"Fran!"

"Okay. He called me when I was out for my run."

"Did he threaten you? Because if he did, I'll …"

Fran's eyes grew wide. "No. You can't. You and Sam and Ben … you have to stop doing … spying on him."

"Spying? Damn it, Fran. He may have murdered our mother!"

"You don't understand." Fran ran to her room in tears. "Just leave me alone."

Nick hammered on the door. "Fran, talk to me."

"Go away. Leave me alone."

§

Nick looked at the clock and picked up his phone. "I will kill that bastard."

He texted Ben: *When you see this, call me.*

Within seconds, the phone rang in his hand. "Ben. Thanks, man. Listen, Henri called Fran twice today, and she is freaked out. She won't talk to me. I think he's threatened her. She says she wants me, us, to stop spying on him? I'm worried. Do you think Sam could talk to her?"

"Hi, Nick," said Sam. "I'm right here. We'll be there in twenty minutes. Just keep her talking until we get there."

"Right. I can do that."

§

The silence was deafening on the drive to the condo. Neither wanted to speculate. Sam jogged to the elevator and held it open with her foot. "Hurry."

Ben quickened his step. "Take it easy. Calm down."

"I am calm," she snapped.

"Okay, okay. I should have said slow down. I'm not the enemy here."

"I'm sorry. Can't this elevator go any faster?" She rocked from foot to foot until the doors opened on the tenth floor. Barging out of the elevator, she rushed down the hall and past Nick in the doorway. "Has she said anything?"

"No." He followed her like an anxious puppy and paced in the hallway.

Sam shooed him into the living room, where Ben had turned on the television. She would apologize to him later.

"Fran? It's Sam. Can I come in?" She stood with her hand on the doorknob, waiting for the click. Hearing it, she nodded to the owl eyes in the living room and opened the door.

§

Fran peered out from beneath her quilt at Sam, reluctant to meet her inquiring eyes. Sam sat on the edge of the bed beside her and said nothing.

She stared at Sam's back for what seemed like a long time before she sat up, blew her nose, and hugged her knees. "I guess you're waiting for me to talk."

Sam looked at her with the gentlest eyes. "So what's this all about?"

How much do I have to tell her to get them to stop? She hemmed and hawed before speaking. "Henri called me this morning on my run."

The expression on Sam's face didn't change. "What did he say that scared you so much?"

Fran shook her head and cringed. "I don't want Nick to know."

"It's as bad as that?"

She grabbed Sam's arm. "Can't we just stop digging around in people's lives? Henri says they were only there to help Dad. I think Mom was being paranoid with these damn quilts." She threw hers to the floor.

Sam picked it up. Placing it on her lap, she smoothed the wrinkles. "She didn't imagine this blue hat, a mistress, and three other children." She pointed to the crows in the border.

"No, but Dad stuck by Mom, even if he was an ornery old reprobate; and he did support Lise and her kids. He tried to do the right thing."

"All true. But Fran, that doesn't tell me what he said to make you want us to back off. Your mother went to a great deal of effort to leave you these clues. I think you—we—owe it to her to find out what really happened. So come on. Talk to me."

Fran jumped out of bed and went to the window, murmuring.

"I'm sorry, I can't hear you."

God, will she never quit? She turned with her fingers stiff and splayed, her jaw clenched, her eyes wide. "He ... got ... pictures."

"Pictures? Of you?"

In a shouting whisper, she spit out the words. "Yes! Of me. He will put them on the Internet if we don't back off." She shook her head in an exaggerated figure eight. "Nick will kill him, Sam. I can't tell him. We just have to stop."

"Come and sit down." Sam patted the bed beside her.

Reluctant to give the appearance of backing off, she perched like a bird on a wire at arm's length from Sam.

"Listen. Why do you think Henri is threatening you with these photos?"

Fran thought she was stating the obvious. "To get us to stop investigating Mom's death."

"Right. And why would he want us to do that?"

She had to concede this point but not give in. "Because there's something to it?"

"Bingo. I can have the RCMP on his doorstep in minutes."

"Please don't do that, Sam. I beg you." She leapt to her feet. How could she convince Sam not to do this? *This can't happen. Henri will tell the police Dad's death was all my fault. That can't happen. That just can't happen. Think. Think!*

She tried to avoid the quizzical gaze following her and paced around the bed, stalling for time. "Can't we just back off a little and not do anything that could get back to him? If we find out she died of an overdose she administered herself, and no one did anything wrong, then this will all blow over."

"We could handle it that way, but you know this threat will never go away unless you deal with it head-on."

"I know, but can you just leave it alone for now?"

"I can for now, but … Nick is out there, beside himself with worry. He has to be told what's going on and why."

Fran stood, blocking the door. She wasn't ready to tell Nick. She wasn't ready!

Sam held her shoulders and forced her to make eye contact. "If you like, I can do the talking. Yes, he will be furious at Henri, but it's the middle of the night, and there are no ferries till morning. I think we can reason with him before he does anything rash."

Crestfallen, Fran let her arms drop. "He'll hate me, won't he?"

"Not for a second. He'll be busy hating himself."

§

Nick stopped pacing when Fran's bedroom door opened. She followed Sam closely, staring at her feet. When he rushed to her side, she rebuffed his awkward attempt to hug. Stung by her reaction, he recoiled.

Sam's motion for him to back off infuriated him. "What is this?"

"Let's just have a seat for now, Nick. Your sister is feeling vulnerable at the moment."

He could see that.

"Fran?" She did not look up or respond. The look on her face was torture. He gestured his frustration to Sam.

"This will be difficult for you to hear, Nick. But I want you to remember it is more difficult for Fran."

"Okay. This is not good." But the look on Sam's face told him to back off. "Okay. Okay. I'm sitting." And he did.

The wait was excruciating. His nails gouged his palms. The seconds felt like hours. Sweat trickled down his neck, but he kept silent.

Sam held her hands up, rebuffing Nick's apprehension. "When Henri called Fran this morning, it was coercion. He threatened to expose her if we didn't stop looking into your mother's death."

"Expose her?" His voice was sharper than he intended.

When Ben touched his arm, he tried to lean back in his chair and look less threatening. "I'm sorry, what does that mean?"

"It seems, when you left for university, Henri took some photos of Fran. He took the first without her knowledge. He then threatened to put them on the Internet if she didn't pose for more. Now, I know you—"

Fran burst into tears. And that was it. He flew to her side, wrapped his arms around her, and held her head against his shoulder. Rocking to soothe her sobs, he said, "Franny, Franny. I am so, so sorry." His tears rivalled hers.

"How could I have been so blind?" Above her head, he simmered with rage. He thought about his phone call to Lise, and all the times Fran had pleaded with him to stay home—not crash at a friend's. "This is my fault."

§

Ben watched the stress building in Nick as he attempted to comfort his sister. He recognized that look; it was guilt. Guilt had been an abscess on his own soul for a long time after his sister's murder, for the exact same reason—because his efforts to protect her had failed.

Sam brought him back to the present with a tap on the shoulder. When he looked up, she smiled and handed him a cup of tea.

"Would you two like a cup? It's herbal," she said. Ben smiled to himself. *That's my girl—divert, distract, defuse.*

Fran uncurled her legs from under her and blew her nose. "Yes, please."

Nick pulled his sister's quilt around her shoulders and looked at Ben. "I will kill that bastard."

Ben waved a finger at him. "No, you won't. I know exactly how you're feeling, Nick. You know, and I know, that Henri is looking at sexual harassment at the minimum." He turned to Fran. "Listen to me. The guy is bluffing. There is no way in hell he will post them. You think he doesn't know he'd wind up in jail? It's not as if he can be anonymous."

Ben could see the wheels churning behind Nick's stare. He knew that look. He had to control the situation before Nick said or did something he'd regret.

"Come with me." Ben took him out onto the balcony. "If you go after this guy, you'll be the one in jail. Then where would Fran be? Not to mention you would never practise law." He let that sink in. "I need your assurance you won't go off half-cocked." He had to ask Nick twice before he agreed.

"Okay, Nick. This is what will happen. Tomorrow, I'll call him, and inform him of the jeopardy he is in. I'll do a little threatening of my own, and he may very well want to destroy those photos before the police are pounding on his door. He is, first and foremost, a coward."

*I*n July, after his high school graduation, when Nick officially moved to the mainland, Franny made him pinky swear he would text her every single night before he went to bed. And true to his word, he did. But when he drove into the yard on Christmas Eve, she leapt into his arms. "I missed you so much. Come and see my room. I've put up a little tree of my own. Tony and Bert laughed at our ornaments."

"Whoa, whoa, Franny. Let me catch my breath. Help me carry this stuff in." He had missed her too.

Their father appeared at the door and held out his left hand. "Hello, son. You look well."

"Thanks, Dad. How is Franny here doing in school?"

She hip-bumped Nick.

Adrian cleared his throat. "Nothing less than a B-plus."

Franny rolled her eyes when Lise appeared in heels, drying her hands on her French maid's apron. Nick tried not to snicker.

"She's settling in very well, aren't you, *petite chèrie?*"

Fran scowled and whispered in Nick's ear. "I'm the lone step-member of this family. I need to 'fit in.'" She made air quotes, mumbling something about Henri that Nick didn't catch.

§

Christmas morning was strained. His father had made no effort to buy gifts for him and Franny, and the ones Lise had purchased were token at best compared to what she lavished on her three. Nick tried to make up for it, and judging by the look on Franny's face, he succeeded.

"A new laptop? Oh, Nicky. Thank you, thank you!" She kissed his cheek repeatedly.

Lise scoffed. "Isn't that a little extravagant, Nicholas?" She looked at Adrian. "It must be nice to have such a generous trust fund."

Nick wasn't about to let her get away with that little dig. "Every student needs a laptop, Lise."

Adrian coughed and said, "Very appropriate, Nicholas."

"Oh! Oh! Wait till you see what I got you, Nicky." Franny dug around under the tree and watched in great anticipation as he tore off the wrapping.

"It's a picture of me for your condo. Do you like it?"

He gave his little sister a big hug. "I love it, Sis. Thank you."

On Boxing Day, he decided to retrieve his things that had been stored in the garage. He was settled in the condo well enough now that he could deal with them.

He groaned when he saw the stacks against the wall. Picking through them, he found none of his. "What the hell is going on here?" He could hardly prevent himself from growling as he yanked the door into the house open. Lise and his father were watching television. "I can't find those boxes I left with you when we cleared out the house."

Lise's eyes never left the television. "I took some books and blankets to the thrift shop last month."

"You *what*? Were they your books and blankets?"

"No, I thought they were your father's."

Nick stepped in front of the television. "Lise, you had no right to dispose of my things or my father's without checking with us."

Lise tried to see around Nick. "There was nothing in those boxes of any value. Out of the way, Nicholas. I can't see my program."

Nick grabbed the remote and shut off the television. "The only reason I brought those boxes over here was because I planned to rent out the house. I see now that was a mistake."

"That house should have been your father's. Why your mother left it to a sixteen-year-old boy ... *incroyable*."

"Well, it's obvious to me. Dad, don't you have anything to say?"

"I'm sorry, Nick. I didn't see any harm in having Lise sort through that old stuff."

"That old stuff, as you call it, was important to me. So don't you dare throw any more of my family's possessions out, Lise! They aren't just my father's, you know. Dad, for Chrissake, think of Franny. And come to think of it, why aren't our ornaments on this fucking tree?"

SECRETS

*H*enri knew the girls on the swings were deliberately letting their skirts fly in the breeze for his benefit. Glimpsing their thongs and hearing the fear in Fran's voice had given him an erection. He gunned the motor rhythmically, flicked his butt out the window, smiled, and waved as he drove away. It was enough to know they knew what it meant.

His mother was in a panic when he got back. "Where have you been? What have you done?"

"I've been dealing with our insurance." He turned a kitchen chair around and straddled it.

"Insurance? What are you talking about?"

"I'm talking about a little arrangement I have with Franny. She will make sure Lenore's death remains … accidental."

"Vraiment? Comment?"

"Enough with the French, already. Let's just say I've got something to bargain with."

Lise frowned. "What have you done?"

Henri grinned to himself. "You got anything to eat? I'm starving. I worked up an appetite making that call." He poured himself a cup of coffee and watched Lise slap a sandwich together.

She plunked the plate in front of him unceremoniously and sat opposite her son. "Now."

Henri started with his mouth full. "You remember when those two moved in, I had to give up my room to that little bitch and share a room with those two little shits and Nick."

Lise became indignant. "What did you expect? We had to take them in. They were his children, and if we wanted to inherit anything, we had to be one big happy family."

"I get it. We did it for the money. And how did that turn out?"

Lise looked around as if the walls had ears. *"Ferme-la!* He doesn't have as much as I expected, but we still have the courts. What has this to do with insurance?"

"Well, on those sweaty summer nights after Nick moved out, I used to visit my old room." He paused for effect. And he got it.

Lise leapt to her feet and came around the table at him. She smacked his head again and again. "You little shit! What have you done? Did you rape her? She was fifteen! A baby!"

Henri tried to fend off his mother's attack. "No! No! I just watched her sleep." He laughed at her pathetic attempt to hurt him. "She had the beautiful breasts of a virgin. I took photos."

Lise screamed and covered her ears. *"Voyeur! Pervers"*

Henri grabbed her by the wrists. "You're no better. You think a mistress is respectable. Think again, Mother—you are nothing but a whore, and me your bastard son."

Lise sank to her knees, wailing. "You know he loved me first. You are his first-born. You are not a bastard. He would have divorced her if he could. I've done this all for you." She clawed at his pant leg, but he shook her off.

Henri's lip curled. "You're a fool, *Maman.* I'm the only one who can save your ass."

§

Nick couldn't sleep. Yesterday, his world had fallen apart. Henri.

Fucking Henri had been abusing Fran. How could he not have seen it? His hatred for the guy grew as the sleepless hours dragged on. He tossed and turned in his bed until he had to do something, anything, to clear his mind. After a warm shower, he sat in the dark on the sofa, listening to the nighttime hum of the sleeping city. He heard Fran get up, but could not face her.

His thoughts were still festering at first light. On the balcony, he lifted his face to the cool breeze off English Bay. Pulling his robe around his neck, he stood at the railing and watched the morning light across Burrard Inlet bathe Cypress Mountain and West Van in gold.

He wished he could kill Henri, or at the very least beat the living shit out of him. But his cooler head prevailed; he would have to stick to imagining. Still, he could not let Henri think he had succeeded—if success was threatening Fran with blackmail. He made a decision. He could still catch the 8:25 from Tsawwassen for a face-to-face. "Let's call it a countersuit. Sorry, Ben. I have to do this."

The line at the cashier was long for a Sunday. It crept forward at a snail's pace. He'd had time to think on the way to the terminal. *I wonder if the asshole is even there.* He moved ahead one car-length and picked up his phone.

§

Henri knew from the ringtone it was Nick. He wiped the sleep out of his eyes. It was 6:45.

"Fuck, man. What do you want?"

"You called Fran yesterday."

"So? Franny and I are tight."

"You son of a bitch. I'm on the next ferry."

"Great. Don't forget the beer. We'll have a family reunion. Why don't you bring Franny?"

"You'll never see her again."

"That's what you think. I've got pictures, but then you already know that. Don't you?"

"I do. And soon the police will know too. You can hit delete all you want. You sent them to Fran. You are going to jail."

"Is that right? If I do, I'll be taking your precious little sister down with me. Ask her how Adrian died." Henri stood up and stretched. "Stay on your side of the pond, you fuck." He tossed the phone on the bed and glared at it.

§

Fran thrashed in her sleep. Inches from her face, Henri's distorted sneer leered down at her. Nick's head floated above, frowning in disappointment. She woke with a start. It was after three in the morning. Hot and clammy with sweat, she crossed the hall to splash water on her face. She saw the faint silhouette of Nick sitting in the dark on the sofa. His head turned, but he said nothing. She tiptoed back to bed and stared at the ceiling. When she thought of him seeing those photos, she cringed. She hated Henri for all the sleazy ways he had intimidated her. If she hadn't posed, he would have told her father she had willingly slept with him. She pulled the sheet over her head and hummed. That couldn't happen.

A siren woke her from her fitful sleep. The face in the bathroom mirror looked like hell. *I need to go for a run. Damn. I will not let Henri spoil running for me.* Slipping into her tights, she brushed her teeth and whipped her hair into a ponytail. Nick said all she needed was a pink bow around it to make her a champagne poodle of the highest pedigree. As if! She frowned at herself in the mirror and stuck her tongue out before leaving.

As she passed his door, she called out to him. "I'm going for a run. Have the coffee on when I get back?" No response. "Nick?" She opened his door. He was gone.

Where would he be this early? She remembered him sitting in the dark in the middle of the night. One glance at the key hooks told her Nick hadn't gone for a walk or a run. *Henri. He's gone after Henri. Oh god, no.*

"Come on, Nick—answer your phone." It went to voicemail twice. She pleaded with him to pick up. She texted. No response. Fear rose in her throat until she was gasping. She stared wide-eyed at her phone. *Ben.* Yes, Ben would know what to do.

He answered with an early-morning frog in his throat. "Hello?"

"Ben! It's Fran. Nick is gone. I think he's going after Henri. He won't pick up or answer my texts. Can you guys come over? I'm so scared."

"We're on our way, Fran. Keep trying to reach him. If it goes to voicemail, tell him, from me, to come back. Not to do this. We'll be there in twenty minutes."

§

Nick scowled as he drove into the underground parking. There was Ben's car parked in a visitor's space. He had heard Fran's messages. He bristled when she ran to him at the door.

"Nick. You had us scared to death. Where were you?"

"I was on my way to defend your honour, Fran, but something came up."

Fran recoiled at his coldness. "When you wouldn't answer, I called Ben. I was so worried."

He brushed past Ben without a word or acknowledgment of Sam sitting on the sofa.

There had been plenty of time to contemplate Henri's cryptic accusation after he left the lineup with only one car ahead of him. But now he wanted to stall. Did he want to confront Fran in front of Ben and Sam? It looked like he didn't have a choice. Before speaking, he helped himself to a beer.

"Last night, I had this crazy idea. I could scare Henri into deleting the photos. I was in the lineup at Tsawwassen when I decided, hell, I should call first—make sure he's there."

Ben opened his mouth to speak, but Nick shut him down.

"He wasn't the least bit intimidated by my threats. And do you know why?"

No one spoke.

"Because he's got more to bargain with than just some salacious photos. Tell me, Fran, how were you involved in Dad's death?"

BLAME

*F*ran curled up beside Sam, anxious to avoid Nick's contemptuous gaze. She pulled her quilt around her shoulders. His face was so full of rage she could not look him in the eye. "If only you hadn't left me there. I could have gone to school in Vancouver."

She flinched when Nick half rose out of his chair.

"What does Henri know that I don't?"

Her eyes darted from Ben to Sam, and Ben extended his arm across her brother's chest. Sam sliced the air with her hand. "Both of you, just take a breath. You don't really believe Fran is responsible for your dad's death. This is just a cruel mind game Henri is playing."

Fran couldn't stop trembling, even wrapped in her quilt. She wiped her eyes on the edge. She hesitated when Sam looked at her and nodded.

"Take your time. If you tell us everything you can remember, I'm sure it will be obvious."

Fran began in a timorous whisper. "That day, I was in my room studying for finals. I heard Lise call out that she and Dad were off to a doctor's appointment." She snuffled. "I knew Henri was watching

TV downstairs, so I locked my door. It had a loud click, and I could hear him laughing. About an hour later, I had to pee. When I got back to my room ... he was on my bed."

Nick tried to push past Ben's arm. "Why didn't you tell me, Fran?"

Sam held her hand up to him. "Nick. She's telling you now. Sit down and just listen."

Fran took a few deep breaths before beginning again. "I was going to leave the house, but he caught me by the arm and held me back. He wanted to take more pictures ... from ... from a certain angle ... up into my face." Her voice quavered.

She glanced up at the fury in Nick's eyes. She felt Sam's arm around her shoulders.

He opened his mouth to speak, but a look from Sam stopped him.

"We don't need to know the details, Nick."

Fran looked into Sam's eyes and fell into sobs. It took her a few minutes to rally, but when she did, she stuck out her chin. "I cried and pushed the camera down into his face. He got mad and grabbed my arms. I was trying to scratch his face and his eyes when the door flew open and Dad charged in, screaming at me."

Fran shook her quilt from her shoulders and flailed her hands like she was shaking off sparks. "Before I knew what was happening, Dad grabbed me by the arm and threw me across the room. My head slammed against the dresser so hard I think I blacked out. When I looked up, Dad and Henri were fighting, and I mean really fighting. Dad pushed me down again when I tried to get up. Henri blindsided him hard, and he fell. I thought he was going to kill him. Then Lise clobbered Henri with something. He got off Dad, holding his head. Everybody was screaming and shouting, including me.

"Lise yelled at Henri in French, and he took off. She helped Dad up, and he came at me, yelling and calling me ... names. As soon as Lise pulled him into the hall, I locked my door."

Exhausted, Fran fell back on the sofa, panting, tears of anger and relief running into her ears. She grabbed Sam's hand when she touched her arm.

"I think Fran needs a break. Nick? Why don't you and Ben bring over the coffeepot and some mugs. And there are some muffins in that bag on the counter." Sam smiled and gave her a hug. Over Sam's shoulder, she could still see the rumbling volcano that was her brother.

They sat in stony silence until Nick, gripping his mug in both hands, ventured to speak. "How did I not see what a pervert he was?"

"Dad said I was the pervert. Even Lise was screaming that if I wasn't such a slut, Dad would still be alive." Fran ran for the bathroom, slamming the door on her words.

§

Sam had to intervene. She coaxed her way into the bathroom. Fran's face contorted in pain, she sagged into Sam's open arms.

Sam stroked her hair. "What they said was wrong. And cruel. You are guilty of nothing. Do you hear me? Nothing. Why don't you have a shower? You'll feel better."

Fran nodded, released her grip on Sam, and turned on the taps.

"Take your time. I'll save you a muffin."

In the living room, Sam, Ben, and Nick drank their coffee in silence. When she heard the shower stop, Sam said, "Fran has more to say, so don't interrupt her and don't react negatively. If she's calm and you want to ask her something, get her permission. Do you understand?" Ben and Nick looked at each other and nodded.

She wondered if Ben was remembering the horror that was his sister's marriage before her murder. *Is he going to dredge up the guilt he felt then? It so much resembles Nick's.*

She snapped out of her dark moment when Fran came out. Looking much more composed, she sat apart from Sam without her quilt. This was a good sign. She drank from her coffee before she spoke.

"I don't know how many hours I stayed locked in my room. I could hear them yelling and fighting for a long time. Then it went quiet, and I heard Lise scream at Henri. That's when I ran downstairs.

"Dad was on the floor in the bathroom. Lise was kneeling beside him, holding his hand. Henri grabbed my arm and wouldn't let me near Dad. He said, 'This is all your fault, you little bitch. Get the hell back in your room and stay there.' Lise came at me, screaming as if she were going to scratch my eyes out. I ran to my room and called you.

"It seemed to take forever for the ambulance to come. And when it did come, it took them a long time to get Dad out of the house. I watched from my window when they put him in the back. They left with no sirens—just lights.

"I saw Lise pacing outside for a long time, but Henri was in the house. My door was locked, but I was still terrified. It wasn't long before you arrived."

Nick nodded. "I remember. I was on the next ferry. When I got there, Lise and Henri swarmed me like angry bees. I dodged past them. I just wanted to get you out of there. I don't know where the hell Tony and Bert were during all this. Did you see them?"

"I don't know where they were."

Sam urged Nick to continue. This could help him on so many levels. Fran was reliving those hours waiting for him, needing him; and he could rescue her again, empathize with her, and ease his false feelings of guilt and Fran's as well.

Nick's eyes darted between Ben and Sam. "When she opened her door, she literally dragged me in and slammed it. She had texted me on the ferry, so I was expecting her to be ready to leave, but this was bizarre—there she stood, wearing her winter coat and boots, with an overstuffed carry-on in one hand and her quilt rolled up under her arm. It would have been funny under any other circumstances. I pulled her past those two hyenas and out of there."

He knelt in front of Fran and took her hands in his. Although he was looking into her bleary eyes, he was speaking to Sam and Ben.

"I had finished my semester, so we stayed in our house until Fran wrote her exams. I'd taken most of the furniture across to the condo, but it was good enough. Then I brought her over here. I'm so sorry. I can't believe I doubted you, Fran."

"That's okay, I did too."

Sam took Ben by the hand and led him out onto the balcony and closed the sliding door. She needed a hug and a little cry herself.

MOTIVATION

*D*eep in thought, Sam stared out the window at the darkening sky. Grey clouds threatened more rain. It was going to be one of those dreary days. The spreadsheet of missing documents in their research filled her screen. She clicked on the photo of Henri's birth certificate that Fran had taken in the attic. It confirmed what Ben had found in his research for Nick—where and when he was born in Paris—but there was no signature beside Adrian Bennett's name. She wasn't that surprised not to find a baptismal record for Henri. However, the birth certificates of Antoine and Bertrand, who were both born in Vancouver, were equally elusive. Surely Adrian would have been there?

Frustrated, she scoured the BC regulations. "Listen to this, hon. It says here that Fran and Nick can apply to the registrar general with 'a reasonable purpose' for the birth records of Antoine and Bertrand because they are half-brothers. I'm calling Nick."

He answered on the first ring. "I was just about to call you. What's up?"

Sam tapped speaker and related what she had discovered—or, more accurately, what she couldn't discover. Sam put her feet up on the coffee table. "What were you calling us about?"

"Right. I got this message from Dad's lawyer, George Collins. Apparently, Lise is threatening to go to court to get access to our trust. He said there is no way in hell. Well, he didn't say that exactly. There is no way she can get at an irrevocable trust. Besides, Dad provided for her and the boys' education in his new will after Mom died. I know because I am co-executor with George. The boys won't get the balance of their inheritance until they are twenty-four.

"But that's not the most interesting part. Lise claims to have done DNA testing of her kids years ago."

Sam sat up and glanced at Ben. "Really? She must have felt she needed proof at some point."

"It must have been when Dad had his stroke."

Ben spun around at the desk. "Let me get this straight. In her mind, in her bid for access to the trust fund, Lise needed a DNA match for Henri because Adrian did not sign his birth certificate. But, if she also had DNA matches for Antoine and Bertrand, I would think Adrian's name on their birth certificates would make it a moot point. Why are we looking for proof that Adrian is the father of those three? Doesn't that help her case?"

"No, Ben, she doesn't have a case. She may have thought she was holding an ace with the DNA, as if proving they were his sons would entitle them to a share in the trust. I think her suit is a hollow threat. No lawyer would tell her she would win. This idea may have been festering in her mind since Mom died. The trust fund was set up after they sold the company, with Mom's share in the proceeds of the sale. Dad was in pretty bad shape, so Mom must have felt the future was uncertain."

Sam paced around the room. "Okay. We know your dad wouldn't divorce your mother. And now, with his disability, she was his primary caregiver. But he was also living in his in-law's house. I think Lise could see the writing on the wall. What would it mean for her if he died before his wife? It was possible, even likely, that he could have another stroke. Your mother would inherit everything. There's Lise's motive."

"Right." Ben stopped Sam from pacing. "I think she was in a

panic to establish parentage in case he died. Would she take the chance that he would remember her in his will? And he wasn't likely to carry any life insurance with her as a beneficiary."

"Exactly. And if Dad didn't marry her, the DNA would help her get child support at least. Think about it. Go back to Dad's stroke. He's sold the company; Lise is out of a job. She sells their house in Vancouver and buys on the Island—closer to him, although he was too disabled to come to her. As far as she knows, he's got a hefty little nest egg somewhere.

"But then Mom dies first and he marries her, so she doesn't need the DNA for the child-support angle. She would have felt betrayed big-time, learning that half of his estate was in this trust. That gives her motive for a second ..." Nick's voice trailed off.

Sam could hear that Nick was getting emotional. "I think we've discussed this enough for now. Why don't you and Fran come over, have supper with us, and we'll just hang out?"

Nick's goodbye was barely audible, but he said they would come. When the call ended, Sam set her phone on the coffee table and leaned back on the sofa. "I'm worried about Nick. He sounds detached. He is clearly repressing his polarized emotions."

"Maybe it's just his way of coping. If he thinks from an analytical point of view, he can distance himself from the fact that these are his parents."

"I guess, but he sounded emotional just then. That's why I broke it off."

"I'm glad you did." Ben kissed her and headed for the kitchen to make lunch.

Raising her eyebrows at him, Sam rested her chin on her arm on the back of the sofa. "You know, if I were in Lise's stilettos, and Adrian was never going to divorce his wife, I'd be adding up his assets."

"You greedy little thing, you."

§

Sam put the lunch dishes in the dishwasher and returned to her computer. Scanned pages scrolled across the screen. "What do these inconsistencies in Lenore's insulin diaries mean?" She looked over at Ben, who was seasoning a roast for supper. "I had Nick submit the requisition for the coroner's report on his mother's post-mortem. And I'm drafting the same for his father." She stared at her screen. "So it has come to this. I can't believe Lise could have murdered both of them ... And then there's Henri."

"That's premature speculation, Sam. Lise claims Lenore's death certificate said 'accidental insulin overdose,' and we know Adrian's said 'myocardial infarct.' Why would the coroner's reports be any different?"

"True. But the coroner didn't have these diaries, and she didn't know Fran was there when Adrian died."

Ben slid the roast into the oven. "If Lenore was murdered, my guess is it was opportunistic. But ... with Adrian, it could have been premeditated."

Sam spun around in her chair. "I don't agree. After Adrian's stroke, I think Lise went into survival mode. She could have been planning Lenore's demise for a long time. But I don't think she planned to murder Adrian. If, or when, Lenore died, Lise expected to marry Adrian and inherit everything as his wife if he should die. But until then, she would live off his fortune, and their children would have a full-time father."

Ben set the oven timer before joining Sam at the desk. "I agree with some of what you are saying. It's all about the money. But when she found out about the trust after Lenore's death, her perceived inheritance halved. It wasn't enough that she had waited all those years to marry him. Now she would not reap the benefits until he died. Sure, she had his financial support, but now she was more of a caregiver than a wife. They wouldn't be planning any trips to Puerto Vallarta anytime soon."

"I see your point, hon, but I still don't think it was premeditated. I see it as an opportunity that arose when Adrian had the heart attack after the fight—they just had to delay calling the ambulance until there was no chance of reviving him." Sam turned her screen to face him.

"Look at these Coroners Service inquest reports. None of them are for home deaths except this homicide, and I don't see any that show the response time of the paramedics or the coroner. That information is crucial in both Lenore and Adrian's deaths."

Ben sighed. "Okay, I concede the point. But let's not bring up any of this unless they do. I'd like to just relax and have a social evening. Today has been pretty intense." He reached over and hit the power button on Sam's computer. "Nick said they'd be busy on campus until about four thirtyish. Are we going to eat off the coffee table?"

"I guess that will work. You know, if we have a family, we will have to get a bigger place."

Ben turned Sam's chair to face him. He leaned down and kissed her. "We'll just have to board that ferry when we come to it."

Sam smiled and looked at the clock. "There's plenty of time to negotiate."

§

When Howard buzzed at a quarter to five, Ben rushed out in the nude to answer it. Still in the shower, Sam snickered to herself. *Thank goodness they're late.*

Nick and Fran knocked on the door as Sam and Ben, now fully clothed, stole one last kiss. He swept the hair off her forehead and grinned. "You look a little flushed—must be the heat in here. I'll get the door."

Sam splashed her face with cold water at the kitchen sink and turned when they entered. "Hi, you two. I hope you're hungry."

Fran looked at the coffee table set with plates and cutlery. "Outstanding. Nick, look at that. And no takeout cartons."

Sam watched with amusement as the two of them scarfed down the meal she knew had taken Ben all afternoon to prepare. Afterwards, Nick sank onto the sofa beside her. "Excellent meal, Ben. That should hold me for a few days." He turned to her. "Now that we're all fed and watered, Sam, where are we with the coroner's reports?"

Her mouth fell open in surprise. "I thought we weren't going to talk shop tonight."

"I know I got a little emotional this morning, but we really don't want this thing to drag on for months. If what we suspect is true, I want Lise and Henri on trial. Geez. Every time I say his name I want to spit. But not on your carpet."

When she looked at Ben, he shrugged and rolled his eyes. Sam reluctantly retrieved documents from the desk and dropped one on the coffee table in front of Nick. "There's this." She handed a copy to Fran. "I've drafted this letter to the coroner's office requesting the report on your dad, and I'm reminding them there is a similar request pending on your mother."

Fran read the last paragraph aloud. "We have information from other sources, including transcripts of our recollections. After examining your reports, we will likely apply for a review of the circumstances surrounding the deaths of both of our parents, Lenore Bennett and Adrian Bennett, as we feel you have not been apprised of all the facts."

Nick read through the letter and signed it. "Thank you for doing this for us, Sam. I couldn't have done any better myself. This should get their attention."

"That was the straightforward part, guys. When would you like to record those recollections?"

Nick looked at his sister in that gentle way of his. "Fran, why don't we do it right now?"

"Sure, I'm game."

Sam placed her phone in the middle of the coffee table and pressed record. "Okay, I think we'll just free-wheel it here, and both of you can talk whenever something occurs to you. Fran, why don't you start from when you heard the siren on the night of your mother's death. You went to the top of the stairs, and your father shouted at you to go back to your room."

As if on cue, from the street below, the sound of an approaching siren rose to a mournful wail then faded like a ghost. Fran was not the only one unnerved by the déjà vu. Sam looked apologetically at Ben. She couldn't tell if he was hiding a reaction or not. He nodded, so she pressed on.

"Take your time, Fran."

With a brief hesitation but no tears this time, Fran retold the story. At the point where Nick heard loud shouting downstairs, he took over the narrative. He became agitated describing his fight with Henri, but remembered details 'like it was yesterday.'

"Did the two of you discuss what happened the next day?"

Nick said, "No, I don't think so. We were kind of in shock. I remember asking Dad about those two, but he was in shock too, I guess."

Fran recalled that she had asked Nick what had happened. "But he just said Mom died."

Nick shook his head. "What a stupid jerk I was. I was sixteen, she was fourteen. I didn't even understand what had happened myself. When Lise showed up at the memorial service, and then when she began coming around to the house, I was suspicious and got right in Dad's face. He almost hit me. I backed off and never pursued it again."

Sam watched Fran twist her hair and stare at the recording phone as if it were a coiled snake ready to strike. Sam reached over and shut it off. "Let's take a break and have a glass of wine."

When Nick mentioned Lise being at the memorial service, she recalled the line from Fran's quilt: *The crow perched on his grieving shoulder / And my tombstone bear my name.* She rubbed the goosebumps on her forearms. *Poor Lenore.*

Later, during Fran's recounting of events the night their father died, Nick got jagged, but not ballistic like the first time. An emotional discussion ensued about whether to include the sexual misconduct in the transcript. They decided it was integral to Fran's account because she had locked herself in her room after the fight. What she heard, and didn't hear, during those crucial three hours was part of the whole timeline.

Sam turned off her phone. "I think that's enough. I'll transcribe all this and email it to you for your input in case you think of something else. The more information we collect, the better."

Ben pointed out that they also had the interviews with Adrian's old warehouse manager and Sherry Baker. "And you have the quilts."

Fran paced around the room, wringing her hands. "What's going to happen, Sam? I'm scared we will not find enough ..." Her voice choked.

Sam motioned for Fran to sit beside her. "Listen. We're making progress. After we get the coroner's reports and glean whatever facts we can from them, we must submit our evidence to the coroner. She'll compare our submission to the 911 transcript, the paramedics' response, and her own response time if she came to the house, and put it all together. If she thinks there should be further investigation, it will happen. She will refer any possible criminal act to the RCMP."

Nick clenched his jaw and pointed at Sam's phone. "If she doesn't see the evidence, I am going to launch a civil suit."

"No, Nick. It won't bring them back." Fran jumped up and ran to the bathroom.

Sam stopped him from following her. "Nick, you're thinking too far ahead. It's going to be hard enough on her if this goes to trial."

INHERITANCE

$\mathcal{I}$t was the day after Lise's unsuccessful attempt to learn the details of Adrian's will that he received the phone call from his lawyer.

"Oh, hello, George. Problems with my trust babies? ... Oh, did she?" Sensing treachery, Adrian turned to see Lise's apron strings disappearing into the kitchen.

"I see ... Yes. I'll see you then ... Goodbye."

Lise appeared at his elbow, startling him. "That was your pathetic lawyer. What did he want?"

"He was just reminding me I needed to update my will."

"I should have mine drawn, too. *Nan?*"

"No. Find your own lawyer, my sweet."

When Adrian returned that Friday afternoon, Lise had worked herself into a lather.

"*Mon cher*, I should have come with you to see these changes. I am your wife and mother of your children. I deserve to be your beneficiary."

"My sweet, you will get what you deserve." He kept a straight face, which wasn't difficult since the stroke. *Let her sweat about that.*

§

Lise hadn't been able to work her feminine wiles on Adrian's lawyer, and now she paced in front of her husband. "I'm telling you, *mon cher*, your darling Nicholas has designs on your estate. Surely that little tantrum at Christmas was proof."

"For heaven's sake, Lise, you threw out things that were special to him. What did you expect?"

"I expected you to be more supportive, *mon cher*. Your precious Nicholas and Frances have been against me ever since we got married, and neither one of them can get along with Henri."

"He hasn't exactly been easy to get along with for any of us, including you. I'm sure you recall how terrified you were the night Lenore died."

"What do you mean? I was not."

"No? When you arrived, what did you come to warn me about? You were so afraid, you didn't care if Lenore saw you or heard you. I know he arrived after I fell asleep in my chair. I woke up when I heard you fighting in the hall. I wonder, did Henri come to kill me or Lenore? I'll never know, will I? Lucky for you she died."

She raised her arm to strike him, but he caught it with a back-hand. "*Mon cher*, how can you be so callous?"

"I've learned it from you, my sweet."

§

A week later, Adrian paid the cab driver and dragged his leg up the stairs and into the office of George Collins, LLB.

"Afternoon, George. I'm glad you brought this to my attention."

"Well, I wouldn't have noticed it if Lise hadn't called inquiring about your will and the trust. I realized then that we hadn't updated it since Lenore's passing."

"I don't want her to know what changes I've made."

"That's a given. Take your time." George placed a copy of his new will in front of Adrian.

He read through the document, signed, and returned it to George. Lenore was no longer the sole beneficiary. His estate would be divided equally between Lise, Henri, Antoine, and Bertrand. The boys' inheritance would be placed in a trust for their education and administered by George until they graduated from university or reached the age of twenty-four. George and Nicholas would be the executors. Lise would get their loveless house. Their home in Vancouver was the only place he remembered playing happy family with Lise and the boys. It was a sad irony that, at the time, Lenore had been alive. Now that she was dead, his life with Lise had lost all its allure.

Adrian wondered if Lenore had known about them when she left her entire estate to Nicholas and Frances. They understood he was making no provision for them in this one.

He shook his head. "I'll probably hear her swearing in French from my grave when she sees her inheritance check signed by Nicholas." Adrian thought about Lenore's jewellery—he'd have to look for that. He should have given it to Fran long ago. He hoped he still had a few other personal items in storage. His conscience twinged, thinking of their Christmas ornaments which had never graced a tree in his home for Nicholas and Frances since their mother's death. "George, I'd like to attach a codicil with a few specific items for each of the children. I'm afraid I don't trust my wife."

CORONER REPORTS

*N*ick checked his mailbox in the lobby. He tossed the flyers in the wastebasket. Shuffling through the few envelopes left, he spotted *Office of the Coroner* in the return address and almost ran into the door.

Fran laughed at him and held it open with a flourish.

Nick waved the envelope in her face. "Here it is."

"Really? Open it, open it."

"Wait till we get in the car." Throwing his backpack in the back seat, he slid behind the wheel. His hands trembled as he slit the envelope open with his thumb. He paused and looked at his sister. This was going to be hard, especially for Fran, but there was no going back. He held the report between them.

Fran began to cry. "Accident? Self-administered overdose?" Fran grabbed the sheet from Nick's hand and ran her finger across the lines. " ... toxicology indicates ... blah ... blah ... blah ... Found unresponsive by the family. This is bullshit, Nick."

"It's what we expected, though, Fran. I'm texting Sam."

§

Nick was stoked as they headed for Ben and Sam's apartment in the rain. It was getting to be a habit: after class on Fridays, they inevitably found themselves on this trajectory. Tonight was Nick's turn to supply the food, and he was feeling smug about his choice. Well, maybe his mood had something to do with the coroner's report, too.

He burst in with a cheeky grin on his face, shaking the rain off his hair. He set two bags on the coffee table. "It's deli tonight—clam chowder." When he unzipped his backpack, Sam almost snatched the envelope from the coroner's office out of his hand. In minutes, she had the document scanned and copies printed.

All four sat around the coffee table, slurping their soup and reading. Fran pointed at her copy with her spoon. "I don't understand this part under 'Investigative Findings': 'All three parties present in the home were interviewed and none had administered insulin to Mrs. Bennett.' We know that's not true, because Nick and I were both there. Dad must have lied to the paramedics."

Nick shook his head. "Neither one of us actually saw Lise give Mom the injection. All we've got is Dad's word, and since he's gone, that's hearsay. Dad had trouble loading the syringe with one hand, so it makes sense she would have helped him. Dad must have lied for her sake. And then there's the reference on the quilt. Although we think the quilt implicates Lise, it's doubtful they would consider it evidence. They didn't take fingerprints that night, or even later as far as I can tell. It will be crucial that we give them reason to compare the fingerprints on the vial, the syringe, and Dad's cane."

Sam nodded. "Exactly. Fran, it will be the accumulation of suspicious facts we present that will give the coroner cause to reopen the investigation. When your dad's report arrives, hopefully things will add up."

Fran tucked her legs up under her. "What will the coroner do?"

Nick could see her shifting uncomfortably. "She could call an inquest to introduce the new evidence. It might not change the CODs, but it may instigate a police investigation."

Sam looked at Ben and raised her eyebrows. "My, my. We have been doing our homework, haven't we?"

Nick took his laptop out of his backpack. "I *am* studying law, you know. But I confess I have been doing some extra reading."

Fran looked over his shoulder at the screen. "You're reading about serial killers?"

"Yes, hear me out. Serial killers all start with the first one. When they get away with that one, the second one comes easier. If they are really sick, they get a thrill or something out of the first one, which causes them to go looking for the next one."

Ben scowled. "Lise is not a serial killer, Nick."

"No, I'm just saying that if she got away with Mom's death, then not calling 911 right away for Dad was probably easier for her. We have to be careful about making accusations, but the thrust of our application should be to link the two." Nick closed his eyes as he wrestled with his argument. *I need to rein in my level of malevolence.*

§

Stepping off the bus, Sam put up her collar against the stiff breeze and shivered. It had been two weeks since they had received that coroner's report, and fall was surrendering to winter. Howard looked up from his station in the lobby and smiled. *Aw, Howard. A smile and a friendly greeting, no matter what the weather.* He held the door for her as usual.

"Hi, Howard. Ben home yet?"

"Yes, he went up about twenty minutes ago."

"Thanks, Howard. Good night."

As the elevator doors closed, her cell phone rang. It was Nick.

"Hi, Sam. Did you get my text this morning?"

"Yes, the coroner's report on your dad. Anything interesting?"

"She mentions rigor set in shortly after she transported the body."

"That means he had been dead for a couple of hours. She would have followed up on that."

"She did. It looks like she interviewed both Lise and Henri. There's more detail, so I'll scan it and send it to you."

"Good. I'll call you after we've looked it over. Bye." She opened the apartment door.

Sam gave Ben a quick kiss and dashed off to the bathroom. "I'll just get out of my scrubs and have a quick shower. Nick is sending over the coroner's report on Adrian."

"Great. It's about time. Nothing fancy for supper. I just thawed some stew and put some garlic bread in the oven."

Sam called from the bathroom. "Perfect, honey. It smells terrific." She stepped into the warm stream and lathered up. *It's good to see him so engaged lately. He didn't seem to be overly triggered by those encounters with Lise or Henri, or even Lenore's coroner's report. That's good, but ... We should probably have a session with Gwen ... PTSD can be so fickle.* She dried off and dressed quickly.

After supper, Sam printed off the report from Nick and settled on the sofa beside Ben.

He handed her a glass of wine. "Let's have a look."

After reading the report, Ben looked pensive. *Uh-oh.* "What?"

"Wasn't Fran upstairs all this time?"

"Yes, we've always known that."

"But this coroner didn't. And didn't Fran say Adrian was on the bathroom floor? Lise and Henri had to have moved Adrian to the bedroom and waited at least two hours before calling 911. And look —Lise even had on a nightgown."

Sam shivered, but not from the weather this time. She gave Ben a generous thank-you kiss and picked up her phone.

"Nick, I think Ben has just found the smoking gun."

GRANT

Sam had lingering misgivings. She felt certain they had all the elements they needed to push for reopening the investigations into the deaths of both Lenore and Adrian. But was it enough for the coroner? It was time Nick and Fran had the benefit of legal counsel.

They arrived at Humphreys and MacGregor Law Office a little after ten. Sam greeted Grant with a smile. "Thank you for coming in on a Saturday. I'd like you to meet Nick and Fran Bennett."

Grant Humphreys had been her lawyer since the Pomeroy murder and had helped Sam through Ben's disappearance just two years earlier. He had become a friend, not just her lawyer. When Sam approached him about Nick and Fran, he didn't hesitate to take them on as clients.

Grant extended his hand. "It's good to meet you. Sam has told me about your problem. Have a seat." He looked at the two carry-on suitcases that rolled into his office. "What's all this?"

"This one is full of documents, and Fran's contains the two quilts."

"Well, well. This should be interesting. Do you want to spread them out over on the conference table?"

As Fran unfolded the quilts, Sam explained how she and Ben had come by the Attic Windows quilt for Christmas, and how she had tried to track down the quilter, L. Bennett. "Then I saw Adrian's obituary and got in touch with Nick through Fran on Facebook. It took about six weeks because they were in Europe for the summer."

Grant ran his hand over the stitching. "So, Fran, tell me about these clues your mother stitched into these quilts. This is very fine work. I have a few of my mother's quilts from the 1960s, and I treasure them."

With everyone seated around the conference table, Fran pointed out the details Sam had found. "You know, I received this quilt on the day Mom died. It was my fourteenth birthday."

"I'm so sorry to hear that."

"Thank you. Back then, I only ever noticed one blue hat. That's it. All this other stuff was just stitching. I never took a real close look at it, but now …" Fran scrunched up her face. "I can't believe I didn't notice."

Grant walked to his desk and picked up the phone. "Joan? Thanks for coming in. Would you bring the camera into my office, please?" He took a legal pad from his desk drawer and a few pencils before returning to the table.

Sam unzipped her suitcase and stacked documents in several piles in front of Grant. She handed him a flash drive. "We have scanned and categorized them on a spreadsheet and copied them onto this."

Grant looked at Sam with a wide grin and then at the Bennett's. "So, basically, I'm just here to dot your i's and cross your t's?"

Nick shook his head. "I don't know where we'd be if it weren't for Sam. I know we never would have been seeking justice for our parents, that's for sure. When Mom gave me that quilt, she made a point of telling me it would be more important to me after she was gone. I wonder if I would have examined it more carefully if Lise hadn't gotten rid of it. We owe you so much, Sam."

She shrugged off the praise. "If Grace hadn't found your quilt in the thrift store, we wouldn't be here."

Joan came in and photographed the quilts—full length, front and back—including close-ups of the blue hats, the ring of three crows in the borders, the verses on the backs, and Lenore's labels.

Sam pointed out the subtler clues to Grant. "These quilts are rife with symbolism. The quilters I've spoken to tell me the quilt patterns on the back are called Double Cross. They also thought the rows of crows on the back looked like hieroglyphics and symbolized a hidden message. And that the black and white stripes could mean jail bars."

Grant took copious notes. "I will read everything you've brought me, and then I'd like all of you to come back for another meeting before I draft this letter to the Coroner's Office."

Nick stood to shake his hand. "Do you have any first impressions, Mr. Humphreys?"

"Call me Grant, please. And yes, I do. Being the son of a woman who made many quilts for specific people and who chose every detail with them in mind, I respect your mother. These coincidences occurred over many years, and this was her way of documenting her suspicions, just in case. And, as you say, she did make some reference to her death to you, Nick, but did not have that chance with Fran."

When Nick and Fran left the office, Sam hung back. She put her hand on a stack of folders. "Grant, I hope there's enough evidence here for the coroner to reopen both cases. I know what it's like to lose both parents, but that was a car accident. It breaks my heart to think those two have lost both parents with no one suspecting foul play."

§

That Friday, the four of them arrived at Grant's office at eleven o'clock. He greeted them as they stepped off the elevator. "Thank you for coming in. This timing is inconvenient for all of you, I know, but we should move on this as soon as possible. I've ordered in lunch to save time."

Sam squeezed Ben's hand. She was already feeling the burden of responsibility lifting.

Nick smiled at his sister. "We're just happy to see this progressing."

They sat at the conference table with Grant at its head. "Help yourself to the coffee, everyone, and we'll get started."

Once settled, he began. "I've drafted a letter to the Coroner's Office based on the information in the files you gave me, but before I show it to you, I have a few concerns I think we need to address.

"First, Fran, I need to talk to you about Henri Richard. Would you like to talk in private?"

"You mean for them to leave?"

"Yes."

"No. I need them with me." She looked at her brother.

Nick gave Fran's arm a little squeeze.

"All right, then. Now that we're all settled, I've read the transcript of your conversation with Sam. You say several times that he never had sex with you but he blackmailed or coerced you into posing for photographs. Is that right?"

"Yes, but he knew I could tell he had an erection, and I was scared he was going to rape me."

"He also threatened to sell the photos and post them on the Internet?"

"Yes."

Grant explained to Fran the gravity of Henri's crime and her options, considering she had been a minor.

Fran shook her head. "What will the coroner do with this information?"

"If we don't go to the police with your case, the coroner will. An inquest is not a trial, it only establishes the cause of death. If her verdict is homicide in one or both cases, the RCMP Integrated Homicide Investigative Team will take over. Are we all clear on that point?"

Everyone agreed, and Grant continued. "Now, the pivotal piece of evidence we have in your father's case is the fact that you were upstairs, locked in your room, listening the entire time after the incident with Henri, correct?"

"Yes. I heard them fighting and yelling. I texted Nick. He said he'd be on the last ferry. It was quiet for a couple of hours until I heard the sirens."

"That had to be when they moved his body to the bedroom. And the coroner didn't know you were upstairs?"

"That's right."

"Lise and Henri both stated that Adrian went to bed and that she did not go to bed until two hours later, whereupon she discovered he was unresponsive and called 911. They don't mention the fight or Adrian having his heart attack in the bathroom much earlier."

Sam held Fran's hand. "Grant, what about the first responders' report? Wouldn't Fran's statement be corroborated by that?"

"The coroner will have all that information in her notes, and I'm confident it will corroborate Fran's version of events. She'll take a dim view of not being told of Fran's presence that night."

Sam still had the nagging feeling they had overlooked something. "Do you think the first responders collected the vials of insulin the night of Lenore's death?"

"Without a doubt. But if they didn't check for fingerprints, it may be hard to prove someone else gave her the overdose. And as you saw in her report, there was injection site bruising from previous injections, not just one. She was having problems injecting herself."

Grant handed Fran and Nick copies of the letter. "Read this over and see if you have questions."

Nick made a circling motion with his finger. "Give Sam and Ben copies."

At that moment, their lunch arrived. Joan refilled the coffee carafe and left.

Nick had Grant clarify a few legal points over lunch, but otherwise agreed the letter presented their claims accurately.

Grant gathered up the letters. "You're asking all the right questions, Nick. I'm surprised you didn't tackle this yourself."

Nick waved him off. "Too close to it, Grant. I needed to focus. Third year, you know."

"Understandable. I'll get this package off to the Coroner's Office today. It includes the photos we took."

Again, Sam stayed behind to speak to Grant alone. "Besides the responsibility he feels for Fran, Nick has one big fear on top of all of this, and I can't think of anything worse." She took a deep breath. "Although he hasn't actually stated it, I know he's afraid his father might have been a co-conspirator in his mother's death—maybe not premeditated, but covering for Lise or Henri."

JUSTICE

etween lectures, Nick received a call from Grant. The coroner had posted a date for the inquest and referred Fran's case to the RCMP.

The news hit him like a freight train. He tried to hide his emotional response from the students streaming past him in the hall. He dithered back and forth before placing his hand high on the wall and tucking his face under his arm.

"Are you all right, Nick?"

He cleared his throat. "Mm-hm. Yup."

"All right. You can expect a special unit to investigate this crime. When they interview Fran, I'll be there with her."

"That's good. Have they arrested Henri yet?"

"I don't know, but I expect they will move quickly on this."

Nick knew if Henri incriminated himself at the inquest, he couldn't then be prosecuted for the crime. "Let's hope there are no slip-ups. I don't want Henri to get away with this."

"My experience is, he will lie and perjure himself rather than admit to a crime."

"This has been such a strain, especially on Fran."

"Inquests are usually quick, so I'm thinking you'll be in and out.

You don't have to sit through the whole thing. Tell Fran I'll be in touch. There's a lot we can do to prepare her for this."

"All right. Thanks, Grant. Have you contacted Ben and Sam?"

"Not yet, but I will."

Nick looked at the time. It was two thirty. He would have to sit on this until he and Fran were back at the condo. His jaw ached from grinding his teeth.

§

It had been a long month. Sam didn't know how she felt now that the inquest was over. She sat at the computer in her pajamas, nursing her morning coffee.

"Listen to this, hon. 'The inquest into the death of Lenore Bennett in 2015 and her husband Adrian Bennett in 2018 ended today, after three days of testimony by nine witnesses.' They list them all, including four emergency response personnel.

"It says that although an inquest is only to determine cause of death, i.e. fact-finding, not fault-finding, the RCMP are investigating the roles Lise Bennett and her son, Henri Richard, played in the deaths of both Lenore and Adrian Bennett."

Ben was flipping pancakes in the kitchen. "Does it say anything else about Henri?"

"Yes. That they've charged him with 'sexual interference with a minor in an unrelated case.'"

"Unrelated? Yeah, right. Except for the blackmail to get us to stop investigating."

"That will all come out in his trial, hon." Sam could smell the pancakes. She put her computer to sleep and spun out of her chair. "What time are Nick and Fran getting here?"

"In an hour, so eat up and get dressed. What did that article say about the verdicts?"

"There was no change from the original CODs: Lenore died of insulin overdose, and Adrian died of a myocardial infarct."

"Grant warned us that might be the case."

"You know, I'm having the same anxiety I had in the Pomeroy case. You think it's over after the arrests, but there's no letup until after the trial, and even then ..."

Ben came around the counter and took her in his arms. "I know. I thought you were going to run up there and hug Fran when they questioned her. You have a propensity for taking on other people's pain. Including mine."

Sam sighed. Why didn't she feel that was enough?

§

Ben checked the weather channel while Sam dressed. It would be sunny but cool. Great. He would take the gang out to the Pacific Spirit Park for a long hike. He took a deep breath, anticipating the smell of sea air.

With the inquest over, the stress of waiting for the trials weighed heavily on all of them. They needed a mental health day, and this one was perfect.

The past few months had been hectic. He worried about Sam. There had been no reprieve from her dogged pursuit of the truth, for Nick and Fran's sake. He regretted not having supported her from the beginning—but when she received those threatening phone calls, everything changed.

When he suggested this hike, Sam seemed to shed pounds of stress and gain a spring in her step. This would be a day to commune with nature, relax, and enjoy themselves for a change.

The intercom buzzed, interrupting his thoughts. "They're on their way up, Sam. Are you almost ready?" A few minutes of silence followed. "What's keeping you?" Ben started for the bedroom.

"Ta-dah!" Sam tried to slide out of the bedroom in her sock feet, but she stumbled into Ben's arms. "Oops. I saw that turning out differently, but this is okay."

Ben kissed her and set her aside to answer the door.

Nick didn't come past the doorway. "Fran stayed in the car. Are you guys ready? I'm pumped."

"As soon as my lovely wife finds her runners?" Ben caught Nick glancing at Sam's behind protruding from the closet and laughed. He wagged his finger, making him blush.

As he locked the door, he said, "You need a girlfriend."

Sam pressed the elevator button. "What?"

Nick and Ben replied in unison, "Nothing."

§

Sam climbed into the back seat, sliding to the far side. "Morning, Fran. Ready for a good hike?"

"You bet."

In no time, they were in the parking lot on campus. It was an easy walk from there to the beach. Sam thought she could almost see Nick's shoulders relax as the water came into view. Fran gave him a playful shove and skipped on ahead, grinning.

They huddled around the map on Ben's phone to decide which trails they would take. For a moment he seemed to be far away. Sam remembered Ben had mountain-biked the Powerline Trail with Gerry a few years ago. *You don't see your best friend murdered and then not experience some anxiety when things remind you of him.* She squeezed his arm. He did a quick double take, smiled at her, and refocused on the map.

"We should have worked up a good appetite by the time we get back to Acadia Beach here," he said.

Fran seemed to be on the same wavelength as Sam. They picked up smooth rocks, sea glass, and seashells on the beach and sat on a sandy log to examine the life in a small tidal pool.

Miniature creatures waited there for the tide to come in. No panic, just waiting. The tide would never let them down. No rescue needed here. Sam shook her head. *I'm not going down that rabbit hole.*

They dusted off their backsides and picked their way down the beach. A curious seal entertained them for a while until he lost interest. The waves lapped at the shore, sneaking around their feet.

Except for the seagulls and the wind in the trees, there was silence. The guys were a long way ahead.

The peaceful togetherness she and Fran had been enjoying was in sharp contrast to the high-intensity conversation the men seemed to be having as they approached.

"Hey, what happened to the quiet solitude—the mental health day?"

Nick grinned. "Just getting the expert's advice on some software I downloaded."

"No shop talk, guys. Come on." Sam twitched her eyebrows at Ben as she put her collection of small things in his pocket.

He fished them out and examined them. "What are these?"

She skipped backwards ahead of him. "They're memories."

He put them back in his pocket and looked at Nick. "You don't suppose I could *download* these to the beach, do you?"

Nick waved his hands in surrender. "I wouldn't if I were you."

Leaving the Foreshore behind, they crossed Southwest Marine Drive and picked a trail on the other side. It wasn't long before the sound of waves lapping and the city traffic thrum gave way to a distinct silence. The occasional chirp or rat-a-tat drifted through the trees. Sam scuffed at the damp earth with her heel. The petrichor reminded her of Chambers Lane Cottage, and she felt a twinge of homesickness.

She dropped back to walk with Ben and took his hand. "Why don't we all spend Christmas this year out at the cottage?"

"What brought that on?"

Sam took a deep breath. "Can't you smell it?" Grinning, she jogged backwards until Ben winked at her.

Catching up with Fran, she turned to wave at the men. "Come on, fellas. Let's pick up the pace. We're hungry."

Sam claimed a picnic table at Acadia Beach while Ben retrieved the basket from the car. As they waited, Fran linked arms with Sam. "Thank you for today."

"You're welcome, but we all needed this. I want to remember this perfect day, enjoying our lunch in the sunshine."

Ben spread the table and summoned Nick from the shore.

Fran munched. "I wonder why food tastes so much better outdoors."

Sam fished her memory tokens from Ben's pocket and spread them on the table. "It was a good day, wasn't it?" She smiled. Snuggling up against Ben, she sipped her coffee and gazed out across English Bay to the high-rises of downtown Vancouver.

Fran tugged on Nick's sleeve. "Come on, walk with me."

Sam thought they looked happier than she had ever seen them. In August, when they'd met for the first time, it had been just three months since their father's death. They had returned from their trip, prepared to focus on the upcoming term, until she brought her suspicions to their doorstep.

The trials would begin in a few weeks. She wished their nightmare would end there, but she knew it wouldn't. Yes, this peaceful day was worth remembering, but a twinge of self-recrimination lingered.

Ben kissed her cold fingers. "I've been thinking of your suggestion back there. It would be good for them to have a family-centred Christmas with us. Mom and Dad will be there. It'll be great."

CHRISTMAS

$\mathcal{I}$t was the weekend before the holidays, and Nick sat staring at his computer. His phone rang. *Shit. How am I going to get this case study done this weekend with all these interruptions?* Without looking at the call display, he answered it. "Hello?"

It was Lise. "Your little slut sister lied! She took those pictures herself! They were selfies. She'd better not lie when—"

Click. Nick had heard enough. His hands shook with rage as he blocked her number. Should he call the police? No, he had no proof she was threatening him. But Grant? Yeah. First thing Monday.

He stared at his computer screen again, drumming his knuckles on the desk. This was no good. He grabbed his jacket and headed out to walk off his anger and focus on his case study.

When the elevator doors opened, he dashed out, almost colliding with Fran. Sobbing uncontrollably, she collapsed in his arms.

"What's happened?"

Fran lifted her head and pointed to the street. "Henri and some —some other guys."

His head swivelled to fixate on the truck idling on the street. He charged across the lobby, his heart in his throat. "Get in the elevator, Fran."

"No, Nick! There's three of them."

Her words fell on deaf ears. Henri's sneer turned to fear as Nick barrelled through the shrubbery in his headlong rush towards him. The coward sped away, leaving Nick cursing and breathless in the street. *You fucking piece of shit. This will bury you.*

His rage now doubled, Nick returned to the elevator to find Fran cowering in the corner. He pressed ten and knelt to take his sister in his arms.

"They threatened to ..." But she couldn't finish. When Nick got her upstairs, he coaxed her to have a shower. The running water did nothing to muffle her sobs. *This can't wait till Monday.* He called Grant at home.

"Grant, I'm sorry, but we have a situation here."

"No problem, Nick. What is it?"

"Lise called me earlier and was saying Fran lied about the photos. That they were selfies. I hung up on her and blocked her number. I was going for a walk to clear my head when I ran into Fran. She was hysterical. Henri and some of his buddies harassed her, threatened her, and followed her ... in his truck! She couldn't outrun the truck and fell."

"Is she hurt?"

"She's skinned a knee and an elbow, but mostly she's terrified. I need to call the police."

"Wait until I get there. We'll call the police and have him picked up."

"Thanks, Grant. Goodbye."

Fran appeared in the hall, wrapped in her fleece housecoat. "What did Grant say?"

"He's coming over. Come and sit by me. I'll pour us a glass of wine."

"I want to call Sam."

"No, Fran. She and Ben are out at the cottage this weekend. You know she'll turn around and come right back into the city if you call. Let's handle this ourselves. Grant will be here shortly, and he'll call the police. Henri is digging the hole deeper, and Lise gave him the shovel."

§

On the drive out to the cottage, Ben pulled into their favourite Christmas tree farm. This place would buoy their spirits. Families were having varying degrees of success strapping trees on top of cars. Their laughter was contagious. Red flags tied to treetops waved over tailgates as pickups bounced over the uneven ground in the field, the chaotic rows of vehicles defining the makeshift parking lot.

"I love this place. It hasn't changed a bit since Mom and Dad brought me when I was a kid."

He pointed out familiar sights as they neared the hub of excitement. The same Christmas music blared from speakers outside the gift shop. The same horse-drawn wagon ferried laughing families and their perfect trees out of the lot.

"I wonder if that could be the same horse." He squeezed Sam around the shoulders as they walked.

Multi-coloured lights festooned the split-rail fence. The Christmas shop sparkled with wreaths, garlands and ornaments. A tiny elf served hot apple cider from a huge copper kettle suspended over an open fire.

Sam grabbed his hand and headed for the cider. "Let's have some."

"After we get the tree, Sam. Let's follow this elf." He pulled her in the opposite direction.

Voices around them hemmed and hawed about the height, the girth, and the distribution of branches. Children darted among the rows, hollering, "This one! No, this one!"

Ben turned full circle. "I can't believe I've been coming to this tree lot for over twenty-five years. How long do horses live, anyway?"

"I don't know. How long do horses live?" Sam stopped at a nice, plump tree. "This one looks about the right size. We can put it in the middle of the sunroom."

"No, over by the west fireplace."

"No, in the sunroom."

The saw-wielding elf preparing to scooch under the tree shrugged at Ben. He'd probably heard that argument a few times. Ben caught the tree as it fell and grinned at Sam, warming her fingers with her breath. "Come on. Help me throw this onto the wagon."

With two heaves, it was up. Ben jumped up beside it and held out his hand for Sam. The elf clicked his tongue, and the horse walked on, the sleigh bells taking Ben back to an innocent age.

As they passed the shop, Sam pointed. "Ooh. We have to come back and get an ornament to commemorate this year. And some cider. You promised."

With their perfect tree strapped to the roof, he felt a spontaneous burst of joy and swung Sam around until she squealed. "All right, you. Let's get that cider and hit the gift shop."

The window displays summoned them inside, where thousands of pegs lined the walls, each one holding a dozen unique baubles just begging to be that special one.

The search began. Sam held up a crow in a top hat with a red bowtie. He scowled. Definitely not a crow. He offered the scales of justice? Sam shook her head. She dangled a miniature quilt beside her coy smile. Uh-uh. Ben sighed.

He stood admiring the splendiferous tree in the centre of the shop. There was a sign that read *You may shop from the tree*. He grinned at Sam. "I have a plan."

"Of course you do."

They walked in opposite directions around the tree, wanting that special twinkling ornament to jump out at them.

There it was, near the top of the tree. He grinned at her and pointed. The two ribbons had caught Ben's eye. Luckily, it hung out of reach of most. This was the one.

Sam opened his hand. "It is perfect, isn't it?"

He nodded. "This half is for Nick and Fran."

§

They hadn't been out to the cottage since the summer, having been so caught up in the tumultuous lives of the Bennetts. As he drove the last kilometre, Ben's chest tightened. The contentment he had felt at the tree lot was gone. It had been two years since Gerry's murder, but still the memory of his best friend sinking beneath the waves triggered his anxiety.

Sam's hand caressed his knuckles on the wheel, bringing him back. "Stop for a moment, Ben. Let's breathe and remember the great times we've had out here. Think about the days you spent making the table, the hours kayaking, our honeymoon." Her eyes twinkled.

She was right. He stopped in the middle of the lane and shut off the engine. He closed his eyes, took a few deep breaths, and let his hands slip from the wheel. Aw, yes. The honeymoon. He thought back to the day they met, and how lucky he was to have been on that bus on that miserable night when Sam leapt through the doors. He could still see her tripping on the front of her coat, landing in the muck at his feet, her beautiful hair hanging in wet strings across those frightened green eyes. Well, her hair hadn't exactly been beautiful at that moment, but he'd seen the potential ... He opened his eyes and smiled at her as he turned the key. "I'm okay now."

Ben pulled up behind the sleeping cottage and turned to Sam. "I'll get the firewood."

She winked at him. "And I'll get the groceries."

Inside, Ben could almost see his breath, and he hurried to set the fire.

"I hope your mom brings that dark fruit cake and those date rolls."

Ben smiled. "I was thinking the same thing. And maybe some walnut fudge for my sweet tooth?"

"Not just yours." She rubbed her hands together.

His fire crackled to life. Satisfied it had taken hold, Ben went to the kitchen to prepare supper. As he worked, he watched his wife wrestling the fitted sheet onto a hide-a-lump mattress in the sunroom. After beating the second kinked mattress into submission, she folded them back into sofas and replaced the cushions. She glared at her last quarry, which was not quite flat, and sat on it, hard. "The skills you learn from living in a studio apartment."

She paused for a moment to warm her hands at the fire before coming up behind him and slipping them under his shirt. She peered over his shoulder. "Smells wonderful."

"Thanks." Ben prided himself on his chicken curry. "Remember we had it cold in sandwiches the night we met?"

"I remember it well. And I made the mistake of asking which deli you bought it from." He feigned lingering indignation to elicit insincere and oft-repeated apologies from his wife. Sam set their places at the table side by side, facing the river so they could enjoy the curry and the view.

With the dishes done, Ben handed Sam a glass of wine and sat in the sunroom with his arm outstretched. "Come. We'll put up the tree in the morning."

Sam snuggled against him. "I don't know how those kids have coped with everything these last two months. We should take them skiing up Mount Washington over the Christmas break— rent a chalet for the week—because they will still have another six weeks to endure before the trials, and god knows how long that will drag on. I remember all too well what waiting is like. Waiting for justice. Waiting to feel safe again." She looked up into his eyes. "What if I ask them to come out here on the weekends with us?"

"Leave it up to them, hon. There's a fine line."

"I know, I know. I'll try not to be smothering." A heavy sigh blew a sassy strand of hair off her face. "Let's just concentrate on Christmas right now. When they get here, I want this place decked out with all the trimmings. Let's even put lights out on the lane. And all across these windows."

Ben kissed her forehead. "Absolutely. Not a single dark corner where a ghost could hide."

§

It was the Friday before Christmas. When they had left Vancouver at ten, the traffic was already heavy. The Christmas migration to the interior and the prairies was well underway.

Sam wished she had driven. Ben didn't need the added stress. He had even left his laptop at home. She worried. "Is Zack covering for you this week?"

"Of course. I promised you I'd log off for the holidays, and I have." Without taking his eyes off the road, he reached for her hand. "I'm sorry. I didn't mean that the way it sounded."

Sam squeezed back. "It's okay, Ben. I understand." But the stress of worrying about him was making her stomach ache.

He looked at the sky. "We'll be lucky if we make it before those clouds open up."

He took the off-ramp to their favourite market for the fresh fruits and vegetables they'd need for the week. When they arrived, the bins were already getting low. Even Dorothy, the check-out girl, was surprised.

Sam pushed their purchases along the counter. "I'm glad we got here early. You've been busy."

A tremendous rumble was the only warning before the sky broke open like a breached dam. The wind came up, throwing sheets of rain through the front of the market. She rushed to help Ben push the heavy panels together across the open wall. The rain doused the open bins until the very last crack closed. She laughed.

Ben shook his head like a wet dog and grinned at her. "I wish I'd parked closer."

Dorothy whipped Sam's purchases over the scanner. "Thank you, guys. I struggle with those panels on a good day."

There were only a handful of customers left inside, and they were in no hurry to leave. "Not to worry, folks. I'll check you all out, and then we'll have a nice hot chocolate in the back by the fire. How does that sound?"

That sounded good to Sam and all the other nodding heads. She hugged herself, and they shuffled into the back.

With all the stories of waiting out flash floods in the desert and holing up at truck stops for blizzards on the prairies, the time passed quickly. The rain let up just long enough for everyone to gather up their bounty and dash to their cars. The hot-chocolate bunch said their goodbyes like old friends.

The lot had filled with vehicles off the highway, waiting out the worst, and they all took the break in the rain to get back on the road.

Ben shivered behind the wheel as they waited in line. He turned on the heat. "Friendly bunch, weren't they?"

Sam smiled. "Uh-huh." The rain and the Christmas spirit had worked their magic. This was a happier man.

§

It was Christmas Eve morning. Sam jostled and bumped with Ben in the kitchen, sometimes even accidentally. She held up a spoonful of wild rice. "I'll taste your sauce if you'll try my stuffing."

"It's a deal." He snapped her spoon with his teeth and dramatically withdrew it. He pulled her to him with exaggerated sounds of ecstasy as he chewed.

Sam rolled her eyes and giggled. This was her Ben—relaxed, kibitzing, and cooking. She wriggled free. "So? Your sauce?"

Ben scooped a spoonful of whole cranberries from a bubbling pot and blew on it. "You're incorrigible." Grinning, he held it to her lips. "Be careful. My sauce is pretty hot."

"You can say that again." She savoured it on her tongue and tried to upstage Ben's dramatics.

"Okay, okay. You don't like my sauce. Give it back."

Before she could react, Ben was kissing her. He held her head in both hands and looked into her eyes. "So there. Behave yourself, you."

Sighing, she opened the fridge door and swung it back and forth to cool off, but she spotted Ben's apron strings dangling as he stood at the stove. She crossed them and wrapped them around in front. As she did, she rested her face on his shoulder, breathed in his ear, and fumbled with the bow accidentally on purpose.

Ben took his time turning. He kissed her, then held her at arm's length. "You're a minx. Get out of my kitchen. Mom and Dad will be here any minute. I don't want to go to the door with this." He lifted his apron and groaned. "And I don't even get to sleep with you for the next two nights."

Sam agreed. There was just too much heat in the kitchen. She took her coffee to the sunroom to sit by the Christmas tree. A smug smile crept over her face. Ben had to admit there was more feng shui there than inside by the fireplace. She texted Grace. "They're just leaving Tsawwassen. I'll see where Nick is."

Two hours later, a loud and persistent honking announced his folks' arrival. Ben smiled. "We should do that in their driveway."

"We could, but your mom has a sixth sense or something. She's always standing outside as we drive up. It's a little freaky."

Grace had a trunk full of food and a back seat of gifts. It took the four of them to tote it all inside. As usual, Grace had to check out the shrubs and the woodpile. She walked into the great room and set her parcels with care on Ben's table.

"Oh my, what a beautiful tree. And look, Lenny, how it picks up its own reflection in all three windows. Just gorgeous."

Sam elbowed Ben, who rolled his eyes. "Let me take those to your room, Mom." He picked up her parcels and headed around the sunroom to the bedroom Ben had used as his home office.

Sam couldn't help checking his expression when he came out. He winked at her, which helped. It was the quilt in there that was ruined with his blood that day. He still found it difficult to work there, but he got better each time he tried.

Sam had just set the hors d'oeuvres and wine on the coffee table in the sunroom when she heard a car drive up. "Nick and Fran are here." When she opened the back door, Grace was already standing there in the cold damp air, waving at them before the car even came to a stop.

She pointed at Grace's back when Ben came up behind her. "What did I tell you?"

Nick and Fran swung their backpacks over their shoulders and lifted several festive bags brimming with glittery tissue paper out of the back. Fran bounded up the path. "We're here! Hi, Grace, hi, Ben, hi, Sam."

Sam grinned at Nick, plodding up the path behind her, crossing his eyes. "She's been like this for a week. My god." He reduced his voice to a whisper. "Now that Henri is in custody and Lise is on a short leash, she's almost back to her former self. It's almost ironic."

"I hear you. Come on in. Ben almost has supper ready."

Fran twirled around in the great room, oohing and aahing. "This is amazing. I love the fireplaces, and the table! Is this the one you made, Ben? It's so cool! Nick, look at the carving on the feet and all around here." She traced the carvings with her fingers.

Sam picked up their backpacks. "I'm just going to put them in our room, Fran." When she returned, Nick had settled his effervescent sister by the tree.

Lenny was already sampling the hors d'oeuvres. He handed a naan samosa bite to Grace. "I'm going to have a cucumber slice with falafel."

The flavours of Ben's signature dishes wafted from the kitchen. Nick took a deep breath. "Man, this all smells so good."

Ben came up behind his mom and kissed her on top of the head. "She dragged me kicking and screaming into the kitchen when I was ten."

Grace patted his hand on her shoulder. "That's right. If I had waited until he was thirteen, he would have been bigger than me."

Sam felt her cheeks flush when Ben twirled his apron strings at her.

Lenny took charge of the wine and made sure the hors d'oeuvres made the rounds. "Just wait till Boxing Day. You will love my hot turkey sandwiches. Isn't that right, Sam?" He winked at her.

She and Grace exchanged knowing glances. "You've got that right, Lenny."

Standing at the tree in animated conversation with Grace, Fran held Sam's favourite ornament—a city bus with a tiny bride and groom painted in the front window. Sam caught Grace's smile as she told the story of their wedding.

Fran turned, wide-eyed, to Sam. "That is sooo romantic." With a resigned sigh, she said, "We lost all of ours in the great 'purge' after Dad's death."

Grace patted her arm. "I'm so sorry. I know how precious these can be." Sam sipped her wine, frowned, and set it down.

Lenny was quizzing Nick about the law when Ben called. "I think we're ready here, people." He set the curried chicken platter in the middle of the table.

Fran was the first to her place. "Wow! I haven't seen a table like this since we were in Paris. Ben, this warrants two Michelin stars." And it did. The table was resplendent with savoury dishes and sweet. Candles glowed and crackers popped with multicoloured paper hats. Laughter and lively conversation filled the air. The wine and conversation flowed until the last crème brûlée vanished.

Nick rose with his glass in the air. "Ben, this meal was magnificent. A toast to the chef." Sam lifted her glass to Ben and then to Grace. She understood.

Nick was not finished. "I also want to thank Ben and Sam for allowing Fran and me to share this time with you. This is our first Christmas without Mom and Dad. It would have been difficult to find joy in our hearts without you. So thank you."

Sam nodded as she struggled to hold back the tears. Ben took her hand and kissed it.

"It was Sam's idea, and we're happy you're here."

Grace added her approval with a touch to Fran's shoulder and a smile. Lenny pushed away from the table and loosened his belt. "Hear, hear. Next year you'll have to come over to our place. That was a wonderful meal, Son. I think I'll waddle into the sunroom and let this settle. I need to make room for a nightcap. Excuse me."

Sam looked around the table at the people she loved and counted her blessings.

§

When his dad got up around one, he was tiptoeing past Ben and Nick in the sunroom, but stubbed his toe in the dark. Ben raised his head.

"Sorry, Son. Bathroom."

"It's okay, I was awake. We have to put out the gifts anyway." Ben shook Nick. "Hey. It's time for Santa to do his thing."

He retrieved their gifts from their hiding place in the pantry. One by one, he arranged them around the tree. Nick yawned and crouched beside him. "I've never been Santa before. You know what this means, don't you? Fran will insist on being Santa next year."

Ben nodded and raised his eyebrows. His dad shuffled past them back to his room, muttering some unintelligible apology. Ben grinned to himself, hearing his mother's familiar voice. "It's right there on the dresser. No, not that one—that one."

Lenny emerged and hung something on the tree before crouching beside them. "You know, Nick, when Ben and Sandra were kids, they'd sleep right here on foamies. In those days, I had to set the alarm to do this. I don't have to do that anymore."

Ben stood back and admired their tree. There was the little sailboat with 'Sandra' painted across the sail. He gazed at it for a while. "I think we're done here. Let's get some sleep." From the sofa, he could still see the white sail of Sandra's boat in the moonlight, and beyond that the stars. *Goodnight, Sis.*

§

Christmas morning smelled good. Grace had taken over the kitchen, so Sam knew a stack of crepes was waiting in the oven. She

roused Fran. "Wake up. We have to get out there before the guys."
She tossed Fran her robe.

Ben and Nick didn't even look up. They were too busy scarfing
down Grace's crepes, stuffed with her blackberry sauce and drizzled
with cream.

Sam sat next to Ben at the counter. "What are you grinning at?
You've got blackberry sauce on your chin."

Fran leaned on her brother's shoulder and climbed up beside
him. "Traitor. Merry Christmas, Grace. Did they leave any for us?"

Grace pulled the platter out of the oven. "Sam can tell you. I keep
making them as long as people keep coming. Did you sleep well?"

"Like a log. It's so quiet out here. And it was nice to sleep next to
someone. It reminded me of sleeping with my mother when I was
small. No offence, Sam."

Sam grinned. "None taken." She spun around to speak to Lenny.
"I suppose you were the first one at the trough this morning?"

Lenny lit up the tree and sat next to it. "You betcha. Hurry up,
you guys. I never used to have to wait around like this on
Christmas morning. Remember, Ben? You and Sandra used to
bring your stockings into our bed. You'd dump yours, but Sandra
would take things out of hers one at a time. She loved the
suspense."

When Grace folded her apron and joined them with her coffee,
it was time for Lenny to do his thing. He donned his Santa hat and
ho-ho-hoed. "Mother, this one is for the both of us, from Nick and
Fran. Here. You open it."

Grace lifted the tissue and peered into the bag. "Oh my. Lenny
dear, you'll have to help me with this." Together they unfolded an
Attic Windows quilt. Grace gasped. "This is the view from our
living room. How did you get it?"

Nick pulled out his phone. "When we were there after the
mantel clock caper. I took that photo with my phone. We had it
printed on the fabric, and Sherry did the magic."

Lenny placed his hand on Nick's shoulder. "That is a fine thing,
Son, a fine thing. Thank you." He straightened his Santa hat and

took the next parcel from beneath the tree. He cleared his throat. "So, what do we have here? It says, 'To Nick and Fran, love Mom.'"

"Love Mom?" Nick looked around at the innocent faces. "What is this?"

Fran grabbed it away from him. "Well, open it, silly!" She tore the wrapper in a second and revealed a framed photo. "I don't believe it." She dropped it in Nick's lap and stared at it through tears. It was a photo of their mother marvelling at the lights of Paris from the Eiffel Tower. And superimposed on it was a picture of Nick and Fran standing beside her.

"See, you aren't the only ones who sneak pictures. The one of your mother was in that album you rescued, and the other one—"

Fran finished her sentence. "The other one we Instagrammed from the Eiffel Tower that night. Grace, Lenny, thank you so much. Nick?"

Nick nodded. "It's almost as if she's imagining her future children as adults in that moment." He started to get up, but Lenny protested.

"Could we leave all the kissing and hugging until we're done? At this rate, we'll be here till next Christmas. Let's see here. This one is for Sam and Ben from Nick and Fran with love."

Sam put her coffee down and placed the bag on the floor between them. When she pulled out the glittery tissue, she clapped her hand over her mouth to keep from screaming. Ben had to help her lift out the double wedding ring quilt. She unfolded it onto their laps. Overwhelmed, she cried.

Fran said, "We asked Sherry to make this for you too, to replace the one you gave back to Nick. There's a bunch of happy symbolism in this one. I hope you like it."

Ben shook his head. "We love it. Thank you."

Sam managed to choke out, "Yes, what he said." She nodded at Lenny. He seemed to be waiting for her to get a grip.

Lenny retrieved a small gift from the heap. "Okay ... This little one is for Nick and Fran, from Sam and Ben."

Sam hugged their quilt to her chest while they opened the gift.

Nick didn't seem quite sure what he was looking at until she pointed out their half on the tree.

Then he turned it over and read, "Family by Choice, Ben and Sam." He took a few minutes to compose himself before he spoke.

"You know, when we were young, we had some good Christmases with Dad and Mom together. It seemed, every second year, he was 'away on a business trip.' Of course, now we know the truth. Those were the Christmases we spent at Granddad and Grandma Allen's place. They overindulged us, and now we know why." He pinched the tears from his eyes. "This past year has been the year from hell. I've been so worried about Fran and my responsibilities. You've helped us in so many ways; I can't begin to express my gratitude. Your kindness has lifted a tremendous weight from my shoulders." He looked at the ornament in his hand. "Thank you for choosing us. The feeling is mutual."

Sam hoped the strength of the bond they had forged would sustain them in the coming months, when the trials of Lise and Henri would disrupt their lives yet again and drag them back into heartache.

Ben made everyone laugh through their tears when he grabbed a box of tissues and passed it around. "Welcome to the family, you two."

TRIALS

Sam arrived home late. It had been a long day. Exhausted, she took a deep breath before turning the key.

Ben muted the television. "So how did it go?"

She sloughed off her shoes and plunked herself beside him in her coat, her purse still hanging from her shoulder. Closing her eyes, she sagged into the cushions. "I didn't want to leave Fran until Nick got home. She was very emotional."

"I don't doubt it. Waiting for a conviction, the tension builds and builds and then *boom*, the dam bursts?"

"That's the thing. This isn't the end of it. Henri will be out in five years unless he gets convicted of murder, or conspiracy to murder, on top of this. And the photos he sold will always be out there. Fran will always feel violated."

"Poor kid. Is she going to see Gwen?"

"Yes. I told her how much she has helped us."

"You didn't tell Fran about my time in hell, did you?"

"She only asked about your PTSD, and ..."

"Damn it, Samantha. I wish you had asked me first. I mean, you know you're the only other person besides Gwen I've told. Even my mother doesn't know the full extent of—"

"No, Ben. She only wanted to know how you are dealing with it. I didn't tell her anything about your ordeal. I promise you." She turned his face to hers and kissed him. How could she have been so cavalier?

Beads of sweat glistened on his forehead. "Good. You know how I feel about it."

"I know, hon. Fran was just comforted to think she had a kindred spirit in you. And a big tough one at that."

He gave her hand a gentle squeeze. "I'm glad she didn't have to take the stand and face that asshole. God, I wish I'd been a fly on the wall the day the RCMP knocked on his door."

An overwhelming feeling of sadness came over her. *Poor Fran.* She closed her eyes to hold back the tears.

§

A month later, Sam sat in the courtroom with Nick, watching him twist in his seat and rub his sweaty palms on his thighs. It was the last day of Lise Richard and Henri Richard's trial for conspiracy to commit murder. Crown counsel was just wrapping up her argument.

"On the charge of conspiracy to commit murder in the death of Lenore Bennett, you have heard the testimony of Lenore Bennett's son, Nicholas Bennett, describing the events of the night of January 5, 2015—the night of his mother's death.

"You have heard the testimony of the defendants, Lise Richard Bennett and Henri Richard, her son. You have heard the testimony of the first responders and the coroner. And you have heard the testimony of Sherry Baker, a close friend of the deceased.

"The facts are these: On the night of January 5, 2015, the victim, Lenore Bennett, recorded in this diary an insulin injection at 6:00 p.m., twenty minutes after celebrating her daughter, Frances's, fourteenth birthday at a restaurant." She paused before continuing. Her point was not lost on the jury. "Nicholas said good night to his mother and went upstairs to study and go to bed. He never saw his mother again."

The prosecutor paced in front of the jury until they shifted uncomfortably in their seats. Then she said, "It wasn't until 11:30 p.m., five hours later, that Henri Richard called 911. What happened in those five hours?

"First responders report attending the home at 11:30 p.m. to find Lenore Bennett in a diabetic coma. Intervention was unsuccessful, and she was pronounced dead at the regional hospital at 12:15 a.m." As she spoke, she held up each item of physical evidence. "These *three* empty vials and these *two* used syringes were found on the bedside table. The third syringe was never found. The fingerprints on one syringe belong to Lenore Bennett, which correlates to the diary entry. Although Lise Richard Bennett claims to have helped Mr. Bennett give his wife an insulin injection, the fingerprints on the second syringe belong to Henri Richard. This discrepancy in Lise Richard Bennett's statement to the first responders was discovered when her fingerprints were found on this cane ... which, you have heard, she used to assault Nicholas Bennett more recently.

"When questioned, Adrian Bennett told the paramedics he had asked Lise Richard—*his mistress*—to come over because he thought his wife was, in his words, 'out of it.' Lise Richard admitted to administering the second vial because Mr. Bennett was, in her words, 'shaking too much.' You will recall that Mr. Bennett was suffering the effects of a stroke. After she gave Mrs. Bennett the second injection, Ms. Richard told him his wife was asleep. Now, Lise Richard *Bennett* has no explanation for either her son's fingerprints being on the syringe or the disappearance of the third syringe.

"The defendants neglected to tell the first responders there were two children in the house who could have shed some light on events, and there is no explanation for the delay in calling 911, or for Henri Richard's appearance there at all. When questioned, Henri Richard said he called 911 as soon as he arrived on the scene; however, the time of his arrival could not be verified. The records show he received a call from his mother at 7:30 p.m. and a neighbour observed a truck of similar colour and make as his in front of the Bennett house 'around 8:00 p.m.' That is the extent of the first responders' report.

"Frances Bennett awakened her brother, Nicholas, when the flashing lights of the ambulance and shouting frightened her. Nicholas states he observed an altercation, from the top of the stairs, between Henri Richard—whom he did not know—and Richard's biological father, Adrian Bennett, now deceased, whose death on June 11 of last year the defendants are also on trial for today.

"Nicholas Bennett intervened in the altercation and, quote, 'threw Henri Richard out of the house,' end quote. His mother, Lise Richard—now Bennett—who was the mistress of Adrian Bennett at the time and was also a stranger to Nicholas Bennett, was standing outside the front door. The defendants left the scene in separate vehicles."

"The initial coroner's report states Lenore Bennett died of cardiac arrest from insulin overdose. However, due to an application by Nicholas Bennett and his sister Frances Bennett, which provided additional information, the coroner deemed the new evidence worthy of investigation by police. And she was right."

An hour into the details of his father's murder, Nick shook his head. "I can't take any more of this. Let's get out of here."

On the courthouse steps, they ran into Sherry.

"Nick, your mother was a fine woman. Let's hope we got her some justice in there." Sherry pulled her lapels together at her throat.

Nick looked up at the grey, threatening sky and turned up his collar. "Thank you for all you've done for us, Sherry."

She squeezed his hand. "You're very welcome, Nick. When the prosecutor asked me about quilting with her, and the business about the blue hat, I think the jury realized how tormented your mother was."

"Yeah. Lise made a big mistake wearing it that first day."

Sam nodded. "I think that was the turning point, if there was one."

"Yup. Who would have thought a witnessed embroidered signature was a legal document?" Nick looked up at the imposing facade of the courthouse with a clenched jaw. "This wasn't exactly how I'd hoped to get my courtroom experience."

Sherry waved her key fob at the parking lot. "Ah, there's my car. I have to catch the four-o'clock ferry, so you'll let me know?"

Nick tucked in his scarf. "You can count on it."

He turned to Sam with tears in his eyes. "They have to find them guilty, Sam. They have to. I could hardly look at her, sitting there with her nose in the air—and Henri?" He shook his head. "I hope they throw the book at him." Nick swayed, rubbing his fist.

An uneasy feeling in the pit of Sam's stomach had persisted throughout the trial. Maybe it would subside after sentencing. Fran had suffered the same nausea at Henri's first trial. She wouldn't even come to the courthouse today and subject herself to the sight of him sitting there, so smug.

Sam wrapped her arm around Nick's shoulders. "I'm sure they'll both be convicted. But, you know, it could be on a reduced charge, and they are likely to appeal."

"Can you imagine what an appeal would do to Fran? And she could never appear at a parole hearing."

"Listen, Nick. When Lise tried to implicate your dad in your mother's death, saying he wanted out of the marriage? And then to suggest that your mother was trying to frame her with the quilts? I think the jury viewed that as particularly repugnant. I think they can smell a rat—or two."

EAGLES

It was May. Nick stood behind Fran where she knelt at the foot of their mother's grave, the early morning sun warming his back. "I was thinking of having Dad's body moved next to Mom's. What do you think?"

Fran jumped to her feet. "No! Absolutely not. He was never beside her in life, really beside her; so why would she want him beside her in death? That's the stupidest idea you've ever had, Nick."

"So we're just going to leave him over there in Lise's plot, with her name beside his on the tombstone?"

"Yes. That's where he wanted to be, anyway. I just wish we could fix this headstone."

"What's wrong with it?" He furrowed his brow.

"Beloved wife of Adrian Bennett? Come on. Get real."

"I think he loved her. Otherwise, he would have abandoned her when Henri was born, and you wouldn't exist."

"Puh-leeze. When he found out about Henri, you were already born."

"You don't know that."

"You weren't paying attention. She's been on the payroll since you were just a few weeks old. Henri would have been one. She probably came to your baptism."

"How do you figure?"

"Remember the line on your quilt about 'fledglings' rites'?"

"Yes. I do." Things were becoming clearer to him.

"Rites? Baptism? What's with you, anyway?" Fran put her hands on her hips. "I thought you hated him."

"I did. For all the years of lies and unhappiness. For the pain it caused Mom, knowing about the lady in the blue hat for so many years. But when Lise said at the trial that he had always wanted to get out of the marriage, I realized that he didn't. He could have, at any time, but he didn't. He had some sense of responsibility for twenty years."

"Pfft. He was a monumental coward. When I think of all the times I sat on his lap begging him not to go away again." She shook her head. "Knowing what I know now—I don't feel the love anymore. Nick, look at me, really look at me. What do you see?"

He hesitated, confused. "I see my little sister?"

Fran stood beside her mother's grave and placed her hands on the headstone. "Look again, Nick. I'm a woman, this woman's daughter—both of us betrayed by that man over there. And after Mom died, he took me out of my home and placed me in the hands of a predator, and he was so self-indulgent, he couldn't see it."

"I'm so sorry, Fran." Nick nodded and hung his head.

"You didn't know. You were just a kid like me. But now you need to see him for what he was." She stood beside him and stared at the headstone for a moment before she hip-checked him. "Why don't we scratch out *beloved* and engrave *first* above it?"

He walked out of the cemetery beside his little sister, the woman. It was pride he felt in his chest. "Come on. I want to catch the next ferry to Tsawwassen. It's another hour to the cottage."

§

Sam heard Nick's car drive up behind the cottage. "They're here,

Ben." She opened the back door and stood on the stoop, waving—just like Grace. She smiled, more to herself.

"You're right on time. Lunch is ready. I hope you brought your swimsuits. The water is perfect."

Fran swung her backpack off the back seat. "I'd like to kayak upriver to see the eaglets."

Ben appeared in the doorway. "We can do that. You made good time. Did you leave right from the cemetery?"

Nick followed them inside and set his backpack in the bathroom. "Yes, we caught the nine-thirty ferry at Duke Point."

Fran dropped her backpack and sat at the table. "Nick and I had a great row at Mom's grave."

Tension crept across Sam's shoulders. She frowned at Nick. "This doesn't sound good."

"I was just thinking of moving Dad over by Mom, but Fran straightened me out."

Fran huffed. "Yeah, I put the kibosh on that idea."

As she dished out the salad, Sam looked across at a grinning Ben and nodded. They had just been talking about Fran, wondering how she'd been coping since the trials.

Ben said, "So exams are over. How do you guys feel?"

"I don't know about Nick, but I nailed mine. Except maybe pharmacology—there are so many new drugs with a lot of contraindications."

Nick chuckled. "The jury's out for me. I should get my results next week."

Sam passed the platter of sandwiches and seized the opportunity. "Speaking of juries, I worried you wouldn't be able to concentrate on studying during the trial."

"Whenever I'd check on Fran, she had her head buried in a book, nodding to whatever music was in her ear buds. But for me, it was as if I had been holding my breath for a year. Sometimes I read the same paragraph three times and didn't remember a word. I'd go for a run to clear my head."

Fran munched on her salad. "It wasn't always music. Dr. Pravir gave me some audio cues to help me refocus if I slid back into an agitated state. It worked." She smiled at Nick. "I was okay ... most of the time."

Ben was refilling their mugs. "I'm glad Gwen could help you. Now that you've had a few months to reflect on the trial, what are your feelings about their sentences?"

"Well, for Fran's sake, I'm glad Henri's sentences are consecutive and not concurrent—twenty years on top of the first five. And for Lise, two consecutive twenty-year sentences for conspiracy to murder was perfect. Because of the fight with Dad, the jury believed Henri had administered the third dose but disposed of the wrong syringe. Lise didn't look too comfortable covering for him. I'll bet she regrets admitting she administered the second dose ... Poor Mom."

Fran stuck out a quivering chin. "Well. By the time he has a parole hearing, I've promised myself I will be ready to face him."

"I know she can do anything she sets her mind to." Nick helped himself to another sandwich. "I don't think the judge gave Lise any leniency for being a mother. I think the jury believed she had insti-gated the conspiracy and pulled Henri into it." Nick shrugged. "Two life sentences even without her fingerprints on a syringe. I was a little worried they might be convicted of the lesser charge of negli-gent homicide."

Sam couldn't help but think of Antoine and Bertrand—the inno-cents. "What will happen to those boys? They are your half-broth-ers, after all."

Nick set his sandwich down and leaned back in his chair. "Dad's will left his estate to Lise and each of the boys equally, since we already had Mom's half in our trust.

"Lise and Henri can't inherit because of the forfeiture or slayer rule: the Latin legal doctrine 'ex turpi causa non oritur actio' declares that a person cannot benefit because of their crime.

"We think Antoine and Bertrand will get to keep their trusts. But, since we are beneficiaries of 'the residue' of Dad's estate, the courts may award Lise and Henri's share to us.

Alternatively, they could split it four ways, which would be fine by us.

"And, interestingly enough, the insurance company is suing for recovery of proceeds of the policy she took out on Dad. Their position is that since Dad paid the premiums on the policy through his support payments, the proceeds also fall under the forfeiture rule."

Fran pointed her fork at her brother. "Listen to you, sounding all lawyerly. I feel sorry for Tony and Bert. We didn't get along very well, but they don't deserve this."

Nick started clearing the table. "They want to live with their grandparents in France and, ironically, they need my permission."

A feeling, almost of parental pride, welled up in Sam. "Which you will grant, of course?"

"I don't have any problem with that." Nick stretched and took a deep breath. "Come on, guys. Let's get those kayaks in the water."

§

The afternoon was sunny and warm. The spring freshet was over, and the river had settled into its banks. Ben jogged down to the river with his kayak. As he approached the shore, he resolved he wouldn't let the river trigger his PTSD today.

Holding the kayak steady for Sam to climb in, he hoped an upstream paddle would release those endorphins for everyone.

The water sparkled and gurgled with every stroke of their paddles. Their voices bounced off the mountainside in the quiet. As they approached the rocky outcrop, they could see the pair of eagles perched near the nest.

Fran whispered, "OMG, look at them. How many years have they been returning to this nest?"

Ben shielded his eyes from the sun. "As long as I can remember. I don't know how many pairs there've been. They can live up to thirty years, so I guess it could be the same pair."

Fran waved at them. "What do you call them?"

Nick laughed. "My guess is 'eagles'?"

Fran tried to splash her brother, but that did not go well. "Okay, okay. Whatever." She shook her hair in his face.

"All my life, no one has ever suggested naming them. Why don't you choose something?"

Fran thought for a few minutes as they paddled. "Okay, I'll call them Maximus the Strong and Sophia the Wise—my aspirations if not my affirmation. Which one is which, Ben?"

"The female is always larger."

"I wish it were the same for humans."

As the kayaks turned downstream and headed home, Ben fought the tension building in his body. He knew exactly what Fran meant. They paddled on in silence.

§

Sam's arms ached from paddling, but she wanted to rinse off with a swim before supper. "Come on. It's invigorating."

The others followed her like lemmings, howling at the initial shock. It only took a minute to feel refreshed. Sam climbed the embankment and grabbed her towel from a log at the firepit.

"Hey! You suckered us into this." Nick tried to splash her.

"I'm going up to get supper started. I'll call you."

From the kitchen, she watched the three of them swim against the current in a game to stay stationary. Ben had thrown a weighted rope out at the foot of the property in case someone tired in the current. Nick was the first to give up.

Tiptoeing through the room to the bathroom, he said, "I can't keep up with Fran; she's a fish."

"Those two were messing with you. Look. Here they come."

After supper, they sat in the sunroom and watched the sunset.

Nick stood up, looking quite stern, and cleared his throat. "I've got an announcement."

The hair stood up on the back of Sam's neck. *What now?* She heaved a sigh of relief when Nick broke out in a broad smile.

"Grant called me. He wants me to do my articling at Humphreys and MacGregor next year."

Fran slapped her brother on the arm. "Get out of here. You didn't tell me this."

Ben reached over for a fist bump. "Congratulations."

The mix of joy and relief made Sam tear up and hug him. "This is fantastic news. I think this calls for a toast. Ben, how about some wine?"

Nick puffed out his chest. "Thanks. I guess I'll be working on the mainland. We have to decide what to do with the house in Nanaimo. We stayed there last night, but let's face it, how often are we going to use it? Renting doesn't appeal to me. I'd rather sell it."

Sam's interest was piqued. "What are your thoughts, Fran?"

"Well, I love the house. It's where I got to spend those last years with our grandparents. But it's also the house where Dad left us so often to be with *her*. I'm glad I was so blissfully unaware at the time, but Mom knew, and I can't forget that. So I don't think I'd ever want to live there again. And, who knows, I might meet someone who will take me down under." She gave her brother a coy look.

"Hang on. Is there something I should know?"

"Maybe, maybe not." She rocked her hands at him. "We'll see if my Aussie is still keen on me in September."

Nick rolled his eyes. "Our decision is … no decision then?"

Sam recalled a similar conversation over lunch at Grace's. She caught Ben's eye, but she didn't see what she'd hoped for.

HOME

*B*en flipped the crepe sizzling in the pan. He had opened the windows to the river to let in the crisp morning air. He listened to the crescendo of birdsong. They always started just before first light. First one, then another. By sunup, there was a multitude in full song.

Pouring the next crepe, Ben contemplated the future of Nick and Fran. He remembered his anticipation at graduation, the plans he had made; and how it had all come to fruition with Keith, the winery, and his job at Cumberland. He saw the same hopes and dreams in the faces of Nick and Fran.

The coffee had just finished dripping when Nick yawned from the sofa bed in the sunroom. "What a way to wake up. I should set my coffeemaker at night." He pulled on his jeans and a T-shirt.

Fran emerged from the far bedroom. "Man, I love this place. It is so quiet. I mean, no city noises. Just birds and the wind."

Nick thumped on Sam's bedroom door. "Get up, Sam. Ben's got a stack of crepes and fresh fruit out here." He added in a sing-song voice. "And there's coffee."

He grinned at Ben. "How did you like the new sleeping arrangements?"

Ben pretended to smack him with the spatula.

A few minutes later, Sam plunked herself on the stool between Nick and Fran, yawned, and put an arm around each of them. "Good morning, you two." They were already on their second crepe.

Ben leaned over the counter and kissed her. "Good morning, beautiful." He winked at her. They had made love last night, without a sound—or so he hoped.

Removing the platter of crepes from the oven, he placed them on the counter in front of her. She looked thoughtful as he heaped a crepe with fresh fruit, rolled it up, and drizzled fresh yogurt on top. "There you go, Sam. Your favourite."

"Thanks, hon." Sam cut the tiniest slice and placed it on her tongue. Her eyes grew wide and her cheeks puffed out. She tore into the bathroom and retched.

Nick and Fran looked at each other, their mouths agape. Nick bobbed his eyebrows at Ben and grinned.

"What? What?"

Nick took a set of keys from his pocket and gave them to Fran. She nodded, reached for Ben's hand, and closed his fingers around them.

"What's this?"

"The keys to the house in Nanaimo. Congratulations. You're going to need it."

THE END

ACKNOWLEDGMENTS

It was my regular Friday quilting day at Jonanco when the idea of clues to a woman's murder embroidered into a quilt occurred to me. I am grateful to my fellow quilters at Jonanco for their friendship and encouragement to write this book—especially Sherry, who made a cameo appearance in *Murder by Pins and Needles*.

Donna Barker, Eileen Cook, Crystal Hunt, Stephanie Candiago, and the members of the Creative Academy for Writers have been my mentors and cheerleaders. Seven days a week, they provide me with hours of online sprints, master classes, guest presenters, advice, technical support, and companionship. I am so fortunate.

Luckily, I met my editors, Tracy Thillmann and Amanda Bidnall, through the Creative Academy as well. Their advice, and that of my beta readers Natasha, Jacqui, Ellen, and Kevin, has given me the confidence to type "The End." It was my good fortune to have the benefit of a male perspective in Kevin. Thank you, Kevin. You made me brave.

But most of all, I thank you, my reader. I write for you.

Sincerely,
Ardelle Holden

P. S. Please stay in touch. You can sign up for my newsletter and catch my blog on my website:

https://www.ardelleholden.com

OTHER BOOKS BY ARDELLE HOLDEN

A Person of Interest

"Within the first two pages of *A Person of Interest*, I felt my heart racing in empathy with the main character, Samantha Bowers! I was hooked. The integration of digital technologies and social media brings a very contemporary feel to *A Person of Interest*." *Valerie Stowell, BS Computer Science Software Engineer, retired, Kelowna, BC*

"Cover is well designed and appealing ... it matches my favourite line from the book: 'Raindrops still glistened like scattered pearls across the glass' (p. 49). It's wet, moody, and gloomy with a hint of sparkling light (hope) coming from within city buildings." *Whistler Independent Book Award book evaluation*

Murder by Bits and Bytes

"A romantic get-away weekend erupts into a nightmare of greed, treachery and murder. Ardelle Holden writes with the skill of a screen writer as her tale unfolds like a movie. Readers are held hostage with the relentless emotional storm of terror faced by Samantha and Ben." *Whistler Independent Book Award book evaluation*

"*An emotional murder mystery* – Author Ardelle Holden has crafted a murder mystery exploring the effect of an ambush and kidnapping on the families and friends of the victims. Along the way you can enjoy skillful, evocative descriptions of the Canadian wilderness in its many moods." *Susan Craig*

ABOUT THE AUTHOR

Ardelle Holden was born in Sioux Lookout, nestled in the woods of Northwestern Ontario. She grew up in Hudson, just a fifteen-mile bike ride from Sioux. She spent her summers biking and swimming off the docks at Bowman Fisheries, Starratt's boat ramp, and the beach at camp—Bow-Manor—on Vermillion Lake.

She dreamed of destinations east and west when the trains rumbled through town in the night. Loud shunting told her they were picking up boxcars of fresh fish on ice or flatcars of pulpwood. Under the covers with a flashlight, Nancy Drew, the Hardy Boys, and Trixie Belden also fed her imagination.

That imagination filled notebooks. As the years rolled by, the 'what-ifs' of life crept into her stories. She imagined extricating herself and others from every dangerous situation, whether real or imagined. Her life as a writer of mysteries had begun.

She and her husband, Patrick, raised their two children while working in aviation, mining exploration, and the wild rice lakes of Manitoba. Retired in Nanaimo, BC, they winter in Mexico where Ardelle solves mysteries and chases rainbows.

www.ardelleholden.com

facebook.com/ArdelleHoldenAuthor
twitter.com/AuthorHolden
pinterest.com/ardelleholden

CPSIA information can be obtained
at www.ICGtesting.com
Printed in the USA
LVHW040814090222
710496LV00017B/816